Founded by the wealthy Miss Angela Childers, the purpose of the Society for Single Ladies is to solve crimes. But its intrepid members are just as fascinated by the mystery of love. . . .

Virginia, Lady Dulverton, has long felt safer keeping the world at a distance. One man sees through her reserve to the woman beneath: the infamously rakish Francis, Earl of Wolverley. Now a widow, Virginia is wrangling with the terms of her late husband's will. When she realizes Francis is in danger because of his connection to her, she feels compelled to help, regardless of the hazard to her own heart.

Francis has worked hard to strengthen his inheritance. But he's also found time to play. Despite his many dalliances, his affections have never been involved. Those belong entirely to a woman he could never have. When he's attacked in the street and told to leave Virginia alone, he decides to do exactly the opposite. . . .

With the help of the Society for Single Ladies, they set out to discover who is targeting Virginia, and why. It's a race that will lead to the Devonshire coast, a smuggling ring, and a love that, however perilous, is worth waging countless battles. . . .

Visit us at www.kensingtonbooks.com

Books by Lynne Connolly

The Society of Single Ladies
The Girl With the Pearl Pin
The Making of A Marquess
Virginia and the Wolf

The Shaw Series
Fearless
Sinless
Dauntless
Boundless

The Emperors of London Series
Rogue in Red Velvet
Temptation Has Green Eyes
Danger Wears White
Reckless in Pink
Dilemma in Yellow
Silk Veiled in Blue
Wild Lavender

Published by Kensington Publishing Corporation

Virginia and the Wolf

The Society of Single Ladies

Lynne Connolly

LYRICAL PRESS
Kensington Publishing Corp.
www.kensingtonbooks.com

LYRICAL PRESS BOOKS are published by
Kensington Publishing Corp.
119 West 40th Street
New York, NY 10018

All Kensington titles, imprints, and distributed lines are available at special quantity discounts for bulk purchases for sales promotion, premiums, fund-raising, educational, or institutional use.

Special book excerpts or customized printings can also be created to fit specific needs. For details, write or phone the office of the Kensington Sales Manager: Kensington Publishing Corp., 119 West 40th Street, New York, NY 10018. Attn. Sales Department. Phone: 1-800-221-2647.

Lyrical Press and Lyrical Press logo Reg. U.S. Pat. & TM Off.

First Electronic Edition: November 2020
eISBN-13: 978-1-5161-0954-8
eISBN-10: 1-5161-0954-6

First Print Edition: November 2020
ISBN-13: 978-1-5161-0957-9
ISBN-10: 1-5161-0957-0

Printed in the United States of America

Author's Foreword

Sometimes, when you're looking for something, you find something else that you lost years ago instead. And what you find is better than what you thought you wanted. This book is for everyone who has ever done that.

Chapter 1

Virginia, Lady Dulverton, glanced up from her book and scowled. That cherub was definitely out of place. Rising, she went to the mantelpiece to straighten it.

She'd never liked the thing. Somebody had exerted all their skill to make the outrageously expensive and ugly figurine. It scowled at her. She scowled back and laughed a little at her own foolishness.

The doorbell clanged, and her mock scowl became a real one. She was not at home to visitors on Wednesdays. Everybody knew that. Perhaps a delivery had arrived, and they were using the wrong door. Her staff could take care of that.

When the sound of raised voices drifted through the closed door, her hand stilled on the porcelain cupid. She knew that voice—

Lord Wolverley. The only man who stirred her senses was standing in her hall. Her pulse rate increased, but she had to face him. He wouldn't leave until he'd seen her. Twitching the skirts of her apricot silk gown aside, she made for the hall at speed.

And there he stood, his London finery barely making a dent in his rampant maleness. The Earl of Wolverley spun around, as if he sensed her standing there.

"Good Lord, madam, who is this dolt?" he demanded.

Virginia stayed in the doorway as he raked her with his gaze. Sparks lit his pearl-gray eyes, but she refused to acknowledge the effect he had on her. She took a couple of deep breaths. Only some quirk of nature, to be sure. "It's Butler."

"I can see *what* he is, but *who* is he?"

"Butler, my new butler."

The provoking earl went off into gales of laughter. His cocked hat, which he'd been trying to hand to Butler the butler, fell to the floor.

"Only you, Virginia, only you." He bent and swept up his hat, tossing it on the hall table. The tiny diamond dangling from his left ear gleamed as he rose, a flash of defiance all on its own.

What was he doing here? And what gave him the right to call her by her given name? What did he want? Virginia fought to keep her expression calm, to rise above his taunts.

Francis, Lord Wolverley, known in certain circles as "The Wolf," had never been particularly friendly with her late husband, but after Ralph's death Wolverley had returned to haunt her. In fact, the sound of her name on his lips gave her a wholly unwelcome frisson. Being a truthful woman, Virginia could not deny that he was a most attractive man. But that did not make her blind to his faults.

She did not know who Wolverley conducted his affairs with. Neither did she care.

She assumed her protective mantle of frozen hauteur. "Only me what? And I am not aware of us being related closely enough for you to make free with my given name."

In the ten years she had known the Earl of Wolverley, he had never ceased to provoke her. Wolverley found rare amusement in doing so, and every time he did, she rose to the bait. As, she ruefully admitted to herself, she was doing now.

He grinned. "Oh, I think we've known one another long enough to dispense with the formalities. And in answer to your question, only you could find a butler called Butler. Do you have a maid called Maid, too? A lady's maid called Abigail?"

"Not at all. And it is cruel of you to taunt him so. My maid is Winston, and the footman in the hall is Hurst."

She cast the man a wry look of apology, but Butler, who was very good at his job, remained stately and impassive. Of moderate height but considerable presence, Butler kept most of the undesirables from the door with consummate ease. Just not this one.

Again, Wolverley defied convention and turned to the butler, meeting his gaze, which was not at all the thing, and nearly startled Butler into taking a step back. Virginia noted his hesitation but did not hold it against him. Wolverley had a vitality that startled many people.

"Indeed, I beg your pardon. But it is most unusual. I trust your feelings have not been utterly destroyed?"

Butler swept a low bow. He didn't have to refer to the piece of pasteboard in his hand when he said, "Absolutely not, Lord Wolverley."

"You can't come in. My companion is away," she told the earl.

His raised brows told her what he thought of her response. "Don't you trust me to keep my hands off you?"

"You know it's not that." Wolverley could be so irritating.

"I'm as harmless as a mouse. Everybody knows that." His attempt at a pout nearly made her laugh, but she refused to let him see her amusement. It might encourage him.

While her companion, Mrs. Dauntry, was away, Virginia had plans for a quiet life. Paperwork with a little light shopping, because a person should take the air occasionally.

Not entertaining the one man in London who was a danger to her peace of mind. If she wasn't careful, gossip would spread, even at this late stage in the season.

At the end of June, London was thin of company, the theaters were closing for their summer break, and the shops were letting their supplies of luxury goods run down.

Her companion's absence gave Virginia the excuse to live quietly. She would attend the smaller gatherings that she preferred, and one ball she had already committed to.

Virginia planned to leave London at the end of the month, after the last event of the season. After the Conyngham ball, she would kick the dust of the city off her heels and head for Devonshire and home.

"Was there something in particular you wanted?" she asked in her best frosty tone, letting her words drip into the space with disdain.

"Actually, yes." He met her gaze, and his eyes were not sparkling with laughter anymore. "A business proposition."

She gave in. If she did not listen to him now, he would only dog her steps until she did. When she sighed, she let him see it. "Come this way."

She led the way into the parlor, despite her butler's disapproving tongue-click.

Ah botheration, he was beginning to care. That was a shame. All her servants took her well-being seriously, so much that sometimes she felt as if she was living in a house of parents. Although she changed her London servants more frequently than the ones at home, they had that distressing habit she could not break. Other servants were openly disloyal, but hers—never.

She'd hoped the appropriately named Butler would be more indifferent, but apparently not. He was falling into the guardianship the rest of her servants assumed.

"Your companion has a convenient way of disappearing. What happened to her this time?" Wolverley asked her.

"Have you been watching us, waiting for your moment?" she demanded of him. And why should that notion shorten her breath and make her heart beat faster? The very idea of anyone watching her should appall her, but in Wolverley's case, it did not.

He shrugged, but a wary look entered his eyes. Wolverley's gray eyes were strangely expressive, changing color with the light and his mood. Most disconcerting. "And why would I watch you, Virginia?"

She ignored his impertinent question. "Mrs. Dauntry is attending a family wedding in the country," she informed him. She gestured to a chair. "Do sit down."

Virginia chose a dark green velvet chair, putting distance between them. She liked the relative somberness of the furniture in this room. It had a cozy air she enjoyed when the weather was chilly, as it was today. Unseasonably so. The flowers in the garden dripped tears of rain.

Flipping up the heavy skirts of his slate-blue town coat, Wolverley accepted her invitation. "I thought Mrs. Dauntry attended a family wedding earlier in the season."

"She did." Annoyance touched her, but she let it go. Or did her best to. Trust Wolverley to notice. "She has a large family."

"She must have."

"Her absence gives me time for myself," she added. "Which means I would rather you kept your visit brief."

Wolverley did nothing but laugh. "If you were not so beautiful, you would not attract so much attention."

She did not give that any credence, and from Wolverley, who knew her as well as anyone, it came as a tease rather than a compliment. She knew the truth. She had something that drew suitors far more than her looks ever did. "Or as rich."

Wolverley, who could easily double her worth, shrugged. "Most of them don't need money. What they want is a lovely wife, someone to care for them and make them feel important."

"And take care of their estates, and while they're at it, give them an heir or two."

Unfortunately word had spread that Virginia inherited the bulk of her husband's fortune. Only the entailed property had gone to the cousin who inherited the title. That had made her cousin-in-law as mad as fire, but there was little either of them could do about it. Even if she wanted to, which she didn't. She had a purpose and independence she'd never dreamed of having when her parents told her they'd found a husband for her.

There was no love lost between her late husband and his cousins, so how Jamie could have expected more than the bare minimum, she would never know.

Her husband's legacy had bestowed precious independence on Virginia. She had vowed never, ever to be at the mercy of any man again. And the only way to do that was to remain unmarried.

However, the inheritance made her an enticing prospect for remarriage. Suitors had flocked to her until she'd managed to persuade all of them that she was not in need of another husband. Or a lover, come to that.

Her marriage had produced no offspring, and as a result, most of society considered her barren, an opinion she had subtly fostered. That had deterred a few more suitors, but not this one.

"You should marry your cousin." Wolverley drawled the words. He knew perfectly well that she wouldn't do that.

"Dulverton isn't my cousin. He is my late husband's cousin and none of my concern."

"Marrying him would save you from the incessant courting." Trust Wolverley to point that out. Her constant put-downs did not deter him from taking an interest in her business.

The maid came in with a tray of tea and, Virginia was interested to notice, freshly baked scones. The tray was placed on the side table at Virginia's elbow, and the maid disappeared after stealing a quick glance at Wolverley.

The tray held treats galore. Most visitors got bread and butter if they were lucky. Even the most fashionable hostesses rarely served anything else, in deference to the refined taste of their guests. Virginia wasn't ashamed of enjoying a scone or two.

She waited until the maid left before answering her guest. "I am fortunate, or so my mother informs me. She would like me to marry Jamie, too. To listen to my parents, it's my duty."

Finally, they had no jurisdiction over her. She could make her own decisions. That felt so good, she didn't want to give it up. Ever.

Her parents did not come to town, but her mother's frequent letters meant Virginia knew what she thought about every topic imaginable. Her father, too, subscribed to the missives. She did not lack for advice, none of which she paid any heed to. Sometimes she didn't read them at all.

Although her marriage had been the choice of her parents rather than herself, she had welcomed it. She never regretted marrying Ralph. Well, only occasionally. Her marriage had not been a bed of roses, but it was infinitely better than what she had left behind. The discipline, the punishments, the little cruelties all aimed to make her cowed and obedient. They had the opposite effect. Now nobody had the right to tell her what to do.

She would not marry again. She was done with that.

"They'll say you were here for hours, that you're my lover. You know that, don't you?" Her hand was steady as she poured the tea. She was just reminding him that he couldn't stay long, exaggerating to make her point.

Before he could come to her, she rose and went to him with his tea. Wolverley placed the porcelain dish in its deep saucer on the table by his side. She also handed him the small silver tray with the scones and butter.

He crossed his legs, unconsciously displaying his fine calves. Gentlemen prided themselves on possessing a shapely calf. Virginia was perfectly aware that Wolverley did not care. He was merely getting more comfortable.

He gave an unconcerned shrug, the shoulders of his coat revealing very little padding. "I doubt it. Your reputation goes before you, Virginia. Besides, everyone knows we are neighbors in the country. Your reputation will survive spending an hour with me." He nodded to the open door. "That is more than enough. Any gossip will escape like smoke into the air above us when I leave." He flittered his hand to illustrate his words.

He was right. Virginia's solid reputation for propriety and good behavior could easily survive a visit from a friend and neighbor. Even Wolverley.

"Have you no other relatives who can act as chaperones?" he asked. "Mrs. Dauntry has a habit of leaving you on your own."

Mrs. Dauntry's absences gave Virginia a respite from society affairs. They suited one another well.

But she wouldn't tell that to Wolverley.

"I have to shift for myself, since my parents do not come to town. Neither do my other relatives." Exactly as she liked it. Virginia kept a careful distance from her parents.

"I have no relatives, or none who will acknowledge my mother. Therefore *I* do not acknowledge *them*."

Although he finished brightly, Virginia knew how much he cared. His lovely, clever mother had committed the worst sin of all; she was the daughter of a yeoman farmer, and therefore completely unacceptable to his relatives. Wolverley's father had discovered her working in her father's dairy.

The scandal, though old, retained much of its power. Wolverley was grudgingly received at court, though to Virginia's knowledge he had gone only once. His fortune went a long way toward canceling out gossip about his low-born mother.

Wolverley was devoted to his mother. He would not go anywhere the countess was scorned, and he refused to keep her a secret. Society would be happier if he did.

Virginia liked Lady Wolverley and saw no reason to avoid her now that her own husband wasn't here to reprove her. Ralph had disapproved of the upstart, as he'd put it. Virginia had no such scruples, so after her period of mourning, she'd made a point of visiting the lady.

"People are leaving London for the country," he said, reaching for another scone. "Town is almost empty."

The plate contained only one scone now, testament to Wolverley's prodigious talent for making food disappear. If a person did not watch closely, it would appear that the offering melted away by magic.

He put his plate down, then turned to meet her gaze, his own serious. Society would not recognize the amusing rogue in this grave man. But she did.

"To our business, if I may. I want to buy a house that is currently in your possession. Combe Manor."

She heard the words with a kind of dull inevitability, as if Wolverley could read her mind, which was far from the case. He couldn't have Combe Manor, and Virginia could not tell him why. That put her in a devilish awkward position.

"I have not visited it for years," she said lightly, "but Ralph was fond of it. He used to go sea fishing there. It's small but substantially built. Ralph told me smugglers lived there, but I think he was teasing me." Not that Ralph had done much teasing. An army general, already retired when she'd met him, her husband had a stern demeanor that descended into irritability with increasing frequency. "I plan to pay it a visit this summer."

"Why are you going there?" His expression had not changed, but his voice was tighter.

"To assess its condition. I would have my man of business look it over, but I am heading that way soon, so I thought I would do it myself. If you must know, I plan to establish an orphanage there."

"An orphanage," he said, so quietly she almost missed it.

Since Ralph's death, Virginia had made quite a name as a philanthropist. She had opened ten orphanages in Devonshire and Cornwall, and planned to open ten more. In her late husband's memory of course. "You have an objection?" she added frostily. What she did with her property was none of his business.

This grave-eyed, serious man stared at her with none of his usual insouciant protection. His emotions were completely bare.

Virginia swallowed. What had she provoked here?

He was tight-lipped, angry, but a bleakness lay behind his eyes. He wanted this property badly, she guessed.

It was as if a stranger had walked into her parlor, a handsome man she found irresistibly attractive, even more than the carefree Wolverley he showed to society. This revealed his soul, his heart.

But he was gone in a flash. If she had not seen that side of him before, she'd have thought it was her imagination, so quickly did his expression change to his usual mien.

"What is it?" she said softly. "Why do you want that house so much?"

He changed to brisk and businesslike, but although he didn't fool her, she let him guide the conversation and show her what he wanted to. "Combe Manor was my mother's childhood home. Her parents rented it from your husband's family before she met my father. When she was ill in the spring, she spoke of it often. I would like to buy it for her."

Lady Wolverley had suffered a severe bout of influenza, so bad that her doctor had feared for her life.

"She has the dower house. Surely that is better than a run-down manor."

"The house would be my gift to her." He got to his feet and strode to the fireplace, touching one of the two cherubs she had just carefully arranged. As if he'd touched her, Virginia shivered.

"I am not inclined to sell." By the terms of her husband's will she could not, but he must not know that.

"It's a small part of what you own," he said, still not looking at her but staring at the porcelain putto. "The unentailed part of the estate was larger than the tail, and you inherited it all. What is a small Devonshire mansion to you?"

He put the figurine down so carefully, it barely made a sound. Then he turned to face her, eyes hard, lines bracketing his mouth. "I can recompense you handsomely."

His gravity disturbed her. It reached a part of her deep inside that nobody else had even discovered, that core of her she kept to herself.

"I will not sell." Could not.

She could, however, tell him as much as possible, try to make him understand. Because Wolverley was not an easy man to cross, and like a dog with a bone, he would not let go.

"Before Ralph died, he spoke to me about the orphans he'd encountered in his military career. He'd come across a child wandering across a battlefield after the conflict, searching for his parents in the piles of bloody bodies, and the sight struck him to the heart. It was his dearest wish to care for at least some of those children. I establish the orphanages for children of soldiers left alone through war, and I am glad to have the resources to do so."

Ralph had made a bargain with her. When he'd made his latest will, he'd offered her everything he could leave her. In return for the property, she had to create the orphanages for him.

"Promise me!" he'd said, and pushed an old Bible at her. "You will follow my instructions to the letter. In return, you may have everything else. Or I will leave you nothing, and you will have to return to your parents."

That didn't bear thinking about. Life before her marriage had been hard enough. To return to them, a woman too old to marry, with no fortune to offer, didn't bear thinking about.

Placing her hand on the book, she'd sworn an oath to establish the orphanages. Since there'd been no witnesses, the oath wasn't legally binding, but Virginia didn't care about that. She would never renege on her vow to him. Promises were important.

"I can give you a better house in exchange," he suggested. "One more suitable for an orphanage. Or are you intent on denying my mother her wish?"

"I'm sure your mother will be glad to know that her childhood home is being put to such good use."

"I see." His voice was hard now. Virginia could almost be afraid of him. But she did not choose to be afraid of anyone, and for her, fear was a choice. "It isn't suitable for your orphanage. It's too close to the sea and too small. Let me give you another house further inland instead."

"No."

"What difference can it make where you house your brats? Sell to me."

Her brats? The word revealed his annoyance.

She countered with her own annoyance. "I don't plan to sell to anyone. My plans will not change."

"Hoarding your property?" Now he was ice-cold. He stared at her as if she was something stuck to the sole of his boot. "I never took you for a miser, Virginia."

He was inviting her to justify herself, but she refused to do so. Apart from her promise to Ralph, she owed nobody—including the Earl of Wolverley—an explanation. She glared at him.

"Very well." He shrugged as if the matter was trivial, which she knew it was not, and just like that, his flirtatious, warm mood returned. He donned it like a coat.

Virginia felt bereft, as if that brief glimpse he'd given her of the man within was all she was getting. She had offended him, and she was sorry for it.

Rising, she nodded at the door. "They will most certainly talk if you are here any longer. People are always watching."

"I know. And they watch you because you are eligible and expected to marry again soon. Dulverton has been gone four years now. You are, Virginia my dear, ripe for the plucking." A cold smile curved his mouth. A shiver of danger shimmered between them.

She wished he would not use her name like that, but saying so would draw his attention to it, and he would do it even more once he knew she disliked it. So she let it be. "I have no mind to be plucked," she said tightly. "And no plans to remarry."

"Oh, but you must!" Approaching her, he bore a particularly wicked smile, but no humor lit his steely eyes.

Lifting her hand, he pressed a kiss on the back, the kind a suitor would give to a lady he was planning to court. Gentle, respectful, but with an edge of danger. Few men had the skill to do that with one kiss, but Wolverley could. She'd seen him do that often, even though his intentions were never honorable. Now, on the receiving end of that tactic, she understood its power.

He took in every inch of her silk-clad body, scanning her insolently. His gaze stopped at her throat. "What is this?"

Next to the medallion she always wore, the gold coin Ralph had made into a pendant brooch for her, was a new pin, intertwined letters in silver.

"Oh." She put her hand over the metal, then dropped it again. She was dressed perfectly respectably, a fichu wrapped over her shoulders and tucked into her gown, but he made her feel bare, as if nothing covered her breasts at all. She wanted him gone.

"That is the pin of the SSL. The Society for Single Ladies. Miss Childers has established a club for us. Why should we not have somewhere to go, to meet?"

"Ah! I have heard of it. It is not merely to gossip, is it?"

She shrugged. "Some of the ladies engage in other activities."

Society knew about the SSL now. They had not kept their activities secret for long. Two sensational cases, and people had come to the right conclusion about the purpose of the society.

"Terrifying. What can women not do if they discover their collective power?" he said.

"I'm sure people will find out."

If he was trying to distract her, he was succeeding. Her body had come to life the moment he'd touched her. And from the satisfied expression on his face, he knew it. He hated her refusal to sell him Combe Manor, and he was looking for another way to persuade her. She was not so rustic that she didn't know that.

"You should leave," she said abruptly, moving away from him with a swish of skirts and a haughty lift of her chin. She'd learned a few things herself.

"Of course."

She did not turn when he left the room.

Chapter 2

Francis's anger choked him. His mother deserved better. She deserved *everything*. As Virginia's front door slammed at his back, Francis swore he would change her mind.

What was Combe Manor to her? A small, out-of-the-way house with nothing to commend it, too close to the coast for comfortable living. An odd choice for an orphanage, since it was at the top of a cliff. Surely something inland would serve her purposes better.

He strode down the side of the fashionable square, ignoring the calls from the beggar crouched by the railings of a house further up and the jovial greeting of someone across the street. He was in no mood to be social. If he walked down to Tom's Coffee House, he would probably have exorcised the worst of his mood by then. Three miles should just about do it.

Virginia was hugging her inheritance like a child clutching a favorite doll, refusing to release so much as a hair off its head. Estates such as hers were to use, to put to work, to make more prosperous. But her attitude when he'd asked what he thought a modest favor, as if he'd tried to rip the clothes off her back...

The vivid picture of Virginia, silk dripping off her naked skin like petals off a rose in a heavy downpour, came to his mind and he could not shift it. His body stirred, responding to his imagination instantly, as it always did when he thought of her. But that was his secret, and nobody, least of all Virginia, knew of it.

He had started calling her by her first name when he discovered it irritated her. During her marriage, they behaved distantly but with cordiality. He had wanted so much more that he hadn't trusted himself. Even then they had met frequently, mostly at social events. After her husband died, he continued to visit her because—because he found her name on his lips tantalizing. He always had, since he'd first seen her as a new bride of eighteen. But he'd seen the summary dismissal she'd given to the men who flocked around her after Ralph's death, and fearing the loss of the tenuous connection they shared, he'd held off courting her.

Although he dearly wanted to.

Her cool, dark beauty held him as no other woman had ever done. That glossy, near-black hair that she rarely powdered, the glittering blue eyes, the graceful stature—she entranced him, and she had no idea she was doing it.

Maybe he could get his revenge another way. One far more public, and one which suited him better. People did not ignore him these days or treat him as if he did not matter. He'd vanquished that demon years ago. He suspected Virginia was following her husband's directives, not her own, as if Ralph could treat him as inferior in death, as he had in life.

His parents had broken the two rules society lived by; they came from different social spheres, and they were in love. Marriage was a business, not a personal choice. After his father's death, when Francis was eighteen, society had chosen to turn its collective back. So Francis had set out to change their minds.

On his Grand Tour, an event his mother insisted he indulge in, instead of wasting his time with whores and substandard art, Francis had made a number of interesting contacts. And because of that, he was now wealthy, untouchable. He'd turned a venerable title of doubtful value into a glossy, prosperous series of ventures. Society could not ignore him now.

And now he wanted Virginia. He'd waited long enough.

Whether she knew it or not, Virginia had issued a challenge, and he had no hesitation in snatching up the gauntlet.

What possible use would she have for Combe Manor? If she'd seen it, she'd know it was not at all suitable as a house for small children. It was miles away from the nearest village, so supplies would be difficult to obtain, and it was too close to the cliff edge to be safe. On the other hand, if one wanted to dispose of a number of infants, it would be perfect. Perhaps she would change her mind after she'd seen it, but he did not intend to wait on her whim.

When his father had met his mother, she had been living at the manor. Her father was a yeoman farmer, reasonably prosperous, but they rented the house from Lord Dulverton. Celia had control of the dairy after her mother's early death, ensuring that society would forever call her "the dairymaid."

And now Francis wanted the house back. His mother's recent illness made him anxious to give her something that meant a lot to her, and he'd settled on Combe Manor.

He could combine his natural desire for Virginia with his other aim. Perhaps get the manor and the woman.

He would pay Virginia court over the next few weeks. Cling to her, get her to acknowledge they were more than friends, even though they were not. Single her out. In short, pester her until she acceded to his request.

Although the season was drawing to a close, one event remained. He would make the most of Lady Conyngham's ball.

Her response when he'd kissed her hand—that was his clue. Although it was also hers. He'd meant the gesture to be mocking, but it had not ended that way.

When he'd touched her, magic had thrilled through his fingers, chasing his original intentions out of his head. The instinct not to release her hand but to draw her close and find out what her lips tasted like had overwhelmed him. Only his common sense reasserting itself had stopped him from taking it further. Every time he touched her was like that for him. Even though he expected it these days, it still struck him like a mallet to the brain.

Virginia prided herself on her reputation for correctness. Not a stain marked her character, even since she had re-entered society a year after Dulverton's passing. Francis would show her how easily that could be overturned. If he pursued his attraction to her in public, if he made his admiration clear, then others would follow. They always did. London might be thin of company, but it was not bereft of it. And Francis had always led, never followed.

His gamble would not be half-hearted on his part, because he wanted Virginia badly. If his play ended with their union, then he for one would not be sorry.

He'd faced the sorry fact years ago that he had fallen desperately in love with her on sight. Although he'd worked very hard at falling out of love, it had not happened yet.

There was the problem of her fertility. Society had decided Virginia a barren wife, and Ralph had often jokingly remarked that it wasn't for want of him trying. He'd had a particularly carrying voice, so everyone who used the same club as he did knew that.

Even if she was not barren, bearing a first child at the age of thirty would not be an easy thing. And Francis feared for her. The conundrum had tangled him up for years. He knew the ways of preventing conception, but none of them were anywhere near foolproof.

Virginia might not be the wealthiest lady in society, but she had a tidy sum, and it was all disposable. No entails, no compulsion to retain the property for the next heir. The fortune hunters went wild. Again. She had deterred them once, but without his help, she'd find it difficult to accomplish that again, if he signaled that she was ready to be courted again.

He would keep them off her, but only if she asked. And if she did that, he'd tell her his price.

Francis strode around the corner, nearly colliding with a small brat who lay in waiting, presumably to pickpocket what he could. He stopped the lad running away by the expedient of gripping his shoulder while he searched himself. Purse, watch, rings, earring, all present and correct. He let the child go and continued to the house he had hired for the season.

Inside, the residence was in a state of turmoil. Traveling trunks stood in the hall, and footmen were adding to the stack. He had to dodge around them to get to the back parlor, where his mother was enjoying a dish of tea. Obligingly, she held up the pot, but he shook his head. He'd had enough tea for one day.

His lovely mother was as serene as always.

After bending to kiss her cheek, relieved to find her temperature normal after her recent bout of influenza, he took the chair opposite hers. "The trunks are yours?"

"Yes. I'll leave for the country early tomorrow morning, immediately after the Conyngham ball."

He raised a brow. "I thought you intended to do some shopping."

"I've done it." She looked away.

Francis's hackles rose when he saw her defensive move. "Has someone insulted you again? Tell me who, and I will ensure they never do so again."

She smiled at him, her blue eyes shining. "Not at all. And I care very little for that."

"Truth?"

"Absolute truth." She crossed her heart in a gesture that took him right back to his childhood. Society also took it amiss that Celia had chosen to rear her son herself, rather than entrusting him to nurses and tutors, something that had increased their bond.

Francis could not have wished for a better start in life.

"Then why so soon?"

Her mouth flattened. "Since I've just promised the truth, I'll tell you. I'm tired, Francis. I want to go home."

"Then I will escort you."

"No. I know you were not planning to leave so soon. Please don't make a fuss, dear. I'll do very well with my entourage of carriages and servants that you insist on surrounding me with. Truly, I will spend the time sleeping, and I will be better without you. Jane will accompany me."

Jane was the widow of Francis's late uncle, and after his death, she and his mother had become unexpectedly firm friends. She had joined Celia for her month in London, and both ladies enjoyed themselves hugely, or so they said.

Nevertheless, he insisted. "It would be a pleasure to escort you."

She humphed. "No, it would not. You would be bored senseless. Stay and attend a few of those terrible dens of iniquity men frequent when the women are not about." She fixed him with a perceptive stare. "But do not get into trouble."

Just as if he was a recalcitrant schoolboy. He grinned. "I wouldn't dream of such a thing."

"Indeed, dear, but you're in a temper, are you not? Don't think I cannot see you."

He knew when he was beaten. And truthfully, he did surround her with armed guards and provide her with the most comfortable carriage he could find. He would ensure the journey was well planned, and his coachman had the list safe.

"I'll escort you to the Conynghams' tonight and get up early to see you off in the morning."

And not get any sleep, because he would be ensuring her trip would be comfortable and uneventful. His mother was the most important woman in his life, and she would continue to be so for the foreseeable future.

* * * *

Virginia arrived at the ballroom on her own, but as fortune would have it, just behind her good friend Angela Childers and one of her uncles. For the life of her Virginia couldn't remember which one. All Angela's uncles were on her mother's side, the aristocratic one. To do them justice, most did not care about the wealth she had inherited from her father, having, as one told her once, "sufficient." Perhaps being younger brothers of a duke helped. They had all the benefits and none of the responsibility.

Virginia joined Angela, who left her uncle in the card room. The comfortable salon already contained a number of people, who greeted the gentleman like a long-lost friend. They had probably seen him twice already this week.

Progressing to the ballroom proved a little difficult, despite the lateness of the season, because the fortune hunters still abounded. They clustered around Virginia and Angela. The worst compliment the ladies received was something about the extremes of beauty, since Virginia was so dark-haired and Angela so fair. Angela merely glanced at Virginia, who had to fight laughter. No sense encouraging them.

In the far corner of the room sat a group of ladies, most of them sporting the SSL silver pin, as did Angela and Virginia. Angela wore it proudly, along with a set of magnificent diamonds.

Virginia had chosen the center of her stomacher, letting it form the heart of a flower embroidered there. They wore them openly and proudly. With two significant successes to their name, and more minor problems dealt with, people were starting to notice the society was more than the sermonizing club it purported to be.

Spinsters, widows, overlooked daughters who did not "take," all had banded together, friendship first, problem-solving after. Even the august magistrates at Bow Street had noticed, though they publicly scorned the society as amateurs and dilettantes. But the SSL could get to parts of society that Bow Street Runners and magistrates had little chance of breaching.

In the past, the little group of ladies would sit together quietly, unobserved. Not now. The animated gossip and exchange of news warmed Virginia's heart. They were valued, useful, and earning money of their own, which Angela banked for them. A system of trustees ensured the money would stay in their hands, rather than relatives and guardians grabbing the prizes. Virginia was happy for them and thrilled that she'd had a hand in creating the enterprise.

Angela and Virginia had to walk around the edge of the room, since the dancing was about to begin, and although several more gentlemen approached them, Virginia and Angela pretended to be engaged in deep conversation. In fact, Angela was saying, "I'll be glad when I reach forty and men consider me too old to marry."

Virginia laughed. "You will never be too old, my dear. You're too rich for that. Best to find an amenable gentleman who will allow you to retain your property."

Angela's blue-eyed, blond beauty was enhanced by the light of intelligence in her eyes. She would not grow into a pinched and disappointed old maid. She'd be just as lovely at forty.

"I can't trust any of them. Not one. The day I marry, my husband inherits everything I own. How can I let all those people down?"

"Your staff?" Virginia understood that responsibility.

Angela lifted one shoulder in an elegant half shrug. "Staff, clients, everyone who trusts the bank to look after their property."

"You should marry Snell," Virginia remarked, referring to one of her chief managers.

Angela snorted. "And oust his wife and their children? In any case, I don't trust any man not to take over. I won't have it. My father left the bank in my care, and it's my duty to take the greatest care of it."

She paused to glare at an importunate man coming toward them. He spun on his heel and pretended he hadn't meant to talk to them at all but walked past on his way to annoy someone else.

By then they'd reached the end of the room. Greeting the ladies, they took seats where they could, but with the voluminous skirts every woman wore for balls, that task proved difficult. Virginia's white-and-yellow striped gown, decorated with tiny snowdrops around the hem, would take up a sofa on its own. She opted to remain standing and refused to take the seat Miss McLennon offered her.

"I am fine, not at all unable to stand," she protested, laughing. "Did you find Lady Cameron's ring?"

Miss McLennon made a sound of disgust. "It was down the back of a sofa in her drawing room. She accused everyone she knew of stealing it, and yet she had not even asked the maids to do a thorough search! She came to the SSL determined to kick up a fuss, but that was the easiest of tasks. I still made her pay for my time."

"She was looking for attention," Virginia remarked. "Her husband does not pay her a great deal of notice."

Miss McLennon gestured to the people around them. "I dare say she could find solace here. Or another room just like it." Many unhappily married women found solace elsewhere once their husbands strayed.

"Ah, but she adores her husband," Miss McLennon said softly. "I saw enough of that while I was there. She has his picture *everywhere*. He gave her that ring, and I am certain she keeps it as a precious memento of something or other."

A hush fell at the end of the room as Virginia was talking to Miss McLennon, her back to the company. Alerted to the tension around her, Virginia turned around, taking her time. Until she saw who had entered the room.

At the far end of the white-and-gold room, with its feminine curlicues and twists, stood two men. Two extremely masculine men. But they did not look as if they didn't belong there. They looked as if they owned the place.

Despite his elaborate silks and lace, the Duke of Colston Magna fooled nobody. He was no namby-pamby idiot. Inside that outrageous pink silk coat resided a powerful male with a fearsome reputation for never losing a duel, or a bout of fisticuffs. Those lily-white hands had pounded Col's opponent into oblivion more than once in the boxing studio.

"One wonders why he is so angry. Beneath that pretty surface he is *simmering,*" Angela murmured.

The Earl of Wolverley wore scarlet and gold, the brilliants sewn into his waistcoat flashing as he moved. But not as much as his eyes. Those eyes held the promise of murder, and Virginia was afraid it was for her. Although they had parted on ostensibly amicable terms, he had not fooled her with his soft talk of pins and neighborly concern.

Virginia and Angela stood together, facing the incoming storm. The men fixed their eyes on them and did not look away as they made their way toward them past all the other guests.

The diamond dangling below Wolverley's earlobe flashed as he turned his head when a woman laughed nervously. Then he returned his attention to Virginia. As the men walked up to them, the women switched places, a swift rustling of skirts loud in the suddenly quiet room. The quartet accompanying the dancers had paused between sets. Conversation around them was muted. Or perhaps Virginia only imagined it that way.

The men made their bows, beautiful pattern cards of obeisance.

Col asked for Virginia's hand in the next set of country dances. Shooting a triumphant glare at Wolverley, she accepted, graciously placing her hand on Col's chilly satin sleeve.

"Hasn't the weather turned cold?" she inquired as he led her onto the floor.

"It has, and after the wonderful sunshine we've been having lately!" he answered, full of bonhomie but glancing past her to where Angela and Wolverley were standing, waiting for the dance to begin.

When she glanced at Angela, she caught a lovelorn gaze from Wolverley, there for all to see.

Virginia gritted her teeth. That one fraught glance told Virginia what he was at. Retribution would not be long in coming. And well, she would have to learn to live with it. How dare he make his intentions so obvious? The whole of London would be talking about his approach tomorrow. His volte-face would be noted and gossiped about in every house in the country.

Before this night, their connection was known but not remarked upon, since they behaved in a suitably neighborly way. But if he made his change of heart so obvious, that opinion would change in a flash.

Tonight, Wolverley gazed at her from afar, the wistful longing of a suitor. Or a lover. All the way through the dance he never let his attention stray, gazing at her as if she was all he could see, watching her dance with her other partners.

She wanted to slap that stupid expression off his face, and Virginia did not consider herself a violent woman.

Ladies gossiped behind their fans, and gentlemen laughed softly as they watched. By the end of this evening, they would believe that she and Wolverley were lovers.

Damn him to hell and back. She could curse all she liked in her mind, but outwardly she kept the polite smile on her face and her attention on her partner in the dance.

Unfortunately country dances meant changes of partner. They were social dances, until they ended with their original partner at the end of the piece. Short of stalking away from the dance floor, which would create a scandal all its own, she would have to face Wolverley and dance with him. Avoiding gossip was all but impossible.

The remaining company in London were avidly waiting for a scandal, something to enliven the gossip over the teacups. Virginia refused to provide it. Utterly refused.

When Wolverley faced her in the dance, he smiled in that way she'd seen when he flirted with women. No, not flirted, but indicated something deeper.

As they crossed in the dance, she hissed at him, "I am *not* your mistress, and I will never be."

"Did I ask you that?" His deep voice resonated through her, thrilling those parts of her she worked hard to keep dormant. "I would not suggest such a thing." He paused while they executed steps that separated them then brought them back together. "Unless I thought you wanted it."

That last was delivered in such a sultry tone that made her palms itch. That would have thrilled the spectators. Two more measures and she was done with him. "I would never wish for it. You know that, Wolverley."

"I know no such thing. We have been dancing around each other for years, rather like we are doing now. Isn't it time we faced what lies between us?"

For a moment, a fraction of a second, he gazed at her as if she was his world, as if he meant the nonsense he was parroting. Then it was gone, frustratingly covered by a flirtatious smile, as if she'd said something witty.

So she laughed. A little too high-pitched, but it would serve to persuade people that nothing was serious here. *Move along, people, find the next show.* "You're angry with me, but this is unfair."

"Is it? Nothing is unfair in war or love. Surely you know that."

She turned the old saying back the right way. Love came first. "I know nothing of *love or war.*"

She had said too much. Virginia bit her lip, desperately searching for something to cover her sentence. But she was too late.

As she made to move on in the dance, back to Colston Magna, Wolverley said, his voice soft and low, "Then I shall teach you."

His breath grazed her ear, making her gasp.

Somebody else had said that to her once. Revulsion filled her, so sudden that she recoiled from it, and the duke had to catch her elbow to steady her. She pretended she'd stumbled, and thanked him, forcing another light laugh. "My mother always said I could trip on a speck of dust. Thank you, sir."

"Think nothing of it," he said somberly. "Madam, if the Wolf troubles you too much, I will stand your friend."

The last thing she wanted to do was to draw any more attention to this atrocious business. "Wolverley? No, we have known each other for years."

Damn the man.

Chapter 3

After thanking the duke and allowing him to return her to the sanctuary of the single ladies' corner, Virginia determined to surround herself with her friends from the club, but unfortunately someone else approached her. James, Lord Dulverton, the man who had inherited the title when Ralph died.

She gave him a cautious smile. "Jamie, how good to see you. I didn't realize you were still in London."

Jamie's round, open face, enhanced by dark eyes, would be considered handsome by many, but Virginia had known him when his features were less welcoming. He had expected the bulk of Ralph's private fortune to come to him, too, but he had never commented on Ralph's will, not in public at any rate. In private he'd raged. Only once, but that had been enough to show her his real feelings.

Jamie was four years younger than Virginia, but that had not deterred him embarking on a determined courtship, until Virginia told him frankly that she did not intend to marry anyone ever again. The cordiality between them was diminished from what it had been in Ralph's lifetime, but it still existed. She could understand Jamie's sense of betrayal when he'd discovered how Ralph had apportioned his estate, but not his attitude to it.

Truthfully, she was surprised Ralph hadn't told Jamie about his plan. But the secrecy was typical of her late husband, as she had reason to know. These days Virginia and Jamie shared a cautious peace, more in the nature of a truce.

"I should warn you that our mutual neighbor Sir Bertram Dean is in town with his family," Jamie said. "He's at it again. Now he thinks that nobody will notice if he claims the spinney at the bottom of Combe Hill as his own. The deeds to that particular parcel of land remain with you, so I have to ask for your aid in refuting him."

"Old coot!" she said without rancor. Dean had done everything to get that spinney. "I shall certainly provide you with everything you need." Sir Bertram deserved a set-down. "I don't have my companion with me at the moment, so calling on me would be difficult. Is your mother in town, so I may call on you?"

"No, she is still in the country." Jamie's eyes hardened. He had brown eyes, so like Ralph's, and that expression was too reminiscent of her late husband for Virginia's liking. "But that doesn't stop you receiving male visitors, does it?"

How annoying that someone had reported it. "Wolverley, you mean? We had some business regarding the estate."

His lips tightened. "Anything I should know about?"

Now he was really beginning to annoy her. She shrugged. "He wanted to buy Combe Manor. I refused his request. Nothing has changed."

The music changed to a lighter tune, and she glanced over his shoulder. Another set was forming. Wolverley was dancing with the second oldest Conyngham daughter. Her lips curved. He had not escaped Lady Conyngham's clutches, then. Served him right.

"I'm glad to hear it. Mama never approved of him. You do not have to receive Wolverley at all."

She injected a chilly tone into her voice. "Who I receive does not concern you."

Jamie crooked his arm and held it out. Either she laid her hand on it, or she embarrassed him by refusing, and caused more gossip. So she took it and tried not to sigh too hard. He raised a bushy brow. "Do you find my company so tedious?"

Should she tell him the truth and say yes? Instead, she smiled gently. "Of course I do not."

He began to walk, so of course she had to move with him. Casting an apologetic glance behind her at the ladies, she promenaded with Jamie around the edge of the dance floor. People watched them, of course. Since the explosive nature of Ralph's will had become known, they awaited developments. Most had expected a marriage, but Virginia had disappointed them.

They paused to speak to a few people, and Virginia did her best to ignore Wolverley glaring at her from the dance floor like the jealous lover he had no right to be. His partner nudged him, and with a laugh, which Virginia saw rather than heard, he turned back to her.

Perhaps letting Jamie pay public attention to her would confuse the gossips. But she did not want to be labeled a flirt, either. This balancing of attention was so damned difficult. Being aloof was infinitely easier.

Jamie followed the exchange. "You need a large footman, someone to deter him. I am alarmed that someone should barge into your house in that way, Virginia. Would you permit me to recommend someone?"

When he used her first name, it didn't have the same effect as when Wolverley used it. She felt no thrills, no desire to get closer to him.

"I have two burly footmen in my house, Jamie, and if required, they could have dealt with Wolverley. I doubt it would have taken their efforts to persuade him to leave. He is, after all, a gentleman."

Jamie spared a glance to where Wolverley was observing them from the dance floor. "Are you sure?" He smiled at Wolverley and then turned away to concentrate on her.

"Positive, but I thank you for your concern." She wanted only her own servants in her house. They should all answer directly to her. Obviously word had spread about Wolverley's visit, but normally, people would dismiss any concerns. Now, thanks to Wolverley's totally unwarranted attention, it would rise again.

Drat the man.

Stepping onto the floor with Jamie, she passed Wolverley on his way off it. Resisting the temptation to thumb her nose at him, she bestowed a gracious smile on him instead. The man had the effrontery to kiss the tips of his fingers and extend them gracefully, as if sending his kiss to her.

Virginia ignored him.

* * * *

Francis left the dance floor smiling. His gesture had not gone unnoticed. Nor would his future advances. He must take care, lest he seriously compromise her and set her against him. He didn't want to marry her under any cloud.

Lady Dulverton was dazzlingly lovely. Despite her determined attempt to behave older than her years, that only added a gracious elegance to her appearance. And her dark, nearly black hair did not take powder well, so she mostly left it off. That meant she was often the only dark head in a sea of powdered hair. Easy to spot.

"Has her own style, don't she?"

He turned his head to see Col watching him with amusement. "You're still here? I thought you'd taken off for pastures new an hour ago."

Col drew a gold-and-enamel snuffbox from his coat pocket and regarded it critically, tracing the outline of a tiny Venus with the tip of his finger.

"I wouldn't miss this show for the world, dear boy. It's far more amusing than anything that has shown in the theaters this season. I fear Garrick is losing his touch, but you could easily replace him."

The company was so thin Francis could have struck a theatrical pose, arm up, leg back, eyes staring into something in the distance, and not hit anybody. Instead he chose to lift his arm and put the back of his hand to his forehead in the accepted gesture for despair.

"You wound poor Garrick, sir! How could you imagine anything more divine than his Richard III!"

"Effortlessly," Col said, unimpressed. He lifted a minuscule pinch of snuff to his nose, sniffed and flourished his lace-edged handkerchief as he snapped the box closed and returned it to his pocket. "But if you continue to court Lady Dulverton in public, you'll have to propose, you know. What if she accepts?"

Francis gave him a derisive grin. "Maybe I'll let her."

"She might," Col said. "I've seen the way she looks at you when she thinks she's unobserved. You've hidden your tendre very well, my dear, but you don't fool me."

Francis stuck his hands in his pockets inelegantly. "You're deluded."

"No, I'm not." Col moved, his controlled grace the result of hours spent in the fencing salon. "Meanwhile, I must go and worship at the feet of my latest obsession. If I do not make haste, someone else will take Miss Childers in to supper."

"You're wasting your time. She will take no one to husband."

Col shrugged. "I know. I'm not concerned about her fortune, only all that loveliness going to waste." He shot Francis a sharp glance as if about to say something, but then thought better of it and looked away.

Francis's gaze strayed to Virginia, now dancing with the younger Harris boy and trying not to look bored. He knew her too well. The slight movement of her body, the way she fixed her concentration on her partner in the dance told him that whatever young Gregory was saying, she was trying hard not to yawn. He smiled at the slight movement of her jaw.

"Good luck with your quarry," he murmured as Col walked away in the direction of Spinster's Corner. Truly, since the SSL had come into existence, that corner saw more activity than the rest of the ballroom.

* * * *

After an hour, Francis finally made his way into the supper room to find that she was not there. When he found Col sitting at a cozy table for two with Miss Childers, he discovered Virginia had not yet entered the supper room.

Where had she gone? Vaguely disturbed, he took a stroll around the other rooms open to the guests, barely dodging another of Lady Conyngham's daughters. The eldest and most desperate, at that.

While the ladies of the SSL had found something useful to do with their time, the oldest Conyngham spent most of her days whining. That high-pitched nasal tone had found its way into the nightmares of several eligible men. However if he told her she should forget marriage and men would come flocking, she wouldn't believe him and probably accuse him of insulting her.

So he would not. He would merely do as every other man did and take care she did not trap him in a corner.

Virginia was not in the supper room, nor had she returned to the ballroom, where the musicians were taking a well-earned rest. Guests moved onto the floor and stood with glasses of wine chattering, but Virginia was not among them. She had not sought sanctuary in the music room either, or the card room.

His disquiet forced him to continue to search for her.

He was strolling along the hallway upstairs where the ladies had been given a retiring room when he heard the scream. Not loud, and quickly suppressed, but he needed no more than that to recognize Virginia's voice. The sound had come from behind a door further up the corridor. After a false start, he found it.

The room was a bedchamber, from the looks of it a guest room, since there were no personal items on display. When he saw what had transpired here, Francis locked the door behind him and pocketed the key.

This was a trap if ever he'd seen one. The candles set in wall sconces around the room softly illuminated his quarry. Virginia sat on the bed, her cheeks and bosom flushed, her clothes in disarray and her hair tousled, not at all the neat, glossy bun and carefully arranged curls that had been on display in the ballroom.

Dulverton leaned over her, one palm against the mattress, the other gripping Virginia's shoulder. He glanced over his shoulder with a grin of triumph, but when he saw Francis, he lost the smile. Who was Dulverton expecting? His brother, with a troupe of guests to witness his conquest? But he'd tried too hard for the conquest.

Dulverton took his time straightening. He shot Francis a triumphant smile. "Ah, Wolverley. You may congratulate us."

"No, you may not," Virginia snapped sharply.

"Not unless you include me in your charming tryst." Francis added an insulting drawl to his voice, strolling over to the bed as if he truly intended to join them. "Really, Dulverton, you have no imagination at all. Did you truly believe you could shame Virginia into marrying you?"

He stood, staring down at her as Dulverton straightened. His neckcloth was askew, and he had a nasty gleam in his eyes. "I'll thank you to take yourself off," Dulverton said.

Francis continued to give Virginia all his attention. Although she was putting a brave face on, she was shaken. Her breath came in short gasps, making her bosom quiver under the tight lacing, and her hands were trembling. She had lost her famous poise and appeared younger and far too vulnerable.

Francis's heart went out to her. Finally, after sending Virginia an unspoken message of reassurance, he lifted his head and confronted Jamie Dulverton.

He was bright-eyed, glaring at Francis as if he wanted to turn him to stone. Francis was not surprised.

"You may leave us," Jamie said.

"I am not a servant," Francis reminded him. If Dulverton had known Francis better, that quiet, steady tone might have alarmed him. But unfortunately—for Dulverton—he did not. He had never been very good at assessing people's moods.

Francis turned his head, not giving Dulverton the chance to issue a challenge, formal or otherwise, and addressed Virginia. "Do you want me to leave, Virginia?"

"Not at all," she answered instantly. "But I would like Jamie to leave. I fear he's been overcome by the drink—or something."

From the red mark adorning Dulverton's cheek, Francis would put twenty guineas on the "something" being a hard slap. Good for her.

She spoke, her voice firmer than before. "Jamie, while your attention is flattering, I do not want to consider marrying anyone. I am enjoying what I have, and I have—things—to do before I even think about marrying again."

"I'm deeply relieved to discover this was an honorable offer of marriage," Francis said, aware of his own sanctimoniousness, "instead of a dishonorable proposal. However, Dulverton, I fear your time has passed. Would you like me to let you out?"

Plucking the key out of his pocket, he flourished it.

Someone tried the door. Then they tried it again.

"Perhaps we should wait," Francis murmured.

Dulverton swallowed. Then he nodded, flushing even redder than before. He'd been found out and he knew it. The door-rattlers would no doubt be the witnesses invited to force Virginia's decision and then to congratulate the happy pair. They were out of luck.

He seemed almost relieved. Francis marked the swift change of expression but did not comment on it.

"I will let you out now," Francis said. "Five minutes after that, I will follow, and we will tell no one that anyone else was in the room. Lady Dulverton may leave in her own time. If she is discovered on her own, why then, she has mistaken this room for the room set aside for the guests' use."

Dulverton nodded and turned to Virginia. "Indeed, I beg your pardon. I did not intend for this to go so far. I merely meant to appeal to you to consider my proposal. I have the greatest respect for you, and I can only apologize for alarming you."

Mending his boats, Francis thought cynically. So he could come at her again another time. Otherwise, she might bar him from her house. If society got wind of a rift between the two, Dulverton might never find his way back to her.

If Francis had his way, that was exactly what would happen.

He went to the door and waited for Dulverton to join him. Francis unlocked the door and, careful to stay out of sight, let Dulverton leave.

The sound of raucous voices flooded in from the hall.

"Oh, there you are!" in mock surprise, and "Do you have anything to tell us?" put in for good measure.

Touching his finger to his lips to remind Virginia to be silent, Francis let the door swing nearly closed, so he could listen without being seen. If they tried to come in, he would claim he was with them the whole time, and that Virginia had felt faint, so they had together escorted her in here and were about to call a maid.

The voices faded away as the group went up the corridor in the direction of the stairs.

Francis closed the door. Then he locked it.

Chapter 4

Francis turned around to see Virginia huddled on the bed, her arms wrapped protectively around herself. He couldn't bear to see her like that. She'd turned her face away from him, but hair straggled down from the knot at the back of her head to drape over her cheek. Her shoulders slumped in a way he'd never seen on her before, and she looked young and fearful.

Instinctively he knew she wouldn't want anyone to see her like this. Should he leave? No, the very thought of abandoning her made him feel ill.

He crossed the room to her and sat on the bed, giving a good foot and a half of space between them. "What did he do to you? Do I need to call him out?"

She shook her head, releasing more strands of silky hair to join the carefully coiffed curls touching her neck. Earlier he'd watched them teasing her shoulders, longing, as many men in that room did, to touch, to feel the threads of silk running through his fingers, over his skin.

This was about her, not him. Ignoring the wants screaming at him, he gently placed his fingers on her shoulder. "Virginia?"

She spun around and lurched forward, right into his arms. Naturally he closed them around her, all his protective instincts rising to the fore. When she rested her cheek against his chest, the gesture felt natural, as if this was meant to happen. As if she belonged there.

She was shaking, a fine tremor running through her body.

Ignoring the panic rising to shorten his breath, he held her, let her nestle. He touched his lips to the top of her head, so softly she couldn't have felt it. "What is it, sweetheart?"

Damn, he hadn't meant to let that out. Maybe she hadn't heard him properly. If she didn't draw attention to it, then he certainly wouldn't. "Did he hurt you?"

"No." She sucked in a deep breath, her soft bosom lifting. She wasn't wearing a fichu, so the tops of her breasts were bare. Her skin tempted him, drew him, but he kept his hands firmly on her back, supporting her, holding her close.

"He didn't hurt me." Her voice trembled. "No, he did not. But I came to use the ladies' room, and he said there was something he wanted to show me that I would enjoy seeing. So I came with him, in here."

She gave a shaky laugh and buried her face against his chest. The clock on the mantelpiece tinkled the half hour. Neither of them moved. Francis waited until she was ready to speak again. Every one of his muscles tensed, waiting for what she had to tell him.

Eventually she spoke again. "He went down on one knee and asked me to marry him. I told him to get up and stop being foolish."

She dropped her chin, so that Francis couldn't see her eyes. When she looked up again, moving a little away from his chest to look at his face, she was smiling, but those blue eyes were bleak. What had the bastard done to her?

"Jamie got to his feet and dragged me to him. I could hardly breathe. Then he kissed me and tried to force his tongue into my mouth." She shuddered. "How disgusting!"

Disgust was not what Francis had seen. He'd seen fear. Virginia carefully guarded her emotions, and fear was something he had never seen in her before. He wanted to know why. And then he would stop it happening again.

Had nobody done that before with her, or had she just objected to Dulverton doing it? Francis didn't answer her. He had to know more before he gave her his response. He would give her what she needed when he knew what that was.

She went on, sitting very still, her body contained. "I pushed him away, but I lost my balance and fell back onto the bed. I was lying in a tumble of skirts and hoops and trying to make some sense of it when he came on top of me. He nearly crushed me. He was so heavy, and I lost my breath. Then he kissed me again."

Francis tried not to hold her too tightly, but he longed to pull her close, surround her with himself. But how foolish would that be, after Dulverton had mauled her?

"Did he do anything else?"

He held his breath until she said, "Isn't that enough? I could not bear it. He treated me as if I meant nothing, as if I was his to do whatever he wished to. I pushed him away, I sat up, and he got off me. I slapped him. Then you came."

He breathed out very slowly. Dulverton had done no more than behave clumsily. But Virginia was behaving as if nobody had done that to her before, or treated her so roughly. Her husband must have handled her like porcelain if a little awkwardness unnerved her so much.

What exactly had gone on in her marriage? Despite the age difference, Ralph and Virginia had been devoted to one another. Everyone had considered it a love match, like the one between Francis's parents.

Dulverton had been absent for years in the army, and when he'd sold out, he'd visited friends in Nottinghamshire and found a wife. Virginia had put Ralph's nose out of joint. He'd brought her to a local assembly, and there Francis had seen her for the first time.

Francis had taken one look at Virginia and wanted her so strongly the emotion had shocked him. He had never lost that first impression of her, despite the way they had shunned his mother, and his subsequent avoidance of them.

Ralph had been a man very aware of his station in life and how others related to that. A stickler for protocol and detail. That had never suited Francis. The men had held off public antipathy, anything that would have caused gossip, but Ralph had kept Virginia close. Had Ralph suspected Francis's instant and lasting devotion to Virginia? Francis had taken such care not to let it show, but sometimes, sometimes he'd let a little of it out, especially when he was younger.

"Yes, I came."

Aware of the double entendre, as she was not, he touched his lips to the top of her head and gentled his hold on her. She'd stopped trembling, but she still nestled close, and he was forced to admit, if only to himself, that he loved the closeness. She never allowed anyone close, so this was a first for them both. He counted himself privileged. She slid her arms loosely around his waist, under his heavy evening coat, and Francis cautiously let himself revel.

"He was merely awkward. Nothing else," he said, assuring himself as much as her. If Jamie had done more, he wanted to know it.

"And insulting." Her voice was stronger now.

"And insulting. He has no idea how to seduce a lady, does he? I will still call him out if you want me to."

"No, please don't. It would cause the most dreadful scandal."

"In that case, of course I won't. He needs lessons in how to treat a lady, does he not?"

Her eyes widened when she looked at him, but he saw no fear in them now. Not that awful, cringing dread he never wanted to see again. Francis forced one of his easy smiles, allowing his mouth to quirk more at one side than the other. The side with the diamond earring. He needed to ensure she was calm before he would leave her. Needed it as much for himself as for her.

The spark between them had always been there, and now it was clearer than ever, especially in this rare moment of tranquility between them.

"Perhaps we should start again. Would you agree to a visit to Wolverley Court when you go down to Devonshire? My mother would be glad to receive you."

Thus demonstrating peace between them.

She gazed up at him, her eyes drinking him in. "Yes," she said.

He wouldn't mention Combe Manor right now and break this fragile peace. "We should seal this momentous occasion."

"What do you suggest?"

He smiled down at her. "With a kiss."

He feathered a barely there kiss over her forehead. That made her smile back at him. Glad to see that, he touched the tip of her nose with his lips, then waited. Her breath came evenly, perhaps a little heightened, and the pulse in her neck throbbed.

But she did not look away or try to leave his arms. If she had, he'd have released her instantly. He did not take any pleasure in scaring a woman he was making love to, even though he knew some men who did.

"Then this." He bent, his lips close to hers, but not touching, a mere breath away.

Francis waited. She rewarded him by stretching up and completing the connection. One hand slid around his neck, but not pulling closer, only holding him there, making the connection between them more intimate. He reciprocated, moving his left hand up the silk of her bodice, following the deep pleats in the back of her gown until he reached the nape of her neck, and bare skin.

With a shudder, he released part of his desire but kept a tight rein on the rest. Pressing his lips to hers, he kissed her properly. Eagerly she responded, with a hesitation that suggested inexperience. Warmth and desire filled him, and a tenderness that felt foreign, but one he listened to. If he made the wrong move now, she would never come close to him again. And he wanted that, very much.

Tilting his head to one side, he sealed their mouths together more securely. He touched her bottom lip with the tip of his tongue, mutely requesting entrance. Virginia parted her lips and sighed.

Even then Francis didn't take her like a marauding conqueror. Instead, he slid his tongue past her lips, pausing to caress and stroke the tender flesh, teasing and inciting, raising her arousal as his rose to almost painful proportions. His groin was taut, his body so hard he feared he might lose his much-vaunted control.

But he could show her what had always hidden beneath their animosity. Slowly, he entered her mouth for the first time. The experience shook him. The care he was forcing himself to take, her taste, and her trust all overwhelmed him, swamped him in the emotion he usually tried so hard to avoid. But this time he let it in. So far and no farther, because he had barriers he would not allow anyone to pass. Not even Virginia.

He licked his way in, savored her sweet flavor, and invited her to enjoy him in her turn. Tentatively she moved her tongue against his, but she didn't attempt to enter his mouth in her turn, as he longed for her to do.

What in God's name had Ralph done with her? What *hadn't* he done with her? She kissed as if she had never done it before, not a true kiss, an expression of desire between two adults.

Francis had never kissed like this, guiding and teaching. He preferred women who knew what they were doing, who wanted him in a specific way, but with Virginia he was entering new territory, and he wasn't sure of her.

Admiring a lady from a distance was very different to coming close to them. To her.

Her little sighs were followed by a groan. He claimed it, swallowed it greedily, pulled her closer to feel as much of her body against his as possible. But bearing her recent fright, he did not allow his passion to run away with him. Running his finger around the top of her bodice, the lace frill tickled, the silky skin invited more. Such small gestures meant so much more with Virginia.

He wanted her naked, he wanted her under him.

His control was slipping. Francis recognized it and braced himself to finish the kiss, to withdraw and slowly pull away from her, letting his embrace go lax so she could freely move if she wanted to.

Virginia let the hand that was caressing his neck slide away, but she cupped his shoulder instead of pulling back.

She gazed up at him, blue eyes inscrutable now.

Francis forced the saucy smile back to his lips, although inside he was shaking with the intensity of a simple kiss.

"That is what your suitor should have done," he murmured. "But fortunately for me, he did not. Never let a man kiss you again, Virginia. Not unless it's me."

She blinked, breaking the intense connection that for all his self-control, he was finding impossible to cut. She was stronger than he was, or she cared less. Or both. Gently, she slid out of his arms.

"You must promise not to pay me any special attention in future," she said, her voice sharper.

"Must I?"

"If you had not fixed your whole attention on me back in the ballroom, Dulverton would not have tried this. And if he does, other men will. I will not have that, Wolverley."

"Francis."

"Wolverley," she repeated firmly. "One kiss changes nothing."

He begged to differ. That kiss had changed everything for him. It had solidified a distant, dreamy kind of love to a certainty.

She bent to pick something up. Brilliants glittered in the candlelight. Her broken fan bore mute testimony to Dulverton's rough treatment of its owner. With a tsk of annoyance, she pushed it into her pocket. "Drat the man." She turned to face Francis, completely within herself again, in control. Crossing to the mirror, she studied her appearance before plucking a few pins from her hair and setting about refastening it back into its neat bun. Busy at her task, she continued to speak to him.

Francis got the strong feeling she was avoiding looking at him.

"I do not intend to marry again. If I have to repeat it another hundred times, I will do that. I have things to do, ambitions to achieve before I can even consider that."

Francis got up and strode to the wall opposite, so he could see her reflection properly. He leaned against the wall, lifting his leg to put his foot against it in a careless gesture. "What ambitions?"

"It doesn't concern you. But I'm happy as I am. Why would I not be?"

"I don't know, why would you not be happy?"

"I *am*. And with your *stalking* me in the ballroom, you gave all those men ideas they wouldn't have had without watching you. Don't imagine I'm not aware of what you want." She jabbed a pin into the pleat of hair she'd deftly created. Francis winced. "You won't get it that way. Combe Manor will become an orphanage."

Combe Manor did not seem so important anymore.

A pause, while she cast around for something, and then saw it on the bed. She pounced on it with a small cry of triumph, one that spoke directly to his groin. As if sensing his condition, she glanced at him. She was, to all intents and purposes, wholly herself again as she refastened the silver pin to her gown.

"You can go now, my lord. Thank you for rescuing me. I shall take great care not to be in a room alone with Jamie ever again." She paused and lifted the scrap of lace she had been searching for. A lady's handkerchief. "Now I have everything I came in with. I can take care of myself from now on."

She had broken him. How could he cause her such unhappiness? He would have to think of another way to get Combe Manor off her because the path he'd taken tonight would never work.

"I will leave first. You follow in a few minutes." He unlocked the door, opened it slightly, listened for a moment to detect any potential witnesses, and left.

Francis did not return to the ballroom. Instead, he went down to the hall and demanded his hat, gloves, and sword. He was satisfied that Dulverton had done no more than frighten Virginia with his clumsiness, but her reaction still puzzled him. After six years of marriage and four of widowhood, she should know more than she did. Perhaps Ralph did not like to kiss, but he had fallen madly in love with Virginia, so surely he would have wanted to?

Francis wanted to. More than anything else he could think of he wanted to take what they had started tonight to its natural conclusion. But he would not. That path would be too dangerous for both of them. That kiss had more than a physical effect on him. It had opened a door, made him realize that the simmering attraction between them was more than his natural admiration of a beautiful woman, more than simple lust. He couldn't remember the last time a kiss had meant so much to him. If it ever had.

The dreamy boy he'd been had melted away years ago, except for his unformed love for the unattainable girl he'd seen across a dance floor. He'd been happy to live with that. Now he was not. Tonight that love had changed, turned from a dream to an aspiration. He wanted her, and he would have her. Somehow he would.

Leaving the house, he stepped into a wonderfully balmy spring evening. Several people strolled past and a number of carriages were drawn up outside, but there was none of the feverish urgency to go to the next event that marked the season, especially early on. If London was like this all the time, he might consider staying longer. He would walk to his own house, clear his head, and work out what to do next.

Happy with his decision, he turned the corner into Piccadilly.

A voice croaked out from the darkness. "There 'e is."

That was all the warning he got before a man jumped on him.

The man grabbed Francis's upper arms, trying to force his hands behind his back, making Francis vulnerable to another man, who came at him swinging his fists.

Francis ducked and forced his arms out of the first man's hold, the sudden movement taking his assailant by surprise. His head plowed into the other man's stomach, and he pulled his arms free. In an instant he had his sword in his hand, whirling around to make the most of the heavy skirts of his coat, throwing the men off balance. He roared for help.

"To me!" he said as he slashed the air, barely missing one man's hand.

They were big bruisers, and his counterattack did not prevent them coming at him again. Striking out, he found skin, opening up one fellow's cheek, the tang of blood tainting the air. The man came at him again, the blade of his knife gleaming in the moonlight. This time Francis found his forehead. A strategic cut rendered his assailant effectively blind. Blood poured into the fellow's eyes, and he shook his head, cursing.

Francis had concentrated too much on that one; he'd left his side open to attack. A hard punch connected with his stomach, knocking the breath completely out of him. Francis slumped on the ground, trying desperately to suck air back into his lungs, sweeping his sword before him in an effort to prevent the blow that would kill him.

The second man grabbed Francis's wrist in a hold that threatened to break bones. He bent close, his foul breath full in Francis's face. "You're to leave the lady alone. That's all."

Then they were off, the man Francis had marked holding a filthy rag to his eyes, being led by the other. They melted into the night, slipping into the shadows of a nearby alley.

Feet pounded toward him. "Good Lord, are you all right?"

Recognizing the voice of a friend, Francis dropped his sword and tried to sit up, holding his side and waving his free hand dismissively. Agony arced through him when he finally succeeded in dragging in a shallow breath.

"Only winded," he managed painfully, then drew up his knees, resting his forehead on them. He concentrated on breathing.

"It's scandalous! A man can't even walk the streets in safety!"

Col put Francis's hat back on his head and crouched down. "I saw one of them say something to you."

Francis shook his head. "Didn't hear him clearly. Think it was—nothing." He was breathless, not stupid. He'd heard what the bully had said perfectly well, but he wanted time to think about it.

The warning to keep away from "the lady" could mean anyone, but in his heart, Francis didn't believe that. The warning was about Virginia. And who else but Lord Dulverton would have thought to do this? A flash of fury seared him, making him grit his teeth and fight the emotion down. He'd return to it later, and by God, he'd ensure he was in the boxing saloon during Dulverton's next visit. Who else could have set those men on him?

Once he was finally breathing, if painfully, Francis got to his feet and brushed himself down. Gratefully he accepted the support of the Duke of Colston Magna's arm. Col suggested they repair to their club, and he agreed. His home would have to wait. He needed distraction and good brandy.

At the St. James's Club on Pall Mall, Francis brushed his coat down, grimacing ruefully at the smears of dirt that bedaubed the scarlet velvet. The fracas could have cost him a favorite piece of clothing. A couple of the gold buttons had been torn from his waistcoat, but Col plonked them on the table with a grin before lifting his finger to order a bottle of brandy.

The Duke of Colston Magna, dandified in appearance but with much more substance than it first appeared, gave Francis's wig a tug to straighten it. "Why you insist on wearing that thing defeats me," he said.

Francis shrugged. "I like it. It's the most comfortable one I have. And wearing it means I can keep my hair short."

"Several men have taken to growing their own hair and discarding wigs altogether."

Col had done so himself, his brown hair tied neatly behind his head with a black velvet ribbon. He'd kept his hair tucked under a formal wig tonight, but he'd pulled that off when they got to their table and hung it on the back of his chair. In less formal occasions, he created quite a stir when he appeared bareheaded. An affectation, people called it, but quite a few men were following his example.

Picking up his glass, Francis took a healthy swallow, ignoring the fact that good brandy should be sipped. Whoever said that had not been attacked in the street. He'd put a hundred guineas on it.

"They're more devoted to their appearance than I am. I prefer to keep my hair short and use these things when I need to." He touched the edge of his wig.

Col laughed, sharp white teeth gleaming. He reminded Francis of a predatory animal, but for his sins, he was the one bearing that nickname. The Wolf, some called him.

"Those things provide a great deal of employment. Perhaps you should consider cutting those lovely locks and buying a new one."

"You never know, my wife might appreciate short hair," Col said then, as if passing the time of day.

The remark snagged all Francis's attention. "You have a wife?"

"Not yet," his friend replied easily. He took a sip from his glass. "But it is time I set up my nursery. I fear I must think of the estate. And Miss Mountford is an enticing piece."

The heiress, eh? Not that Col would be attracted by that. He was wealthy enough. But her connections were impeccable. Her parents guarded her like the treasure she was, but they would allow Col through the ring of fire they set about their daughter. She was richer, on paper, than they were, having inherited her estate from her grandfather. Francis had considered her for himself, but although he enjoyed her company, she did not arouse him like Virginia did.

He was not unaware of why Col had chosen to make his announcement here. What polite company was left in London would add that to their gossip.

"You've spoken to her parents?"

"They spoke to me." He took another sip, eyes glinting over the rim of his glass. He was fully aware of the silent sensation he was causing. "I have been hanging after Miss Childers this age, but her adamant refusals are wearing me down."

He would not have mentioned Miss Mountford if he was not serious, but Francis had never seen any partiality in that direction. Still, a dynastic marriage had its advantages. "Will you marry soon?"

A slight lift of Col's shoulder indicated a shrug. "Probably. But negotiations are torturous. They have only just begun, and they could break down yet. I shall tell you when you may congratulate me."

When the contracts were signed and the wedding held. Weddings were generally private affairs. Not so the balls and dinners that followed. Perhaps Col chose the end of the season for that purpose. The fuss would not be as great.

They moved to other topics, other sources of gossip. Anyone believing men did not gossip should attend one of the many clubs springing up around town. Francis appreciated Col's chatter, giving him time to calm his senses and recall the attack in peace, although not quiet. As usual, the main room of the club was busy, filled with gentlemen taking a few hours out of their busy days to drink, gamble, and gossip. Ah, but that was the busy day of many here.

A few had stared at him curiously as he'd entered, but he'd given them no clue. They would know soon enough, if anyone bothered to report it. After all, it was merely another small scuffle in a city that saw several every day.

Except it was not.

If Dulverton thought he would keep Francis away by setting a couple of bully boys on him, he had a shock in store. He had agreed to Virginia's strictures tonight, but now he changed his mind. If anyone got Combe Manor, it would be him. And he would thoroughly enjoy getting it, if it meant getting closer to Virginia.

Chapter 5

Virginia could not get that kiss out of her mind. She could taste him, feel him, his breath on her cheek, his heart pounding next to hers. At the moment his lips met hers, everything made sense. It was inevitable, day following night.

She must be mad. The minute Francis—or as she must think of him, Wolverley—entered her life she fell on him like a starving widow.

Even shopping with Angela and buying a completely extravagant fan, all lace and brilliants, which she seriously discussed having inset with diamonds, could not take that one fraught kiss out of the forefront of her mind. When she got home she handed the package containing the fan to her abigail, Winston. Usually she enjoyed her new purchases, but this one had defeated its purpose. She didn't care if she never saw it again.

To Wolverley the kiss was probably little more than a tease, taunting her with what she could have if she asked properly. Or let him have Combe Manor. That had probably been his sole motive. She was a fool, but he still wasn't getting Combe Manor.

She wandered into the parlor overlooking the front of the house, preparing to do a little tea-drinking and people-watching.

She was independent, able to dictate her own fate. In the last four years she'd learned to love it. Why would she want to change that?

Except that she kept thinking of a pair of laughing gray eyes and a wicked smile. And the feel of his hard body against her own. Ralph's body had been hard, but in a battle-scarred, leathery way. Francis would not be leathery. And she and Ralph—that had been different. Completely different. Ralph rarely kissed her, for a start. A brief brush of his thin lips against hers. Once she'd tried to deepen it, but he'd pulled away.

He'd smiled down at her. "You do not want that, my dear. Believe me, you do not."

Being barely eighteen, she had believed him. And also, she'd been deeply in love—or thought she was. That was before the disillusionment. She could see Ralph's face now, rugged, tough, the scar on his cheek a sign of the more serious injuries on his body. She still heard his cries of pain in her head sometimes, and she would get out of bed and reach for her robe before she recalled that Ralph was dead and didn't need her help any longer.

Ralph had taken her from an impossible situation. Because of that she would have done anything for him, and she tried, but it had been hard.

Those moods had not lasted long. And after he died, their bargain meant that Ralph had ensured she would never have to marry for duty again. Or ever, come to that. In fact, he'd said once that he would prefer her not to marry, but the decision must be hers. In any case, he was hardly in a position to stop her.

He must have known he couldn't prevent it. Only make remarriage difficult for her, which, at the time, she'd wanted. Now she wasn't so sure. But there wasn't much she could do about that now.

The clang of the doorbell led to murmuring in the hall. Virginia waited until the footman came in with a card and a note on a tray. She sighed when she saw Wolverley's name, but at least the corner wasn't folded over, which would have meant he had called in person and was waiting for her.

On the note he'd scrawled, "Drive with me today? I'll call at eleven."

Wolverley's bold hand reflected the man: decisive, hasty, and distinctive. But there was no harm in her driving with him in an open carriage, and a distraction would help right now. He could hardly kiss her in an open carriage. She needed to make a few things clear to him, and this was her chance to get him in private.

She would go.

* * * *

An hour later, Virginia was outside the house, dressed in a dashing green riding habit, being helped up to the seat of a phaeton. Trust Wolverley to have the lightest, most dashing vehicle possible.

"I suppose I should be glad you didn't bring your curricle," she grumbled.

As his tiger climbed to his perch at the back of the phaeton, Wolverley swung himself up into his seat with the agility of the natural born athlete.

"Would you have preferred that to the phaeton? I can always arrange it for the next time I take you driving."

"There won't be another time," she said smugly. "I'm traveling down to Devonshire at the end of the week."

"You're leaving without telling me?" He glanced at her as he swung around a corner. "You're looking particularly lovely today, Virginia. That shade of green suits you to perfection."

Ignoring his compliment, Virginia gripped the handrail by her side. "Do pay attention to where you're going, Wolverley, or neither of us will be going anywhere!"

"Don't you trust my driving? I'm accounted a fair whip."

He was considered a superb driver, but the speed and hairsbreadth technique was not one Virginia was comfortable with. However, if she said so, he might take it in his head to go even faster and pay less attention to what he was doing. So she held her tongue.

"At least you'll be out of London." He brightened. "And so will I. I'll make arrangements to follow you."

"Not literally, I trust. London is gossiping enough already."

London always gossiped about young, well-off widows who'd inherited the bulk of their late husbands' possessions. As Virginia had learned to her cost.

He cast her a wicked glance, and she tightened her lips in disapproval. "Why not? We'll be on the same road. How can we possibly avoid each other when we are going in the same direction? London won't be there to gossip."

"I'll be days ahead of you."

The earlier she left the hothouse that was London, the better. In the country she could put more space between them, and matters would settle into their usual course.

"I am not a target," she said bitterly. "Not a thing. You and Jamie will not squabble over me, or rather, over my possessions. Is that clear?"

"For goodness' sake, call me Francis when we're alone. You call Dulverton Jamie well enough."

"He is a relative."

"Only by marriage. Can you not manage to use my given name?"

She shook her head. She dared not. He made free with her first name, and to be honest she liked the sound of it on his lips, but she dared not give him more opportunities to weaken her resolve.

He pursed his lips, and God help her, the slight movement plunged her straight back to that explosive kiss. She could taste him again, feel the melting intimacy of her body pressed against his. He wasn't even looking at her. Lord, she was in trouble. She had to make space between them, or she would be in serious peril.

"As for your possessions…" He paused while he took another corner. "If you sell Combe Manor to Dulverton, I will take that extremely amiss. But the kiss was nothing to do with that. I kissed you because I wanted to. You must be aware how utterly delectable you are, Virginia."

Words failed her. While she was still gaping, Wolverley adjusted his speed and bowled through the park gates. During high season, Hyde Park was thronged with fashionable vehicles and people taking the air, but now, at the end of June, it was much less crowded. Lady Conyngham's ball had ended the main events of the season. Soon the theaters and pleasure gardens would close for the summer, and town would empty of company.

The summer round of house parties and attending to estate affairs would begin, and London would steam under the summer heat. A few people stayed in town year-round, or almost so, but this year even Angela was planning to attend a few summer parties in the country. The SSL was still meeting, though, and she planned to go and bid them farewell tomorrow, Thursday.

Now was as good a time as any to talk to him. "Wolverley, I must speak to you."

"Speak away." He cast her an amused glance. "And don't be tiresome, Virginia. Call me Francis."

Taking no notice, she continued. "You cannot continue to pay me the kind of attention you did at the ball last night. People will notice. People—men—will pursue me. You know the dangers of being taken in by fortune hunters. It is real. Why, Lady Glaston was only rescued from that fate at the last minute by his lordship."

"And now they are happily married."

"But that wasn't her abductor. He was a slimy fellow. If you encourage that kind of person, you will put me in danger. And you cannot say that nobody has noticed your attentions to me."

He said nothing. When she ventured a glance at him, his lips were tight, and he was staring rigidly into the distance.

"Admit it, Wolverley."

He sighed. "Yes, I do. Admit it, that is. People have noticed. But—what makes you think you are not a marked woman already?"

She frowned. "What on earth do you mean?"

He shrugged, refusing to meet her gaze. "I don't know. Forget it."

Why should she? Did he know something already?

About to question him further, she noticed someone waving vigorously. So did Wolverley's muttered curse. "Good Lord, did you know they were in town?"

She waved back. "Yes, Jamie told me last night."

A stout gentleman stood by the path, a lady by his side, their children completing the picture. All were waving.

"We have to stop," he said. "You acknowledged them."

"So I did," she said as he drew his frisky horses to a smooth stop.

She didn't even have to grab the handrail again. As a lady should, she waited for him to dismount and offer his hand to help her down. She didn't see what he was up to until his hands went around her waist and he lifted her off her perch, settling her gently on the ground.

Virginia closed her eyes, giving in to her weakness. He felt so good, warm and strong.

At least he stepped back as soon as she was down.

"Don't mention it," he drawled, so easily that she wanted to put her hands on him—around his neck to be precise—and squeeze hard. He captivated her and infuriated her, sometimes in the same sentence.

He was looking past her, his smooth smile firmly in place. "Ah, Sir Bertram. So good to see you in town this season. Taking the air?"

She had wanted to avoid Sir Bertram. She would see enough of him when she went home.

Their Devonshire neighbor had been a particular crony of Ralph's, and their condescending attitude to her sex had infuriated her in the past. Now Ralph was gone, he had made himself of particular service to her, by arranging a few small matters on her estate. However, he had only done it to further the acquaintance and continue to read her lectures.

His favorite topics were on the decadence of the aristocracy. As if she would know anything about that.

And yet he had brought his daughters to town. Was he planning to marry them off to those decadent aristocrats?

"We had to present the girls sooner or later, so we thought we'd wait until Amelia was old enough and get all the girls done all at once," the man said, the burr of Devonshire evident in his tones. He could speak as properly as an earl when he wanted to, but he liked to remind people of his origins. "We've seen the minster, and the cathedral, and I took them to the opera."

His three daughters bobbed curtsys and fixed fish-like stares on Wolverley.

It sounded like they were getting their cultural education in a month.

"What did you see?" Virginia asked, knowing what he would say, because there was only one opera running.

"Handel's *Rodelinda*. A fine opera demonstrating the danger of despots and the glory of democracy."

Virginia frowned. She had seen the opera, but it had not sent her that message. She was probably too concentrated on the central love story. That was the reason the opera was one of her favorites, not any message it sent.

But before she could speak up, Wolverley added his mite. "I saw Francesco Baratti last month. He was very fine. In an Italian opera, what was it called?" Frowning, he tapped his boot with his whip, as if trying to remember.

Virginia refused to tell him. They had been at the same performance, but she would not play his game and make it appear as if they'd gone together. They'd exchanged brief polite exchanges while waiting for their respective carriages, but that was all.

She had to behave as if she was in perfect harmony with him, and that she was immune to his considerable charm. The task would be more difficult than any time in the past, but she would do it. She'd faced worse.

Wolverley confused her; he fascinated her. She wished she was free to discover which one mattered the most. But she was not.

At least he was provoking Sir Bertram, and not her.

"Pooh!" Sir Bertram said, scoffing at Wolverley's words. "Italian opera cannot hold a candle to Handel! I wouldn't give you tuppence for an Italian aria, or the fancy-boys who trill them, next to a good English tenor!"

The hero of *Rodelinda* was usually sung by a castrato, but Virginia decided not to mention that. Sir Bertram was a defiant Tory, and a supporter of English everything, a sentiment that most county gentlemen shared. The fact that Handel was German didn't seem to matter.

Virginia gave Lady Dean a sweet smile, and even included her three daughters, who, she noted with amusement, were still staring at Wolverley with their mouths half open. As he turned his head, the sunshine caught his diamond earring, sending a flash of brilliant light to temporarily dazzle her.

She blinked but kept her gaze firmly fixed on the girls. Girls? The oldest must be in her early twenties by now. She would find a husband at home, to strengthen the family bonds in Devonshire. Perhaps even north to Somersetshire, if they were more adventurous.

Lady Dean said, "There is an Assembly in two weeks' time in Exeter, if you were thinking of attending."

"I may do that, thank you." She wouldn't put a foot anywhere near Exeter Assembly rooms if she could help it. There were as many young men looking to further themselves there as in London.

"We enjoyed ourselves at Lady Conyngham's last night," her ladyship went on.

"Oh, I'm sorry, I did not see you there. Yes, it was enjoyable."

But she had made an early exit. The reason for that sent heat rushing through her. "I felt unwell, so I left early."

"I wished to speak with you on a matter of business," Sir Bertram said. "We are leaving tomorrow. May we call on you later?"

Regretfully Virginia shook her head. "Mrs. Dauntry is away, and the house is being closed up, ready for my departure. I cannot offer you hospitality. But you are welcome to visit me at home in Devonshire when I reach it."

Sir Bertram shot Wolverley a sharp look. What on earth was that for? "I have heard that you wished to make an offer for Combe Manor, sir."

Wolverley inhaled sharply. "The manor is a lovely spot, perfect for my mother. It was her childhood home, so I wished to give it to her."

Sir Bertram shook his head, shifting his comfortable, loose-fitting bob-wig so it was no longer level. Virginia itched to straighten it, but naturally, she restrained herself from doing so.

"I had thought to make an offer for it."

What was this fuss about Combe Manor about? It had sat there quietly rotting away for many years, its only occupants the old couple Ralph had installed to keep it weatherproof and guarded.

Jamie wanted the manor to complete his holdings in that area. Together with the spinney, that would give him a clear path to the sea and tidy up that part of the main Dulverton estate. But why would the Deans want this place? And Wolverley too? Did he want it for more than sentiment's sake? What was she missing?

"Combe Manor is a relatively small property, close to the sea. The land isn't suitable for crops or cattle, or even sheep, unless the fence at the cliff edge is mended. Sheep would tumble over, and there isn't enough sustenance for cattle," she pointed out.

"You know why I want it," Wolverley said softly, then raised his voice so it was not so intimate. She should be glad of that. "Why do you want the property, Sir Bertram?"

The magistrate shrugged, his well-worn black coat of good cloth revealing the substantial body beneath. The squire was not tall, but he was a man of considerable substance. "It is close to my land. It would be convenient."

"For what?" she demanded. "It's just an old house." And he'd offered for the spinney, too.

"So it is," Sir Bertram agreed. "But it would parcel into my lands comfortably. It's not part of your main holdings, it's separate, so you are hardly using it, my lady. We could tidy up a few loose ends." He shot Wolverley a glare. "I have asked Lord Dulverton to consider the sale of the spinney close by, but he tells me that is in your gift too, my lady. With the spinney giving access to the house, I see it as one parcel."

She smiled. "Indeed. I intended it for one of my orphanages."

Sir Bertram shot her a startled look. "Indeed, my lady? Then I shall trouble you no longer. I wouldn't like to deprive the orphans of a home."

She had no idea he was so concerned about her project, but at least that was one less buyer bothering her.

Not that she would be selling it.

She needed to reacquaint herself with the house and discover why people wanted to buy it all of a sudden. She wanted to know why everyone was so interested in the place.

And she would have to look over this one for herself. If she could trust no one, she'd have to do it alone. No problem—she was used to that. But a sense lingered, something she was unaccustomed to. A moment later, she had it. Loneliness.

How could she be feeling lonely when she'd spent the last four years happily living by herself? Why would she feel the need to confide in somebody now?

Chapter 6

Francis shot Virginia a glance as they bowled around a corner. "You're very quiet."

"Do I have to engage you in constant inconsequential chatter?" She bestowed a sweet smile on him that didn't reach her eyes. "I suppose society expects it. But I find Sir Bertram somewhat exhausting."

He grunted a laugh. "I know what you mean. He never ceases, does he? Everything is about himself."

"In my experience, that is the truth for a great many people," she commented acidly.

Her sharp tone surprised him. "Is present company included?" He kept his voice smooth, fought to retain the edge of humor he usually used as a shield.

"Not at all." But she said the words after a pause, small but significant.

Her comments didn't surprise him. Francis preferred to let events center on him, while he watched events and remarked on them. Surprising what people let escape when they thought they weren't being observed. He could talk and listen at the same time, a skill that did not come easily to everyone.

Least of all Sir Bertram. The man was a boor, convinced the world revolved around him, but Francis had always believed he had good intentions. He leaned to County rather than Country, which was not surprising, but he worked hard and took care of his tenants.

"He only speaks to me when he cannot avoid it."

"Count yourself fortunate," she said. "But I do not snub him."

"Hmm." He paused, thinking.

Virginia's position as a widow meant she was excused a number of activities. It also meant she should not be welcoming single men into her house, but devil take that. He would not be observing that particular rule; he'd just make sure nobody noticed.

"Take care, Virginia, or you'll find yourself sponsoring all his daughters, and you'll find yourself cooking to death in a court mantua. He needs a sponsor to present his wife and daughters. You would be most convenient."

The elaborate, old-fashioned gown women were obliged to wear for court was floor-length and made from a heavy material, with plenty of precious metal and spangles.

"Not like the utterly charming gown you're wearing today."

Light and fresh, her habit was shorter, to allow for walking on grass, and plain in color, enhancing her shape beautifully. Virginia needed no elaborate enhancements.

At the thought, his body flushed hot. Capturing her, holding down a willing Virginia while he explored all the delectable curves beneath her not-so-prim gown had given him far more illicit dreams than he had any right to, especially recently. He'd almost accustomed himself to his body readying itself for something it would not receive when he was in her vicinity.

"What are your plans for the summer?" she asked him then.

"I'm expected at Chatsworth, then I'm planning to visit Dunmore. He has a neat little hunting box in Leicestershire where we plan to enjoy a few weeks at the start of the hunting season."

"You're celebrating the Glorious Twelfth?" The Twelfth of August, the start of the shooting season.

"Yes, why not?"

"No reason."

She sounded subdued, so he risked another glance, although the traffic was getting somewhat thicker. He slowed the horses. They were reasonably amenable now, having had their outing. She was staring at her hands, twisting them together in her lap.

"What's wrong?" Rapidly he reviewed their conversation. "Is it the Twelfth?"

Turning her head, she stared at the passersby, although the people appeared fairly unremarkable. He suspected she didn't even see them.

"I do not celebrate the mass shooting of so many beautiful creatures."

He had to strain to hear her.

"Your husband enjoyed the season thoroughly, and you invited all the neighbors to the estate." Except for his mother, so he had not attended, either.

"Ralph said you were too good a shot," she said with a wan smile.

She must know as well as he did that was not the reason his mother had not been invited.

"But you did not enjoy it." This time he didn't make his words a question.

"I enjoy other things more. If I had made my dislike obvious, I would have been roasted dreadfully for it. The best way to attract attention is to dislike the very thing everyone is there to do. Doing that would have been very unmannerly of me, would it not?"

"I see." Francis seethed on Virginia's behalf. If he had been in Ralph's place, he would have ensured she did not have to be there. He'd have found another hostess, or better still, not held the parties at all. "How about hunting foxes?"

"I enjoy that much more." Animation entered her tones, much more than the slaughter of the birds had. "Foxes are vermin. I confess the kill doesn't interest me, but I enjoy the challenge of the ride."

"Because it requires skill." When there were so many birds provided for guests, shooting them was not the most difficult challenge.

"Yes."

"But you do not have to do that now. You may do as you wish."

"Within reason, yes indeed. I will not be celebrating the Twelfth of August by shooting anything."

They had arrived at her street. Francis tossed the reins to his tiger and alighted from his perch, electing to help her down himself, although one of her footmen had come out of the house to help. He swung her down, enjoying the way his hands spanned her waist. And yet she was not tightly laced. She wore some kind of soft corset, perhaps a leather one, which gave him a teasing sense of her soft flesh.

He would give a great deal to touch that skin, to kiss and taste it, to stroke it with the flat of his hands. Not that the opportunity seemed likely to occur, but a man could dream.

Allowing her time to find her feet gave him time to relish her proximity. Her lush lips moved, and he took a moment to listen to what she was saying.

"I wish you joy of your birds. I shall make a quiet appearance with Mrs. Dauntry at a perfectly staid country assembly." She smiled. "Perhaps not the hotbed of Exeter, though."

"If you let me know when, I will forego the pleasures of the hunting lodge and join you."

"Give up the slaughter for a few hours in an assembly room with indifferent wine and uneven floors?" She laughed him to scorn as she took a step back.

Alarmed he had forgotten he was holding her in the public street, he tried one of his tip-tilted smiles. "Even that. My mother enjoys them."

He'd brought her into the conversation deliberately. Hearing her response might cool him down and remind him of his purpose.

"Then I will look forward to seeing her there." Before he could ask her outright about his mother, she went on. "Though I have heard of the goings-on in those hunting boxes," she added. "You may not see the light of day at all, and not even one feather."

"I shall bring one for you."

Her reply was hasty. "Oh please do not. In fact, after today I would ask you not to come to my house again. People are gossiping, and you have no more intention of offering for me than I have of accepting. The alternative is something I have been avoiding for years. Men feel a widow is there as a personal challenge to them."

Anger suffused him, to think of anyone harassing her.

"Tell me who," he said, baring his teeth. "If anyone dares distress you, I will take them up on it at once."

Her laugh tinkled, but her eyes were grave. "That would be to do exactly what we are trying to avoid. I am perfectly well, and able to take care of myself. I shall travel down to Devonshire smothered in servants. I'll even hire a pair of outriders."

"I see." But he had no intention of leaving her alone, not until he was sure she was perfectly safe.

Leave her alone, the ruffians had told him. Well they could whistle for that. Or did the person who'd sent them know that would act as a challenge and instead bring him closer to her? If he or she had, it didn't matter. Francis's first consideration was Virginia, and despite her annoying propensity to go off on her own without telling him, she would continue to be so.

"I will not do anything scandalous, I promise," he said. "Only I will be a good neighbor."

Turning, she stumbled, her hat pitching backward and her skirts getting tangled around her legs. Quicker than thought, he had her again, catching her by the waist and yanking her upright. She fell against him, her body coming into full, glorious contact with his.

Acting on instinct, he pulled her closer, tilted up her chin, and kissed her. Swiftly, but that burning contact seared through him, pushing him into mindless passion. Was it because they were talking about danger that he went into full protector mode? He had no idea. Because she responded, sighing as she opened her mouth.

That was an invitation if ever he felt one. She wasn't innocent; she was a widow, so she must know that a response like that would drive any red-blooded male to distraction. His basic instincts overtook his sense of social survival. Anyone could see them, and he didn't care.

Dimly he became aware of a pressure against his chest.

She was pushing him away.

That was the only thing that would have stopped him. Reluctantly, he separated from her and let her step back, keeping his hands up in case she fell again.

Virginia looked adorable. Her lips were reddened, her bosom heaving as she drew deep breaths. The sweet curve of her waist, spreading into swelling hips, which were emphasized by the padding of her skirts, tempted him to take hold. All he had to do was to put his hands there and draw her in....

A sharp cry of laughter brought his senses roaring back.

"In the street!" someone cried.

Tears made Virginia's eyes glossy. As he watched, one precious drop spilled over and trickled down her cheek. She didn't have to say anything. He knew what he'd done. And he didn't have to look around to know they had been seen.

He had committed the deepest sin, behaving in a vulgar way instead of merely scandalous.

"Hit me," he murmured. "Slap my face, Virginia."

She should have done it immediately, and then he could take the blame. After that, he'd have to stick to the role of spurned suitor and keep his distance. If he could win back what he'd lost her by that one impulsive act, he would do it, even if it killed him, which it might well do.

After all his good intentions, after his promises, he had let her down.

But she left it too late, and the observers were upon them.

"My word," said Lord Meredith, husband to the biggest gossip in London, "an interesting move, what?"

In a whirl of skirts, Virginia turned and strode up the steps to her front door. It opened before she had time to knock, and she swept in.

"My fault entirely," he said, turning a bright smile to his lordship. "A man has to steal his pleasures where he may, must he not?"

His lordship shrugged. "I dare say, but I never knew you and the beauteous Lady Dulverton were so intimately acquainted, what?" He drew out his snuffbox, but didn't offer it, an omission Francis noted.

"We aren't, but the lady is maddeningly lovely. I confess, frustration drove me to make the move, and I will beg her pardon when I see her next."

He started to stroll up the street, so his lordship had to walk with him. The tiger walked behind, the clop of his horses following him.

"I should not have done what I did, but the fault is entirely mine." He touched his lips with his fingers. "And I cannot be altogether sorry, although I doubt she will let me close to her ever again." He gave Meredith a knowing smile, and the man responded with a smirk.

"But it was a good show," his lordship said, not altogether condemnatory now, but in concert with Francis. If he could turn what Meredith had seen, the incident would still be laid at his feet.

Virginia should have struck him.

* * * *

Never one to hide from her problems, Virginia headed to the residence of Angela Childers the next day.

When she stepped out of her front door, nobody spat at her, not that she was really expecting that, but they did not shun her either.

A couple of neighbors passing by gave her a civil greeting but did not stop. Since they had a dog on a leash that was busily trying to strangle itself in its eagerness to get to the park, they did not stop. Virginia got into her carriage and rode the short distance to Angela's house.

She had spent the night tossing and turning, reliving that kiss, balanced between wanting more and feeling utterly humiliated by what Wolverley had done. Kissing in the street like a common whore! Heat tinged her ears and then made her uncomfortable for an altogether different reason.

He had recovered first. She should have slapped him, as he requested, but she'd been so stunned that her senses had not reformed by the time his friend had hurried up to where they stood, staring at each other. What else could she do than run up the steps as fast as she dared?

Mrs. Dauntry had always said she was too kind to her suitors. But Wolverley wasn't a suitor, although they had become friends since her husband's death. She couldn't possibly see him as a lover.

Except she did.

She got down from her carriage in the courtyard and walked up the steps to Angela's front door.

Since most of her wealth stemmed from her bank, Angela tended to spend more of her time in the City of London. Childer's Bank didn't pause during the summer months. So the house in Piccadilly, hard by Burlington House, served as her main residence. It was much larger than the usual

London house, more of the style of mansion popular in the last century, and since only she lived there, contained a number of rooms she barely used.

One of those, at the end of a wing, she'd given over to the Society for Single Ladies. Since men had so many clubs, why could women not have them? That was her argument, and such was her influence that few caviled at it. Only at the selection of ladies who went there.

The only criteria were that they were single when invited and Angela approved of them, since they were using her house. She provided rooms for their exclusive use. Governesses and princesses had visited the club. Under that roof, everyone was considered equal.

Virginia entered the main room to smiles and nods. Although the club was thin of company at this time of the season, there were still a dozen women present. She loved the lack of ceremony and effusive welcomes. When she flourished the folder she had tucked under her arm, several people lifted their heads.

Miss Manners, a woman about the same age as Virginia but with a less fortunate story, got to her feet, her brown hair displaying gold streaks as she walked through a steam of sunshine. Miss Manners was a handsome woman with a modest dowry, but that had not prevented her failing to find a husband. Becoming a single lady, she was passed from family to family, caring for children not her own or accompanying young women on their dazzling debuts.

However, she was planning a far more exciting future for herself, although few people knew that yet. Angela had helped her, as she had helped others, with advice and finance, and most important of all, confidence.

As Virginia spread the papers on the large table before the window, Miss Manners leaned over. "Oh, maps! I adore maps."

"Plans."

The door opened, the rustle of silk heralding someone else coming in. Virginia did not put her papers away. She trusted everyone here. Glancing over her shoulder, she saw Angela approaching them, a smile on her lips. "What do we have here?"

"Plans to a small house I own in Devonshire. I planned to set up one of my orphanages there, since it is standing empty. Suddenly it's a popular place. Nobody took much notice of it before, and after Ralph died, I had other matters to occupy me with the main estate. It's a modest manor house, in an exposed position on a cliff. When I announced my plans for it, the current Lord Dulverton, Ralph's cousin, offered to buy it. That was just after Lord Wolverley made me an offer. He wants it for his mother, he says, because she was born and brought up there."

"So after years of nobody taking any notice of it, suddenly everyone wants to buy it?" Angela leaned over the plans, studying the layout.

"And Sir Bertram Dean came to London with his family. He is a staid man, vastly prefers the countryside, but he has taken the time to come to town, at the end of the season, when Parliament isn't sitting. He did have his family with him, but this is the wrong time of year to present young women. The last ball of the season was last night. And you'd expect him to call on me. But I heard nothing until we came upon him in the park."

"We?" Miss Manners fixed her with her bold stare. "I thought you told us your companion had already left town."

"Emilia has. She has a family wedding in Devonshire, so I gave her leave to go." Virginia fought the hot flush rising to her cheeks, but her painful awareness of her failure added to her discomfiture. "Lord Wolverley kindly took me out to take the air. I had not intended to stay in London so long, but I had matters to arrange." Helplessly, she smiled at Angela.

Angela turned her attention to Virginia. She straightened and faced her. "Virginia, do you have feelings for Lord Wolverley? You do know what his friends call him, do you not?"

"The Wolf," Virginia admitted. "But that's because of his name. Wolverley, wolf, you see?"

"Partly." From a seat nearby, pretty, blond Miss Maria Mountford smiled. "He's known as a hunter who doesn't stop until he gets what he wants. The story is all around the city that you kissed him in the street."

In stark contrast to Miss Manners, Miss Mountford was a great heiress and in demand for every ball and event of the season. Her beaux were legion, but she took little notice of any of them.

She was attractive and dainty, but she had a spine of pure steel, which helped to make up for her lack of stature. Although she did her best to appear plain, she failed badly at that. It wouldn't have deterred the majority of her suitors in any case.

They were all equal here. That was one of Angela's rules, and one of the best ones.

A sharp gasp came from Angela's direction, but Virginia didn't look. "I would say it was the other way around. I stumbled and then…" She couldn't say it without recalling the touch of his lips, his taste, his body pressed against her. And being wildly aware that she wanted more.

But she could not have it. From now on she had to avoid him. That shouldn't make her feel so unhappy.

Angela watched, her gaze far too perceptive for Virginia's liking. "I see. Do be careful, my dear. A young widow must be beyond reproach. That doesn't include kissing handsome gentlemen in the street." She quirked a brow, making her words a suggestion rather than a criticism.

All the same, Virginia understood her message. She smiled ruefully. "I know. I'm going to Devonshire on Monday, and I will not make a public appearance before I leave. By the time I return to town, gossip will have died down."

"Are you not going to Chatsworth this summer?" Angela asked.

"I had planned to." But Wolverley had dropped the information that he planned to visit. That meant Virginia would not go, after all. "I haven't made any definite plans."

"He took the blame," Miss Mountford piped up. She put her newspaper aside and devoted herself to the conversation. "It's in the gossip sheets this morning. He indicated to Lord Meredith that the fault was all his. He said he would call on you to beg your pardon."

"Well, he won't get inside," Virginia retorted.

Miss Mountford's information relieved her somewhat. However, kissing someone in the street displayed a sad lack of breeding that the sticklers wouldn't long forgive, if they came to hear of it.

Since few people remained in London, she would pray that not many witnessed the encounter. The neighbors on either side of her had left, for sure. Their knockers were off their doors, a sure sign there was nobody at home. Further up, spectators might have a more restrictive view. She could deny that the incident had happened at all.

Perhaps she would get away with it, if she was circumspect.

Something about Miss Mountford's words alerted her. Ah, she had it. "You've been speaking to the Duke of Colston Magna?"

They had danced together three times at the Conyngham ball, and the gossip sheets were full of it the day after.

Miss Mountford's cheerful expression dropped, her mouth turning down. "My parents want me to marry him. They've started negotiations."

"Ah." Never had Virginia appreciated her state of widowhood more. Nobody could force her to do anything, as long as she remained beyond reproach. "You do not wish to marry him?"

Miss Mountford shrugged. "It matters not. I must marry who I am told to marry, and I can only be glad that he is not a monster. My parents find him acceptable. And so do I," she said after a pause, but with no particular enthusiasm.

Colston Magna acceptable? He was one of the most sought-after men in society. Virginia had a suspicion she knew why Miss Mountford found Colston Magna only acceptable.

"You have a penchant for someone else?"

Her gaze fell. "What I want is not important, apparently."

So she wanted someone else.

The worst part of being an heiress was the control parents exerted, to ensure their fortune did not fall into unworthy hands.

"So as a married woman, I will no longer be a single lady," Miss Mountford continued brightly. "And I will no longer be eligible to be a member."

"No matter," Angela said. "You joined the club when you were, so you shall have honorable member status."

"Then I will still have a refuge," Miss Mountford said gratefully. She leaned her elbow on the arm of her chair and rested her chin on her hand, making a pretty picture. "I will send you an invitation to the wedding celebrations, but don't feel obliged to come."

"Please tell me if Lord Wolverley is attending," Virginia said. "Since he's a particular friend of Colston Magna, I imagine he will be, so do not take my refusal personally. I will avoid him in the future."

"I'll be sure to let you know."

Virginia indicated the plan of Combe Manor. "I'll spend a few days assessing the house. Then I'll visit my estate, ensure everything is well, and go up to Lancashire, where I've been invited to visit the Whallers." Dreadfully stuffy people, but so out of the way that Wolverley would not find her, even if he decided to look. "Lord Whaller detests Wolverley, and he returns the sentiment." Not Chatsworth. Definitely not Chatsworth. And not Colston Magna.

Angela pulled a face. "I stayed there once. Old house, uncomfortable beds, as I recall."

"But a small price to pay to live down a scandal."

Constantly avoiding scandal annoyed Virginia, but she couldn't blame anyone except herself. She had encouraged Wolverley, she had to admit.

"Then I'll go too," Angela said. "And we will say 'Lord who?' when anyone mentions Wolverley." After exchanging a smile with Virginia, she turned back to the house plan and the sketch of the place. "Combe Manor is close to the sea. The sea and Devonshire generally means one thing."

She wasn't talking about beauty. "Smugglers," Miss Mountford supplied. They gave the word its due pause.

"So exciting," Miss Mountford continued. "I only have small properties by the sea, and I've never had occasion to visit them."

"But you've drunk smuggled tea," Virginia said. "At least a third of the tea we drink is smuggled. Probably much more."

Angela made a sound of exasperation. "If the government would agree to lower the duty on it, they could put the smugglers out of business. They'd make up the income from the extra, legal tea. But they won't do it."

Virginia flicked the fine lace at her elbows. "We can't tell what is smuggled and what is not. This lace is French, and I bought it in Bond Street, but who knows where they got it from?"

"Tea, brandy, lace, tobacco." Miss Manners leaned over the plan. "So which of those does this house handle? It's close to the sea, on a cliff. And since it's in Devonshire, you can't tell me there are not caves underneath it. It's isolated, not lived in…perfect for the gentlemen."

"The gentlemen" was the deliberately vague term many used to describe the smugglers. Look the other way on a moonless night and a barrel of brandy would appear at the back door.

"We can do little about the trade. The gangs run their communities with fear and reward," Virginia said now. "I will not have any house I own used in that trade."

"If you see anything while you're there, you won't try to act on your own, will you?" Miss Manners said, her frown indicating her anxiety.

Virginia shook her head. "No, and if there's a run or a landing in the bay, I shall pretend to ignore it. I can't fight them on my own. But I can tell the excise men and take steps when I'm in a place of safety. The house is not far from Newton Abbott. I can also stay at the inn there. If there is smuggling going on, then it is because of the caretakers I have there. If I find any evidence at all, they will go."

Miss Manners heaved a sigh but said nothing. She didn't have to. Although a member of a distinguished family and related to the Dukes of Rutland, she had no house to call her own, nor any likelihood of having one. She was one of those poor relations who provided useful services for free.

Unpaid governess, companion, nurse, she went where she was required and received food, lodging, and little else. Nobody noticed her pretty face and lively intelligence because she had no fortune. If she were destitute, Virginia would help her, but she was not, and she never complained. Or gossiped, come to that.

Although Virginia owned a comfortable estate and a number of residences, she'd started lower than Miss Manners and ended higher.

Except their journeys weren't finished yet. She could end up as low as possible. Life had no guarantees; recent events had only reinforced that for her. She was only too aware that her behavior could leave her an outcast, which would mean the several lucrative arrangements she could access through belonging would be denied her. And she would be very alone.

She had to take the greatest care in the coming weeks. The ladies here would help her, and in all honesty, she had come here today for the support and help she would find. That was one reason the SSL meant so much to her.

"Speaking for myself, I would not go within ten miles of the place, sea or not," Miss Mountford said. "The sketches make it look forbidding, and if there is nothing else for miles, your body won't be found for weeks."

"Good Lord, it won't come to that," Virginia protested. "I only mean to stay there a night or two, and I will not disturb a soul. Merely assess it before I carry on. As far as anyone knows, it's a way station for me, a place for me to rest before I reach my ultimate destination."

"You're braver than I am," Miss Mountford commented. "Or more foolhardy."

Demurely, Virginia agreed to take no unnecessary chances.

She might be adventurous, but she wasn't an idiot.

Chapter 7

On arriving back at her London residence, Virginia was gratified to discover Butler had removed the front door knocker, something London residents did to indicate nobody was in. Nobody need know she was at home, so she could have a quiet evening without any visitors disturbing her peace.

The bulk of her staff had left for Devonshire in an unmarked carriage, with most of Virginia's wardrobe and jewels. The London staff had left, all but Butler, Hurst the footman, Mrs. Coble the cook, and Winston.

When she arrived at her Devonshire home, her staff would be waiting, ready to pamper her and treat her like the lady she was. She'd hired a comfortable chaise to take her to her home. No postilions, no grandeur. She wanted to pass as a gentlewoman rather than a viscountess. She longed for a few days on her own, to think and plan, and rest after what had been an eventful London season.

The hired servants didn't care about her. The notion was exhilarating. Not that she did not enjoy having people around her who cared for her, that would be foolish, but the journey was a holiday, a time when she didn't have to think about anyone but herself. A respite, in fact.

She found unlocking the door and entering the house enjoyable, instead of having the door flung open at her approach. Putting her roll of papers down, she instructed Hurst to tuck them in her valise after he'd ordered tea.

The main rooms upstairs were already in holland covers, the sheets on all but her bed stripped. She felt like an interloper in her own home, but she didn't mind. Tea, a book, and an early night were in order. She would enjoy every moment.

After removing her gloves and hat, Virginia turned to close the front door, which she'd left open at her entrance. The trouble with opening one's own front door was that one must close it again.

Wheels rolled down the street. Her senses prickling, Virginia stepped back.

She was right to be cautious. Sitting on the high perch of his ridiculously delicate phaeton, his tiger clutching the back rail, was Lord Wolverley. He glanced at her front door and slowed his vehicle. Damnation. The absence of a door knocker would not deter him.

He leaped from the phaeton before she could move out of sight, and hurried up the steps. Virginia tried to block his entrance, and behind her, she felt the presence of her one remaining footman, the burly Hurst.

"You cannot come in," she told Wolverley. "I am alone."

Wolverley's response was to wave off his tiger. "Wait for me at the end of the street."

"No, you must go."

He ignored her demand but hustled her back so he could kick the door closed. "I had meant to ask you to come for a drive, but I see you're not dressed for it."

How dare he treat her house like his own? "Didn't you understand what I told you yesterday?"

"I did, but…" He flicked a glance at Hurst. "I have something particular I need to say to you." His gaze swept the hall, taking in the packed valise standing there, her traveling cloak and the scarcity of furnishings. "If you mean to travel, then I should speak to you now."

"Society will hang and quarter me," she said, trying to get around him to the door. "Out."

He ignored her imperious demand. "No, they won't. Your neighbors have already gone, and I sent the phaeton to the other end of the street. The area is clear, and there is nobody to see." His brusque words belied the care for her buried deep inside what he said. He had noticed, and he was agreeing not to compromise her respectability. "Ten minutes, Virginia. That is all I ask."

Had he discovered something about Combe Manor, or did he want another chance to buy it? Either way, she should not do this. But if he left now and someone had seen him enter, he'd do as much damage if she threw him out now than in ten minutes. The urgency she saw in his eyes persuaded her.

"Very well, ten minutes. But then you must leave and not seek me out again." She took him to the breakfast parlor at the back of the house. This and the front parlor were the only main rooms left out of holland covers, and after she left on Monday, they would be shrouded too.

As soon as the door closed behind them, Virginia turned to face him. "You cannot keep doing this, Wolverley."

"Doing what?" he asked, a smile curling his mouth.

"You know what." With a wave, she indicated the room, and the lack of company. "Mrs. Dauntry is not here. Nobody is here to give me countenance. If you're not careful, you'll have us lovers and married in a month."

"Would that be so bad?" He asked so softly, sincerity in every syllable.

She caught her breath. "Of course it would. You are foolish." But her heart beat faster, and she became aware of the vital presence of this man. "Tell me what you have to, and be off, my lord." Reverting to the formal title should have made her feel safer. But it did not. Not one bit.

He gave a sharp nod. "I know you intend to avoid me this summer. I cannot blame you for it. But I don't want you to."

Lifting her head, she met his eyes. They were blazing. "We cannot meet again, Wolverley. Every time we are seen together will add to the gossip. Even if we are yards apart all the time." She couldn't stop staring at him.

"That's not the entire reason, is it? You feel it, don't you, Virginia?"

"Feel what?"

"This attraction between us. Dulverton saw it. One look was all it took. It hasn't worn off, has it?"

"No." Unable to speak, she mouthed the word.

For once, she would speak the truth. When Wolverley appeared, the very air stung with intensity. The reaction had frightened her, and Virginia hated being frightened.

Ralph had spoiled her for passion. She never, ever wanted to repeat the events that happened with Ralph, never wanted another man in her bed.

And yet…

When Wolverley took a step forward, she did not step back. Putting up her chin, she dared him.

He dared more. Another step, and he was standing directly in front of her and then, without fully understanding how it happened, she was in his arms and his mouth slammed down on hers.

He groaned into her mouth as she opened her lips, and he was there, thrusting deep, licking gently, tasting her, seducing her with his magnificent body and his kiss, by turns passionate and tender. The care he took as he shifted her so her head rested on his shoulder undid her. He freed his right hand to go roaming. He touched her jacket, slid her neckcloth away, undid a few buttons and found skin.

Her skin prickled, and her whole body came awake. Like a character from an old story, Virginia awoke from her long sleep. And now she was awake, she wanted more.

With a sharp intake of breath, she moved closer, slipped her hand inside his coat, around to his back, where two thin layers, one silk, one linen, lay between her and his bare flesh. By sliding her hand up, she created enough friction to feel the flex of hard muscle.

For this, yes, she wanted this—him—so much.

When he touched the roof of her mouth with his tongue and stroked, so very gently, all her good intentions flew away. Only a whisper of one remained, and she clutched it, held the sentence she must say in her mind, and let him have his way.

More than that. Virginia was no passive participant. As he laid kisses all the way down her throat, unfastening buttons as he went, she delved under the fine silk of his waistcoat. She frantically tugged at his shirt. Men's shirts were voluminous. The fabric pulled up and up. She gasped as he pulled her fichu free and kissed the upper slopes of her breasts, his breath heating her skin to fever pitch.

And they were still standing. The sofa in this room wouldn't take their combined weight. There was only the sturdy table.

She barely had time to think before he had her on her back against the polished mahogany.

"Virginia, Virginia," he muttered, straightening, impatiently tugging at his neckcloth then tossing it to the floor, discarding his coat at the same time.

"You'll be the death of me."

But not yet.

She hadn't been aware of speaking the words aloud until he cupped her chin gently, smiling down at her. That open, loving look seared through Virginia, right to her heart.

"We were always going to end here. With this."

Before her shocked mind could absorb what he'd said, he kissed her again. Curling her hand around the back of his neck, she flipped his wig aside, to reveal his gorgeous thick, dark hair. The strands threaded through her fingers, the texture adding to the bombardment of sensations rioting through her body.

Her hoops, being of the new design, collapsed as he pushed the right place, the clever little hinges giving way, and then, oh then, he dragged up her skirts and slid his hand up her thigh, heading toward the center of passion, the place where he could make her his.

A triple knock jarred her from paradise. "My lady? I have your tea here."

Wolverley lifted off her, cool air sweeping over her. Internal heat scorched her with horror. What had she done? What had she been about to do?

She cleared her throat. "Leave it in the front parlor, please."

"Yes, my lady." Retreating footsteps, perhaps a touch too loud, moved away.

"Oh God, they heard us." Using her elbows, Virginia levered herself off the table and reached for her jacket with shaking hands.

Wolverley ran his fingers through his hair, turning away from her. "Will they tell anyone?"

She shook her head. "Only a few servants are here right now. I can trust them." Or handle them somehow. By now she was certain Butler, Winston, and Hurst would keep their counsel, but the other two, Mrs. Coble and the housemaid, not so much.

"This is impossible."

When she lifted her head from fastening the buttons, she found him watching her. Apart from his coat, he had restored himself to respectability, but he'd changed. He watched her, his eyes bearing a fond expression she had never thought him capable of.

"I want more, Virginia. I want to court you, and I'm willing to make what lies between us respectable. I want to marry you."

For the first time she felt trapped, not freed, by the conditions of her husband's will. She had to tell him, but how, when Ralph had expressly forbidden her to tell anyone? When he'd imposed penalties on her telling anyone?

"I cannot marry you."

He raised a brow. "It didn't feel like that a moment ago. May I ask why?"

His hands warmed her chilled ones as realization hit her. Desperately she cast about for a solution.

He tucked his shirt back in his breeches, then found his wig.

"No." She could not.

"I see." His tone had tightened, but he was keeping control of himself.

"Can you wait for a while?" She should not ask him, but she wanted him so badly, she would tell him that much. Would he do this little thing for her?

"How long?" The lines around his mouth relaxed.

It would be unfair not to tell him. "Would you object to a six-year courtship?"

"*What?*" Dropping her hands, he flung himself across the room and dislodged his wig all over again, by shoving his hands through his hair. "Six years? God, Virginia, why?"

She turned away. "I can't tell you."

She'd signed papers; she was legally bound. "I truly can't." She ventured a small piece of what she had to tell him.

"You can, and you will. You want me, I know that now, so there has to be another reason why you won't marry me. Tell me, Virginia."

She should. He would not leave her if she didn't tell him at least some of it. Although she had avoided his presence, she knew about him. Wolverley had never reneged on a promise, never broken an oath, and always kept his word.

He had developed a fortune on those principles. His partners in business knew he would not let them down. If she did not tell him, he would keep coming back. Either that, or he would leave, and the bad blood between them would worsen. After today, she couldn't bear him to think so ill of her.

She had to tell him. Legal requirements or not. "It's part of Ralph's will."

Wolverley watched her, his intent gaze never leaving her face. He stood completely still. "Go on."

"In six years I will have control over the inheritance he left me. Until then I have full use of it, but I do not own it." She bit her lip. "If I marry before then, I will lose it all."

He breathed out, a great puff of air. "Do you think I need your inheritance? No, Virginia. I do not." He picked up his coat, shrugged into it. "If we pursue this, then I am happy to take you with your dowry and widow's portion."

She stamped her foot in exasperation. "You don't understand. I have to wait for ten years after his death. If I don't, I get nothing."

"Does your cousin know?" he asked sharply.

"God, no!" She gave a shaky laugh. "At least I don't think so. I can't tell him, either. If anyone discovers I have told you, then I lose it all."

"The bastard!" He growled. "A dead man is holding you to ransom! There must be a way out of this for you."

She shook her head. "No, there is not."

"Will you come to me anyway?"

Again, she shook her head, and for the first time, she used his given name. "Six years, Francis."

He framed the name, his mouth silently following her use of it.

"At last," he murmured, as if he understood the barrier she had just let fall.

He caressed her cheek, so lightly she hardly felt it, except she was sensitive to his every touch. Where there had been untrammeled passion, now there was tenderness—and love.

He stared at her, the lines bracketing his mouth graven deep, his neck muscles taut cords. "I've waited for you for ten years. I left the country and stayed away because I wanted you so much. But then, if we'd indulged ourselves, it could have led to disaster. I refused to bring that to you."

"Yes," she said softly. "Francis, yes. I tried, I really did, but I never forgot you. And when you came back…" She bit her lip. "It was worse."

"Much worse," he agreed. "Then your husband died, and I thought I could leave it a year before I proposed." He smiled wryly. "I tore through Europe in an effort to forget you, but nothing worked. It's been four years, Virginia. I swear, I'll settle whatever you want on you. I can put the sum in trust, so I can't touch it. I want you, not your money."

She swallowed, stared at him. Was it possible she could do this?

"Do you trust me to take care of you, sweetheart?"

Virginia couldn't answer. The idea of having nothing, of relying on another person for her existence, filled her with terror, even if that person was Francis.

After her parents, after Ralph, how could she trust anyone again? She opened her mouth, and closed it again. Her heart beat so hard she could barely breathe.

When he spoke next, his tones were level, utterly controlled.

"I can't wait that long. It was all I could do to stop myself taking you on that table, and you were not far behind me. We cannot go on like this, trying to rip each other's clothes off the minute we're alone together. How can I stay close to you and not make love to you? No, it's now or never."

"I understand why you cannot wait. You need heirs." And society considered her barren, a calumny encouraged by her husband. For all she knew, she could be.

"You understand *nothing!*" His lips were still reddened from their kisses, but his eyes spat fire. "Virginia, we can't keep doing this. If you can't trust me, can't come to me, then I don't want anything else. I won't ask you to be my mistress. You don't deserve that, and neither do I."

"I…" He was right. She couldn't keep doing this, either. "I know."

Although her eyes glistened with tears, she faced him proudly. "If you can't accept my terms, then you had better leave now. I only beg you to keep my secret."

Already she regretted telling him. She should have simply said no. That had never proved a problem before.

"Naturally I will do so. I swear it. But I will not come back. We had best keep our distance from now on."

He broke her heart when he left.

Chapter 8

Fighting her tears, Virginia wandered into the front parlor where the maid had left the tea. She didn't want it, but the ritual of pouring and drinking would stave off her grief for a while. Despair hollowed her out. She knew what she had done. He wouldn't come back. If not for that terrible bequest, she could have accepted his suit, allowed him to court her, and she had no doubt, marry her.

Being left destitute terrified Virginia. To have nothing, or to depend totally on the whim of her father or her husband—not again, never again. To be dependent on a man again—any man, even one who loved her—filled her with unreasoning terror.

A rumble of wheels outside heralded the phaeton passing her window. Standing to one side of the window, so he would not see her, Virginia watched him pass out of her life. Oh, she'd see him again, but only at a distance, and never with the intimacy she still craved.

Francis—Wolverley—held the whip just so, but he had not yet urged the horses to a showy trot. He was so close she saw his tight expression. Then the shoulders of his brown coat moved as he shrugged, and he turned back to his horses, lifting his gloved hand, ready to urge them on.

An urchin stood on the pavement in front of the rails of her house, watching the carriage pass. She'd seen that child before, but beggars often had spots they claimed as their own. Dressed in a torn and worn scarlet coat that could have once belonged to a soldier, he could be a thief, perhaps a cutpurse. He held a piece of leather. A sling, the kind boys in the countryside used to scare crows off the crops.

As Francis's carriage passed by, he lifted it. Whipping it around expertly, he flicked, and a small missile sped from the sling, high in the air. A dark spot shot across the blue sky.

A sharp cry and a rattle followed in short order. Francis jerked back as if shot, veering sideways. He tumbled off the phaeton, plummeting to the ground headfirst.

Virginia raced out of the parlor, straight to the front door. Butler stared at her, his mouth open in astonishment, but Virginia did not hesitate, fumbling at the door before wrenching it open.

She took the shallow steps to the street in two bounds and hurried to the spot where Francis lay, his body sprawled at an unnatural angle.

The horses bolted, the rattle of the carriage punctuated by galloping hooves and the shouts of the tiger. She could do nothing about that. Francis was all her concern.

Butler was not far behind. "Get him inside," he snapped, glancing up at someone behind her. Hurst wasted no time hurrying around the prone body and tucking his arms under him.

Virginia got to her feet. Although the day was fine, her hands were cold with shock, her face numb with fear. No thought other than terror that the urchin had killed him filled her mind and urged her body into action.

Francis was not an easy burden. It took Hurst and Butler, both substantial men, to heave him up. He left a patch of blood behind. She swallowed down her nausea.

Virginia picked up a few items that had fallen from his pockets as the men carried him up the stairs and into the house. She hurried after them and kicked the door closed with her foot, just as Francis had done when he'd called less than an hour earlier.

The housemaid stood on the landing staring down at the scene.

"Take him upstairs to my room," Virginia snapped. She was sleeping in the only bed that could receive him. "Get water and cloths," she told the maid. Her mind raced with horrific possibilities.

Only one thing was twisting her insides, turning her heart and mind inside out. He could be dying, if he wasn't dead already. That tore her apart. Rather than that, she would have kept him with her, accepted him. What had she let slip out of her fingers? What had she done, sending him away like that?

Picking up her skirts, she raced upstairs.

Butler and Hurst bent over the body laid out on the bed. Butler had dispensed with his own coat, and they were in the process of removing Francis's.

"He's alive," Butler said tersely. "Breathing, but he's out cold. He must have hit that road hard."

Winston stood to the side, her face a picture of shock. "My lady, you cannot have him here...."

"Quiet," Virginia ordered her. "His lordship has been in an accident. He needs our help." Although from what she'd seen, "accident" was not the best way to describe what had happened.

"He was driving his phaeton," she told Hurst. "He fell about five feet."

Damn all sporting vehicles. Most of all, damn the urchin. She would happily murder him if she ever got a hand on his scrawny hide.

Virginia turned as the housemaid scurried in, a can of hot water in her hands, and cloths and towels slung over her arms. "I thought they might come in handy," the woman said. "My lady," she added, giving a scared glance in Winston's direction.

Virginia waved away her insistence on her title. "You did well, Fowler."

Hurst held out his hand. "I could do with one of them cloths." His polite tones were stripped away in the face of disaster, replaced by the voice of the authentic Londoner.

Grabbing one from the maid, Virginia slapped it in his hand. After roughly stuffing her lace ruffles up her sleeves so they wouldn't get in her way, she took another cloth and went to stand at Hurst's side, ready to render any help he needed.

Francis was so pale, but he was breathing shallowly. Butler was exposing his shoulder by the expedient of tearing and cutting the cloth away, revealing a strongly muscled arm and shoulder. He felt along it, while Virginia turned her attention to where Hurst was attending to Francis's head wound. That was where all the blood had come from, since his shirt was not stained with it.

The footman gently turned Francis's head so he faced Butler, who stood on the other side of the bed. Virginia barely recognized her own voice when she said, "Get a physician. Do it now."

* * * *

Hurst had raced half a mile to find the man, who resided in Red Lion Square, or so his card said. The footman brought the physician straight up to the room, where Virginia and Butler were cradling Francis's head, trying to stop the flow of blood. Winston stood to one side with an armful of bloody cloths.

They didn't bother to correct the man's assumption that Francis was Virginia's husband. He did not know them, which was probably just as well.

She volunteered her name as Durban, the first name to come to mind, the artist who had painted the small landscape by her bed.

The physician had insisted that Virginia leave the room while he and the two men stripped and examined him. Virginia had protested, but the man had been adamant. "I need the space," he'd said. "Pray do not concern yourself. I will do everything I can. But I will do nothing if you remain in the room."

"But I'm his wife!"

The lie had come easily, but it had no effect. The last thing she wanted to do was leave him, but faced with the medical man's intransigence, she could do nothing but obey. Francis was terribly hurt, how much she didn't know, and the uncertainty twisted her stomach into a tight knot.

Entering the dressing room, Winston helped her to strip out of her town finery and don the plainer gown set out for her planned quiet evening at home. What would happen now she had no idea, but if Francis was so ill, she would not be going anywhere on Monday.

Then she found her writing slope and scrawled a note for Francis's mother. The phaeton had gone, so why had nobody called to discover where he was? Had his mother already left town? She'd get Hurst to deliver the note later. She needed the footman to help care for Francis now.

She was emerging from the room when Butler came out of her bedroom. "You may go in now, ma'am."

She appreciated that he'd recalled her borrowed title, but wasted no time going back into her room.

Francis had been put to bed, wearing a borrowed clean nightshirt, presumably loaned by one of the men. His left wrist was wrapped in a clean bandage, and another was bound around his head. He was asleep, his chest moving gently with every breath. Virginia counted ten of them, breathing with him, before she turned back to the physician, Mr. Cunningham.

"Well, madam," the physician said, turning away from the bed and rolling down his sleeves. "I've done all I can. Your husband will do."

She breathed out in a long sigh.

"He must have a very tough hide, madam, because his head is not broken, although he has damaged it."

Cunningham glanced up at her. "He has a gash to his head, which needs cleaning and dressing at least twice a day for the next week to ensure it does not take an infection. His arm is badly bruised where he fell, but nothing is broken. That should heal cleanly in less than two weeks. He is, however, unconscious and likely to remain so for some time. He has suffered a concussion. He needs watching, madam. All night. If there is any change, send for me immediately."

"What do you mean, change?" Fear clutched at her chest.

Cunningham spoke quietly and deliberately. He must have met many situations before where he'd had to impart bad news. "When he wakes, he may be impaired in some way."

"Impaired? How?" she demanded sharply.

"Blows to the skull such as your husband has suffered have unpredictable consequences, especially in the following week or so. He could recover in a few days, or it could take more time. The brain is swollen, you see, and we have no way of curing injuries of that nature. We have to wait and see. Bleeding him will not help in this matter, neither will cupping or any other cure. I speak from experience, madam, not from theory, as more fashionable men would have it."

He paused, watching her carefully.

Virginia steeled herself. "Tell me everything."

He kept a sharp gaze on her while he told her, plainly and clearly. "Very well." He spoke slowly. "He could be blind, either temporarily or permanently. His hearing could be affected, or his sense of smell. Or all three."

She clutched her chest. "Oh, God!"

Cunningham continued. "The most likely outcome, however, tends to affect the memory. Your husband may not know you when he wakes. Or he may remember everything. Generally, a section of the memory is lost, but not all of it."

"He will not know me?" Dazed, she tried to take in what he was saying. Blind, deaf, what could be worse? Oh, a complete loss of memory.

"That is unlikely, madam, or if it is, the most severe effects tend to be less permanent. As the swelling in the brain subsides, the memory may return."

"What should I do?"

"Keep him quiet and calm, and allow him time to recover. Do not alarm or irritate him."

Her mind began to work again. Her plans teemed back. She pushed them aside. She would handle them as she thought of them, but her first concern was for Francis. "What is the worst that could happen?"

"He could die."

Virginia's mind immediately rejected the words. She hadn't heard that word, the most terrible of all. He wouldn't die. He couldn't. Why, two hours ago Francis was perfectly well, in rude health. Nearly making love to her. Would she ever feel his hands on her again? Would he ever wake?

Did the physician have to be so brutal? He would not die. Not here, not today, or tomorrow. Oh, why had she said no to him? Why had her cowardice forced her to turn him down? Yes, cowardice. Fear of the unknown, of giving herself to another man. As if all men were the same.

Her throat tightened, her heart sank, but reason seeped back. "What is most likely?"

"That he will wake late in the night, or tomorrow morning, and fail to remember events from a few days ago to a year or more. If he does, do not try to force him, but tell him the memories will return in time. Let him know what he needs to, and no more. Assure him that rest will restore him."

"I see."

"And don't forget, if there is a change, any change for the worse, send for me immediately."

She did not ask his fee. Instead, she pushed a purse into his hand, fat with coin. He didn't demur.

He left Virginia to her fate.

Chapter 9

Groaning, Francis opened his eyes, then snapped them shut as a shaft of bright light pierced his skull. What the devil had happened to him? This was worse than any headache he'd ever suffered, even after the time he'd stayed drunk for five days in a row for a bet.

A soothing hand stroked his brow. "You're safe."

What an odd thing to say! Nevertheless, he recognized the voice and the touch. Virginia was with him.

A male voice, one he didn't know, said, "Is he awake, ma'am?"

"I think so. He's coming around. Close the curtains, please, Hurst. The light might hurt his eyes."

He smiled. Always practical, his Virginia.

Except she was not his Virginia, was she? Vivid recollections throbbed through his head. He'd come close to making love to her, but something had stopped them. She'd been wearing a green velvet caraco jacket, the color of grass on a spring sky, and he'd done his best to get her out of it.

He had pictures rather than a clear memory, but they were more than enough. The sight of her hair coming down from its pins, the way it felt in his hands, her delectable body, the mouthwatering curves, the taste of her throat, her mouth, and her response…

To his shock, his body stirred. He hadn't thought there was room in his body for anything but pain. And it wasn't as if he could do anything about it now. At least he was safely tucked away, under the covers of this bed. Whose bed? It didn't belong to him. Subtle differences told him that.

After the rattle of curtain rings against a rail, he tried opening his eyes again. It still hurt, but this time he persevered.

There she was, sitting next to the bed, a nightstand bearing a variety of objects, from a decanter of some cloudy liquid to a dark glass bottle containing what he suspected was physic.

"Francis!"

When he tried to reach out to her, his arm exploded in pain. He cried out. She put her hand over his, gently moving it back to his side. "You landed on this side, so it's badly bruised, but the physician says it will be much better in a week and healed in two."

"Physician? Have I been ill?" He searched her eyes, hating the anxiety in them. Had he caused that distress?

"Not exactly. You had a fall from your carriage."

He tried to laugh, but more pain shot through his head, so he stopped. "I've never fallen out of a carriage in my life. Did I hit a rut in the road?"

"No." She sighed. "Somebody tried to make a hole in your head, but you are tougher than that, my friend."

No, not friend. "Who? Someone shot at me?"

"A small boy used a sling. You have a gash on your head and a large lump behind it."

He winced. David had killed Goliath using a sling. Well, at least he'd emerged better off than the Philistine. His head was still on his shoulders, even if it did hurt like the devil.

So he'd been hit, fallen from the phaeton and struck his head. Which accounted for the conviction that his head was splitting in two. Or perhaps into tiny pieces.

How long had that happened after she'd said she could not consider marrying him for six years? He remembered that part. But if he reminded her of that painful conversation, she was likely to close down. He'd seen her do it, but she wouldn't do it with him. He wouldn't give her the chance.

Nor would he mention the attack on him the night of the ball, and the muttered instruction to leave her alone. The determination to remain with her, that someone wanted to hurt her, firmed in his mind.

"What's the date?"

"It's Saturday, the twenty-eighth of June, the day after the attack."

He grunted. Even that hurt.

"Do you think you could drink some barley water?"

"To hell with barley water. Bring me brandy."

The man standing on the other side of the bed laughed. Indignant, Francis turned his head to confront the burly servant and then regretted his impulsive move. His head didn't just throb internally, it hurt outside, too.

Hurst was a footman, he guessed, from the man's size and simple clothing. "I'm sorry, my lord, but my lady is as likely to give you brandy as she is to give it to me."

He raised a brow, an action that froze most servants, but it had no effect on this one. "I see." He had to admit he was thirsty. "I detest barley water. How about a small beer?"

Reluctantly, the man nodded, but glanced at Virginia for permission. She must have given it, because he left the room.

"Where am I?"

A wary look entered her eyes. "In my bedroom at my London town house."

"Ah."

"Nobody from your house has come to see you," she said. "I sent Hurst with a message this morning, but he said it was shuttered and nobody was inside."

He nodded, then wished he hadn't. After gulping some cool air to conquer the rising wave of nausea, he said, "That's not surprising. I only hired that house for the season, and I gave it up after my mother left for the country earlier this week. I used a room at my club instead. Why is this house so quiet and bare? Where are all your servants?"

There were no crystal containers on the dressing table, no scattering of delicate robes. The drapes around the bed had gone.

"I was leaving town, so the house is under holland covers. I have only five servants here, and the doorknocker is off. I was planning to leave on Monday, but I won't do that now."

He remembered, but he chose not to let her know. "Why not?"

She shook her head, smiling. "Why do you think? A man collapses outside my house, and I'm expected to walk away? That is not likely under any circumstances. Much less when it is—" She broke off, biting her lip.

"Me," he finished for her. "Thank you."

"I thought the man who was with you would have driven the phaeton back to your home and reported it. When nobody came, I sent a message."

Damn. The pair of matched grays were the only cattle he'd allowed to be harnessed to the phaeton. "The phaeton has probably magically vanished into the rookery of Seven Dials, never to return. The horses with them."

Her eyes rounded, bless her. "What about your tiger?"

"A new hire from Chambers'. Adequate at his work, but I never intended to keep him on after the end of the season. I told him so a few days ago, so I can assume that he has made off with the phaeton and horses as his reward."

She gasped. "We should send for the authorities, lay a complaint. Horse stealing is a capital offense."

The phaeton and horses were the least of his worries. He reached out, far more carefully this time, and laid his hand over hers. "Normally I would do so, but I fear we'll never see them again in any event. Let it be, Virginia. The long and short of it is that there is nobody in London to ask after me. Nobody who knows where I am."

She swallowed, watching him.

He groped past the pain threatening to split his head open, trying to think. When she'd told him about her husband's will, anger had consumed him. Why should she wait on the whims of a dead man? What was it about her marriage and her early life that had put that terror in her eyes? It wasn't him, he was sure of it. Was it the prospect of losing her wealth? So many questions, so few answers.

Perhaps if she trusted him more, she would let her husband's estate go. He could provide for her, and he had every intention of doing so. But until then, he had to be patient. Not six years patient, but until he regained his strength.

If she knew he remembered everything, telling him the real reason she wouldn't marry him, she might back off again. He'd left her house thinking that he'd handled her badly, that she would never allow him close to her again, and now he was back.

So let her think his memory had been affected by the blow to his head. Let her think she had her secret safe. The next time she told him, he would not be so insistent, nor would he react so angrily.

But he would have her and keep her. He refused to allow her to obey a dead man. The spiteful toad had tried to ensure that nobody would have her but him.

And somebody—would Jamie Dulverton go that far?—had tried to kill him to keep him away from her. He'd ignored the warning from the first attack and been punished for it. He did not doubt that the two incidents were connected.

Anyone desperate enough to attack him was dangerous.

"I will escort you to Devonshire when I'm well." Because she was not traveling on her own.

She patted his shoulder, the uninjured one, as if soothing a mad person. He didn't have the energy to protest now, but once this screaming headache subsided, he'd take her to task. They could not stay here too long. Who knew when the attacker would choose to break into the house?

"How many people are in this house?"

"Apart from us? Five servants, three women, two men."

His stomach hollowed out. They were too vulnerable here. They had to move. But he couldn't do that yet, however much he wanted to.

The beer arrived, along with tea and bread and butter. Content to watch Virginia gliding around the room, pouring the tea and placing a few slices of the food on a delicate plate, he enjoyed the sight and the intimacy of lying in her bed, savoring the simple domesticity. He wanted that to happen again, frequently. He longed for it.

But in order to have it, he would have to deliver her home, alive and well. And that might take a little finessing.

He lay there, trying not to aggravate his headache by breathing too hard, and made his plans.

* * * *

After she managed to get him to eat a little, Francis slept for most of the day. Virginia sat by the bed, watching him.

When night came she stayed by his side, thinking. Her mind raced in circles, and she didn't seem able to keep a thought for long. The servants entered and left and came back. Today was Friday. Tomorrow she would cancel the carriage she'd hired for Monday and stay here until he was well. Leaving him in this state was unthinkable.

Winston had served food to her on the table by the window, but she'd taken care not to sit in front of it, so as not to alert anyone that she was still in residence.

They dressed Francis's wound twice, and once again before Hurst came to relieve her. The gash was nasty, but they saw no sign of infection and only sluggish bleeding when they cleaned it. The tension winding her tight began to dissipate, especially when she heard Francis's yelps and curses. He wasn't too weak to make use of his varied vocabulary, then.

Hurst insisted she left while Francis was still awake, so he could help him with what he called "male necessities." Francis still seemed dizzy and confused, with periods of lucidity, but recalling what the doctor said, she did not push his memory.

Last night she'd used the guest room nearest to his, not bothering to have the bed made, but lying on top of the mattress with a quilt over her. She had not slept well.

She returned in the early hours of Saturday morning and sent Hurst away. She'd listened to the rasp of his breathing and ensured his pulse was steady. When she'd woken him, as the physician had told her to, he'd moaned in pain, but he'd answered when she spoke his name, before subsiding back into sleep.

She was worried for his life. That attack had been deliberate. She'd watched that boy load and aim his sling, not understanding that he intended to use it on a person. It wasn't as if the street was full of vehicles, as it had been when the season was at its height. Only a couple of chairmen were on the street, and when Hurst had questioned them, they'd claimed to see nothing, which was suspicious in itself.

Who wanted Francis dead?

Exhausted by her near-sleepless night, she leaned forward in the chair Butler had found for her. Finding a soft support under her cheek, she drifted off. She'd meant to stay awake to watch over him, but sleep crashed over her like a great wave, and she was gone.

When she woke, the clock was tinkling the three-quarter hour.

"It's nearly nine o'clock," a soft voice informed her.

A gentle hand rested on her back, a weight she only became aware of when she tried to sit up. He rubbed between her shoulder blades, helping her ease her tired muscles. "Good Lord. I had no intention of sleeping like that."

Her back creaked, and the bones in her elbows and shoulders strained as she sat up. Hair fell into her eyes from her destroyed hairstyle. She must look a complete mess.

"Well," she said, "that puts paid to any romantic feelings you might have had for me."

She shouldn't have said that.

"On the contrary," he answered softly. "Seeing you like this makes me more appreciative, not less."

She shook her head, a denial and an effort to wake up. "Don't be foolish."

He was sitting up in bed, a bank of pillows behind him. Someone must have helped him with that, but it had not been her.

Had the servants seen her that way? Someone must have.

"Butler told me you stayed with me nearly all night," he murmured.

Telltales. She hadn't wanted him to know. Did he remember what she had told him on Thursday, before he'd fallen from his phaeton? She should never have explained the terms of Ralph's will. Even telling someone could cost her everything. Her resolve was set, and she would fulfill her husband's wishes. By the time the six years were up, Francis would have moved on and married someone else. Someone who could fill his nursery.

Getting to her feet, she held the arm of the chair for a few seconds to allow her senses to settle.

"The maid brought hot water fifteen minutes ago," he told her. "It should still be warm."

Normally Virginia would strip and wash all over, with her maid's help, but that was not happening this morning, not with a man in her bedroom. She crossed to the washstand and found the can of hot water standing next to it. While she washed her hands and face, and found the brush for her hair, he spoke to her.

"I have a great deal to thank you for, do I not?"

"How are you feeling?" Their eyes met in the mirror above the washstand. Flicking her attention away, she reached for the towel and buried her face in it.

"I still have a headache, but it's bearable. I can sit without feeling sick, and by the end of today I expect I will feel completely well. I have eaten a couple of fresh rolls, and since that experiment was successful, I'll eat more soon."

"And your arm?"

He winced. "Bruised, that's all. And I lost my earring." He said the last in a mock-downcast tone that made her laugh.

"Why did you wear it? Defiance?"

"Of a kind." He grunted, a half laugh. "I enjoyed it. If people were staring at me, I'd give them something to stare at." He tugged his earlobe. "It feels strange without it. I'll have to get another."

She shook her head. "Everybody knows who you are, Francis. You don't need an earring to announce your presence."

He smiled. "Thank you. I think."

"Who pierced your ear?"

"I did."

Now it was her turn to wince. "My nurse did mine. A hot darning needle and a cork."

"I wish I'd thought of the cork. I did it for a wager ten years ago, and then I thought I might as well make use of it."

She pulled a few pins out of the nest of her hair and groped for more, grimacing when they pulled her scalp. "I need only put off my trip for a day or two, then? It is Saturday today." She glanced at the clock. "The carriage will arrive on Monday morning, but I'll send a message to delay it."

"Good." He swung back the covers and lowered his feet to the floor. "I'll come to Devonshire with you."

The brush pulled away and dangled from her hair as she spun around. "What are you talking about? You can't come. You're still ill."

Annoyingly, he stood up perfectly steadily, only one hand on the bedpost for support. "I'll do. You could be in danger."

"Nonsense! I hired postilions, and Hurst and Winston will accompany me. Get back into bed, Francis, please."

The sight of his bare legs from the knees down alarmed her, especially since he was heading in her direction, his tread firm but slow. Gently, he disentangled the brush, showing far more patience than she would have given him credit for. Far too intimate, like a domestic scene.

But then, what would she know about those?

Taking the brush from her, he set about taming her tangled curls. "You have very beautiful hair," he murmured. "Like silk."

"Like tangled wool," she retorted, but she allowed him to stroke the brush through her locks, gently teasing out the knots.

"Silk," he repeated firmly. "Virginia, I have to tell you something. On Thursday—"

"You remember?" she interjected, far too harshly.

"Not everything. There are some annoying gaps in my memory. I don't remember leaving the house, for example."

She breathed a sigh of relief. He probably didn't remember what she'd told him. He might not even remember his proposal. Better that way.

"I do have something to tell you, though."

Oh, perhaps not. "What about?" She tried not to hold her breath.

"Leaving your house the day after I kissed you for the first time— Virginia, do keep still, you nearly jerked the brush out of my hand—I was waylaid by what I guessed were hired ruffians. They warned me to keep away from you."

"What? And you've only told me now?" She forced herself to remain still while he stroked the brush through her hair.

"I regret that omission, but I had no way of knowing they were serious." Before she could scold him further, he continued, "Thursday's attack on me was deliberate, also, obviously. I'm assuming the same person instigated it."

She bit her lip, a sting of pain that reminded her what she should do. "Then perhaps you should listen to them. Stay away from me, Francis."

She couldn't let him face more danger because of her. How could she ever live with herself if she did that? Somehow she had to persuade him to stay away. She'd double her guards if that would satisfy him. But he had to leave.

"I will listen to them, but not like that. I intend to keep closer to you. Someone means you harm. Why, I have no idea, but we can discuss that later."

"But you are the one getting hurt. They want you to leave me alone. So do it."

"I am your protector, or someone thinks I am. So they want me away from you so they can get at you. I cannot allow that."

"They won't hurt me."

He shook his head. "Are you sure about that?"

He would not let her protest, but continued to stroke the brush through her hair, now completely disentangled. She watched him in the mirror. He was totally engrossed in his work. The rhythm soothed her as nothing else had done, as if he was brushing her stress away.

He spoke to her as he brushed. "In this house you are a sitting target, so we must not stay here. The knocker is off the door, but whoever is watching this house knows we're in here. We're vulnerable to attack. If a ruffian breaks down the back door, we'll be overwhelmed in minutes. Besides us, we have two menservants and three women. While I don't doubt your cook could give a good account of herself, we cannot risk it. We must move, and we'll do it quickly and discreetly."

That sounded ridiculous. "Why would anyone want to attack me here? I have nothing of particular value left in this house. The jewelry left two days ago with footmen to guard it in the traveling carriage. I planned to follow quietly on my own."

"And so you will. I have been speaking with Butler, and we agreed that he and Hurst should come with us as footmen. They are healthy men in the prime of life, and I believe you can trust them. We will travel quickly."

"*We?*" When she tried to turn to face him, his hand pressed a little harder to stop her, just enough to keep her in place.

He worked methodically through her hair. It crackled with energy.

"Yes, *we.*"

"I'll hire more men," she said.

"And stick out even more? No, my dear, we'll travel together as a private couple. Hurst has gone to the club for my valise, so I can be respectable."

Her thoughts whirled.

The trip to Devonshire would take the best part of a week. Crammed in a traveling chaise with the man she had dreamed about this last month, even with her maid there? How could she even consider it? "I am sure I'll be perfectly safe."

"I'm not." He put the brush back on the washstand. "There. Now you are more like yourself. Shall I pin it up for you?"

"Can you?" Before he could attempt such an outrageous thing, she grabbed the pin dish and held it to her chest. "I'm perfectly capable of achieving a simple style, thank you."

Chuckling, he stepped back. Apart from the bandage wrapped around his head, he appeared annoyingly normal. But surely his head must be pounding.

"Go and change," he said. "Your maid has left clothes for you in the powder room. I'll shave."

"Just like that, you're taking control of my life?" If she hadn't been wearing house slippers, Virginia would have stamped her foot, but the action would have hurt her more than Francis. "This is why I won't marry any man! They take over, give orders they are not entitled to. How could you think I would do this?"

He couldn't travel with her. He was too tempting, but more important, he was in danger every minute he spent with her.

Stepping forward, he put his hands on her shoulders. She lifted her chin, meeting his eyes defiantly. "I will not leave you. Someone wants you alone, separated from any protectors. I have no idea what they want, but you seem to forget that you are a woman of substance. You know how dangerous traveling on your own can be. Let me do this, or I'll hire another vehicle and follow behind you. Either way, I'll be with you."

This time she did stamp. "How could you? This is intolerable. I'm merely going to my estate." She stopped guiltily. She wasn't going straight there. She would stop at Combe Manor on the way.

He soothed her, stroking her hair as if she were an agitated kitten. And to her chagrin, she melted under his touch, felt herself moving closer—

No. That would never happen again. Yesterday had warned her, she could not allow that situation to recur. She'd been so close to losing— everything on that table.

She stepped back. "I'll dress," she said firmly. "And you'll rest. Then we will talk further." Turning, she made for the dressing room. "That's an order. You may shave and wash, but there is no need to dress, if you don't wish to. I'll have dinner served up here later."

She enjoyed his responsive chuckle, although she gave him no sign that she had done so. That would only encourage him.

When she reached the door, he called her name. "Virginia."

Her hand on the doorjamb, she turned. "What is it?"

"I'm truly concerned for you. This isn't another start, or a jape."

She did not deserve his care. He was courting danger for her sake and had faced it already. Her mind was in complete turmoil, but she was determined on one thing. She would not put Francis into any more peril. If the men wanted him to leave her alone, well, he would do so.

She was quite capable of taking care of herself, as long as she employed more men to accompany her. When the watchers saw her leaving on her own, they would be satisfied. Francis had not said so, but she could guess who wanted to separate them.

Jamie wanted to marry her, so he would want them apart. He had to be the person behind this. If she ever found proof of her suspicion, she would ensure Jamie Dulverton suffered for it.

Turning away, she entered the dressing room and closed the door.

* * * *

They argued all Saturday, until she'd pretended to give in, just to get some peace. But Virginia had made up her mind.

How could she ask an injured man to do more than he had already? And just as much to the point, how could she travel with such a man, when they had let the floodgates open on their feelings for each other?

Better he cooled his heels in Derbyshire and Leicestershire, as he'd originally planned. A period apart would cool their ardor, and when they met again, they could slip back into the guarded cordiality that had marked their previous dealings. No courting, no more thoughts of marriage.

He would always have her grateful thanks.

He'd slept, but a normal slumber. Indeed, she could barely believe he was recovering so quickly, but she felt safe leaving him here.

When she was sure he was sound asleep, she found Butler and told him of her amended plans. She would leave earlier than she'd planned. At half past six the next morning, Sunday, a day earlier than she'd told Francis, she would leave in a hired carriage. She sent her revised orders to the livery stables she usually used.

Not being foolish, she had also arranged for more protection. The carriage she'd originally ordered would arrive on Monday morning to confuse anyone who might still be watching the house. Francis could take it if he wanted to, but she'd prefer he remained in town until he was well again. Preferably at his club, out of danger.

Everything was arranged.

Butler had his orders. He would remain in London, as planned, and keep his lordship in her house until he was well enough to leave. Or accompany him back to his club, whichever Francis preferred.

That night she went to the guest room she was using, leaving orders to be woken quietly at half past five.

The discreet tap on her door had her jolting awake. She dressed simply, Winston helping her in silence and following her down the back stairs. They did not put their shoes on until they were in the garden. Hurst followed with their valises.

They went out by the garden gate and walked up the narrow path between the houses and the stables, to where the carriage waited at the other end of the street. Only then did she breathe more freely.

She let Hurst hand her up into the carriage she'd hired. It was a comfortable but plain chaise, shiny black on the outside with yellow upholstery on the interior, a little worn, but comfortable and well-sprung.

Virginia had donned a plain russet-colored gown and had packed another in dark green in her valise. She had plenty of linen, caps, and a spare hat, enough to render her respectable, but not enough to make her stand out, and she carried her trusty road atlas.

Winston traveled in the carriage with her, and it was furnished with every comfort.

Butler came up behind her. "Everyone on this side of the street has left, my lady. Lady Conyngham's ball was the last event of the season of any significance, and now everyone is fleeing London as if the plague has hit it."

"So Lord Wolverley will not be seen leaving the house?"

"No, my lady. I will make sure of it."

Hurst carried her valise and vanity case to the vehicle and tossed them in the boot, then came back around the side of the carriage and opened the door for her. Virginia's maid settled on the opposite seat with her back to the horses, and they were off.

Chapter 10

"What are you talking about, gone?" Crushing the letter in his hand, Francis glared at the perfidious butler. The clock on the mantel tinkled the hour. Eight o'clock.

"The viscountess decided to leave early, my lord. She asks you not to worry."

"How dare she?" he roared, fury mixed with fear surging through him. Flinging back the bedclothes, he leaped out of bed, flinching when his bruised arm hit the bedpost. "What is she thinking? Do you know how much danger she is in?"

"Danger?" Butler shook his head. "That is you, my lord, surely."

He brought his face close to Butler's, letting the man see the murder in his eyes. "You foolish man! I was attacked because I was getting too close to her. Someone wants Virginia, and they were prepared to stop me any way they could to get to her. They wanted to separate us because they want her alone." He flung himself to the washstand.

"She has increased her guards, my lord." Despite his assertion, he didn't sound so sure.

Francis snorted. "Much good that will do her." He snatched up the razor and began to strop it on the leather, stopping because his arm was stiff.

Quietly, Butler stepped forward and took the razor from him. "She will be safe, my lord, and if you are not with her, whoever wants her will think you have obeyed the stricture. Either that or, pardon me, they will think you have perished."

"Hmm." His temper subsiding, Francis began to think, putting all his energy into it. Taking the seat, he let Butler shave him. But he didn't believe Butler. Alone, Virginia was in more danger.

"Who does she have with her?"

"A coachman, Hurst, four footmen, including a relief carriage driver, and her maid."

He held up a hand in an imperious gesture. "Winston?"

"Yes, my lord."

Francis made his decision. "I will follow her, but I will not let her know I'm doing it. If I trace her steps, visit the same inns, I can ensure nobody was asking questions about her."

He would do her that service, even if she allowed him nothing else. If, as he suspected, Dulverton had paid the bullies to attack him, Dulverton would consider his work done.

But Francis would not follow his original plans. He'd spoken of them in public, so no doubt Dulverton had heard of them. He would travel the same road as Virginia and ensure nobody was following.

No doubt she thought to cool what had exploded around them, but he would not let that fall away. He'd found her, and he would keep her. He'd allowed her to think that his memory of his marriage proposal had disappeared with the accident, but he remembered every word. Every touch. She wanted him every bit as much as he wanted her. That was all that mattered. The rest would sort itself out.

Butler finished his shave. As Francis rose to find his clothes, someone hammered at the front door. He exchanged a glance with Butler. "Who is in this house?"

"The cook, the kitchen maid, and the two of us. The couple who will be taking care of the house in her ladyship's absence will not arrive until tomorrow."

He'd seen something that would aid them in the dressing room, should they need it. "Go and answer it. I'll be right behind you."

Glancing out of the window gave him no clues. A couple of chairmen were running up the street, an empty sedan-chair slung between them. The person at the door must have arrived in that, but no crested carriage or any assistant waiting gave any idea who was trying to break the door down with their thumps.

He seized the cavalry sword that rested by the window and unsheathed it, breathing a sigh of relief when he found the weapon well cared for, oiled and sharp. It must have belonged to Ralph. Still in his nightshirt and with nothing on his feet, Francis ran down the stairs behind Butler, taking his station behind the door as the man answered it.

With a gasp, he flung the door wide.

"You can put that thing down," Miss Childers said, sparing him a glare as she barreled through.

Numbly, Francis closed the door behind her.

Although dressed in her usual finery, the banker had come alone. She led the way to the back parlor, the scene of Francis's near-seduction of Virginia, her steps brisk and no-nonsense. The scent of lavender and lemons still hung in the air, aromas he would always associate with Virginia.

"Here." From under her cloak, Miss Childers produced one of her infernal leather folders. She unfastened the strings and drew out a paper.

Butler, having recovered from his astonishment first, was the first to speak. "Would madam like refreshment?"

"Nothing, thank you. Where is Virginia? This is not a social visit. I need to talk to her."

"She left this morning," Francis told her. "Very early."

Miss Childers uttered a most unladylike curse. "Then there is no time to waste. I believe she's in danger." She gave Francis a more perceptive study, taking in the bruises on his arm and the bandage wrapped around his head. "I see you've been in the wars already."

He gave her a rueful grin. "Indeed."

"And it was for her, was it not?"

He nodded.

"You are devoted to her?"

Not wanting to disturb her flow, he nodded again.

"Then you must listen to me." Shuffling through the papers, she plucked one out and handed it to him. "Here."

Alarmed at her urgent words, Francis glanced down a neat line of figures and saw nothing amiss. "What is this?"

"Not the numbers, look on the left!"

And there he saw it. The name "Wilhelmina Winston," and this address. The name of Virginia's personal maid. He gave the numbers another perusal. "These payments are much too high for a salary."

"But not too high for a bribe," Miss Childers said, her lips firmed in a straight line.

Now he saw the sharp brains behind the beauty. This woman was formidable. He'd always known that but never seen it so clearly before.

She went on. "Those payments arrive on a regular basis from a bank in Exeter. The address seems innocuous. One of my clerks marked it for my attention because of the London address, which he recognized. This kind of money for a lady's maid?" She shook her head. "Added to which…"

Heedless of the ink rubbing off on her white gloves, Miss Childers flourished more paper at him.

It was a London morning newspaper, the kind Francis usually read at his club. "This is an account of the latest scandal to hit London this morning. The whole of the Square Mile is talking about it. Four footmen from Chambers' Livery Stables were found in an alley this morning, their throats cut clean through. Their employer said they had been hired to accompany a lady of fashion on her forthcoming visit to the West Country. The carriage they were to use was missing, and the horses too." She gave a sound of exasperation. "The reporter seems more obsessed with the theft of the horses than the deaths of the poor unfortunates."

Francis snatched the paper from her and scanned it, before handing it to Butler. "Virginia uses Chambers'." His voice shook.

"She used them to hire the carriage and staff to take her into the country," Butler said hollowly. "She planned to travel covertly. I sent Hurst to make the arrangements yesterday."

His narrow face had gone white, his face reflecting Francis's appalled realization.

Someone wanted more than for him to stay away. They knew the carriage Virginia planned to take, not difficult since many members of society used that livery stable. But they were desperate, or ruthless enough to murder four men to get to her.

Francis's mind clicked back from numb horror to action.

Virginia was in danger, from whom he did not know, but he had his suspicions. Who but Jamie Dulverton would want to do harm to Virginia? She'd rejected his suit, so she was no more use to him alive. But if she died, he would inherit the lands he had lost. But would Jamie be desperate enough to murder?

A doubt remained. He had not considered Dulverton a murderer. But perhaps the people working for him had taken his orders too far. However, if Dulverton had started this, he was responsible for everything that happened.

Why had he not thought of that possibility before? From proposing marriage to murder, with nothing in between.

He rattled out a series of orders. There was no time to waste, certainly no time to think. He had to get to her.

Or he might never see her alive again.

Chapter 11

Virginia enjoyed the journey to their second stop at Staines. They had stopped to change the horses and have an hour's rest before continuing.

The route was picturesque, and her map book contained colorful descriptions of the places they passed. A few grand houses and a number of elegant villas, not all of them occupied by perfectly respectable people, met her fascinated eyes. She traveled this route at least twice a year, to and from London, and each time Virginia found something new to enjoy.

Winston slept. At one point she tilted alarmingly close to Virginia's shoulder, but she eased the maid away without waking her. The Great South Road was busy; at this time of year the fashionable were leaving town, and they traveled past a few carriages with coats-of-arms blazoned on their sides. Virginia shrank back in her seat and pulled her hat low every time.

Carters were traveling to London, carrying the food and produce that stopped the residents starving. London was surrounded by market gardens and small farms, all of which serviced the vast open maw of the city. Virginia watched, noted, and enjoyed.

Staines was just over twenty miles from town, so when they stopped to change horses, Virginia decided to take dinner in the pleasant inn. The Three Cranes was busy, but Virginia sent Hurst to bespeak a table, and he returned with the glad tidings that one was available.

"And do you recognize anyone here?" she asked anxiously.

"No, my—ma'am, nobody."

By her side, Winston groaned and blinked awake. "Are we changing horses?"

"Dinner," she said firmly.

The interior of the inn was pleasant, with oak paneling around the walls and enough space between the tables to offer a degree of privacy. A few people glanced at them as they passed, but no recognition lit anyone's eyes. They were safe to eat here.

The landlord settled them at a comfortable table overlooking the yard. Unfortunately, the tables with a better view of the river were all taken. Virginia decided not to make a fuss and ordered their meat pie and ale, with a similar order being sent to their servants. Winston joined her at the table.

The food arrived, fragrant and hot. Since they were traveling privately, they did not have to rush, unlike the passengers on the stagecoach, who had about ten minutes to burn their mouths on the food and dash back to the coach. The stagecoach waited for no one.

By the time they had done, the room was considerably emptier. The stagecoach had left twenty minutes ago, and no more private passengers had arrived. There were perhaps six other people sitting at the tables now.

Virginia stood up, shaking her skirts out, preparing to leave. Hurst should have settled with the landlord. Winston got to her feet as the sound of wheels on cobbles heralded another arrival.

A shout alerted her, then another, the noise increasing so quickly she hardly had time to think. More shouts echoed back to her. The yard was in complete chaos, men fighting, yelling. A riot had erupted seemingly from nowhere. What was going on? Was Hurst involved?

She whipped her head around when someone yelled closer to her. Silver flashed as a man sitting at a nearby table brought his hand down on the wrist of a footman holding a dagger—one of her hired footmen. The man's mouth opened in a soundless cry, heard only faintly above the mess of people in the yard, and the mullioned windows between them. But he dropped the knife.

As she moved to grab the weapon, someone seized her wrist and forced her arm behind her back, wrenching her shoulder. Pain shot up her arm, piercing and momentarily stunning. It was her turn to cry out, but she would not allow her attacker to have it all his way. The man at the table pulled the white linen cloth, sending the dagger and everything else on the surface clattering to the floor.

Gritting her teeth, Virginia turned in the direction of the tug and, before the man could secure her other hand, grabbed something from the avalanche of tableware, and swung it at him.

The teapot shattered against his head, its scalding contents pouring over him. Her would-be captor's scream was totally unnecessary, but the distraction gave Virginia a chance to jerk aside, loosening his hold.

Springing back, she cast about her for another weapon. The man fixed her with a fulminating glare and snatched up a carving knife from the long table running down the center of the room. The woman who had been cleaning it before the riot exploded moved away hastily, the clatter and crash of crockery and cutlery adding to the din.

Everyone was shouting, including Virginia. Winston was nowhere in sight. She had vanished as if she'd never been there.

Backing away from the man wielding a knife, Virginia grabbed plates and whatever came to hand to hurl at him. They shattered against the walls with satisfying crashes as the man ducked and weaved to avoid them. People shouted into the chaos.

She was backing off to the end of the room, and she did not even know if there was a door there. She could be trapped. If she was, she'd make a good account of herself. This man was not planning to capture her. He had murder in his eyes.

A door behind her burst open, hitting the wall behind her, and a voice she knew shouted, "Here! Virginia, to me!"

Butler? What the devil was he up to?

Virginia didn't hesitate. If Butler was in league with the people trying to kill her, she was done for. But if she stayed here, she was finished anyway. People cowered against the walls, watching the man advancing on her. Nobody stepped up to help her. And she was running out of plates.

Virginia flung herself through the door and spun around, hoicking her skirts above her knees in one hand for fear she would trip.

"This way!" Butler called, and caught her free hand, dragging her across the yard at the back of the inn to the river.

She had not noticed the path by the Thames before, little more than a towpath, but it provided an escape route. Butler pulled her along until she caught the pace and ran with him. They hurried in silence for the stretch of several houses, until they paused and looked back. The noise was fading, so the riot had not spread to the rest of the village.

They were both breathing heavily. Butler bent over, his hands on his knees, sucking in air. "I'm too old for this," he said, and straightened, meeting her gaze. "You all right, my lady?"

"Oh, it's 'my lady' now, is it?"

Butler gave a wry grin. "I had to attract your attention somehow, ma'am, and not some other lady."

"What on earth happened? And what the devil are you doing in Staines instead of London?"

Butler turned and led the way along the path at a more sedate pace. The path was not wide enough for them to walk abreast, so Virginia followed, keeping a keen eye on the path behind them while he spoke.

"The footmen you hired were murdered, and Winston has been receiving significant sums of money from an unknown source in Exeter. You were surrounded by traitors, my lady. We had to get to you."

"Good Lord. Murdered?"

"Miss Childers brought us the news the day you left. Chambers is to be trusted, but the footmen were waylaid. Miss Childers is endeavoring to discover who paid for the murders. The chaise, by the way, was stolen, along with the horses."

She gaped at him. "All to get at me?"

"Indeed, my lady."

"How did you get here so quickly? We were many hours ahead of you."

His mouth flattened. "We rode here. We did not stop."

"At all?" Fascinated, she watched this unforeseen aspect of the normally cool, collected butler.

"At all."

Her dazed mind caught up with events. Four footmen dead. Her maid a traitor. No, that did not make sense. "You said 'we.'"

"His lordship and I. We came ventre à terre, as they say."

Her butler had hidden depths. But she still didn't understand. "If Winston wished me ill, why would she not have killed me before? She had plenty of opportunities." She shuddered when she recalled how many chances the maid had to murder her. And yet she had not.

"We believe, that is, his lordship believes, that she was only told to watch you until recently, when the attempts were made on his lordship's life. The connection between you was noted."

That did not make her feel much better. Her mind still whirling, Virginia tried to take stock. But she could make no sense of what had just happened. Someone wanted her badly enough to have four men murdered?

A name lurked in the back of her mind, but she did not want to believe it. Could Jamie really do this?

Even when he'd tried to seduce her at the ball, she never imagined that he would attack her. He only wanted to compromise her into marriage. Not kill her.

Another man occupied her thoughts. "What of Francis? Where is he?"

Butler shook his head. Somehow he'd retained his wig, and the tail whipped his shoulders. "We got separated in the riot. There is another inn about half a mile from here. He suggested we meet there."

Francis! Had she nursed him through the murderous attack only to lose him now?

"Why a riot?"

"The four men accompanying you were assuredly not from Chambers'. As soon as they recognized his lordship, they set up a hue and cry. Yelled 'Stop, thief!' and set the whole yard against us. What could we do but create as much chaos as we could?" He gave a helpless shrug and grin.

"I see." Belatedly she recalled her still precarious situation. "What do we do now? I have no carriage, no way of traveling. And I have no money, nothing more than the purse I carry and the clothes I stand up in. I left all my possessions back at the inn."

Without immediate funds, it would take time for them to get out of Staines, away from the danger dogging at their heels. Money could have bought her a swift exit, a horse or a chaise. She didn't know this area, nor anyone who lived here, so she couldn't throw herself on the mercy of a friend. They were stuck.

She still had the gold pendant brooch her husband had given her, a few coins, and her silver SSL pin. She could use the brooch as surety, until they regained their senses and assessed the situation. She had nothing but those.

The tears finally flowed. They poured down her face until Butler roughly shoved a handkerchief into her hand.

"I've lost my hat. I have no gloves. How are we to persuade anyone we are respectable?" she wailed. "And now I have nothing!"

"Don't worry about that." The deep voice, the one she'd wanted to hear above all others, startled her into flinging herself at him.

Francis caught her, chuckling. Blood was caked on his neck, but his arms were strong and his body was a refuge. Virginia laid her forehead against his waistcoat. "I thought—I feared..." She sniffed.

"It takes more than a riot at a country inn to finish me." His voice, alive and vital, vibrated through her.

Hurst spoke from behind him. "Aye, and if it wasn't for his lordship fighting them off, I wouldn't be here either. He's a demon with a sword."

Somehow that information didn't surprise her. Virginia lifted her head. "Are they still coming after us?"

"No," Francis told her, taking the handkerchief and dabbing at her cheeks. "The inn is in utter chaos. Nobody noticed when we left."

After finishing his task, he handed the handkerchief back and smiled down at her before releasing her. He took her hand. "Come, let's walk to the next inn. Not the one we agreed to meet at, but one further in town, where we can pass unnoticed. It can't be more than a mile. Can you manage that?"

She nodded. A mile would give her a chance to collect her senses. The further away she was from the mess, the better she liked it.

They walked together, the four of them, venturing back up to the street through a narrow alley. A few people stared in the direction of the inn, but nobody went there.

As they entered the High Street a cluster of men on horses galloped past, bristling with pistols and swords. "They're probably from the parish, sent to clear up the riot," Francis said. "We won't be going back there."

They passed a shop, the wares encroaching on the pavement. Old furniture, dented silverware, and a rack of second-hand clothes on hooks above the windows served to enhance the three gold balls of the pawnbroker.

Francis halted them and went inside, emerging five minutes later with a straw hat for Virginia and three cocked hats for himself and the other men.

"We should appear at least respectable," he commented as he paused at a horse trough. Finding a handkerchief, he dipped it in the water and scrubbed roughly at the blood on his neck. "Some of the blood is mine. The wound reopened," he said with a grimace. "I fear my wig is stuck to it, but if I move it, it will bleed anew."

"Oh no!" Virginia shuddered, but Francis caught her outstretched hand as she reached for him. "No, wait until we've found shelter."

"Is there any chance of going back to the inn to retrieve our belongings?" Virginia asked.

Francis shook his head. "No. We are not going back there, nor giving our pursuers a chance to discover where we are. Once that chaos has sorted itself out, we should be long gone."

They walked past a few market stalls. The air was rife with honking from the geese tethered there. Once they could hear themselves speak again, Francis added, "Once we are back on the road, we'll decide how to proceed. We have a few hours of daylight left. Enough to leave the dust of Staines behind us."

They reached an inn set on the main road. The small, timber-framed establishment looked like heaven to Virginia. She was shaking, a fine trembling set up in all her limbs. Francis kept a firm hold on her hand. He strode inside the inn as if he owned the place. "Ho, there!"

A small man as wide as he was tall bustled up to them. "Good afternoon, sir. May I help you?"

"You may indeed. My sister and I would like refreshments."

Oh, good idea. Traveling as siblings gave them a kind of respectability. As long as nobody recognized them.

The innkeeper seemed to have no argument with that. "Immediately, my lord, sir. Did you hear about the fight going on up the road?"

"At the Three Cranes?" Francis said casually. "We passed it by."

The innkeeper rubbed his hands together. "Always been a ramshackle place, the Three Cranes. Only built a few years ago, and they never stop trying to take custom from us."

From the clean but dilapidated appearance of the old inn's interior, the Three Cranes had largely succeeded in its self-imposed task. But they were only too grateful to have a seat in a private parlor. Francis saw them ensconced there, then took Hurst off.

The landlady brought them a hunk of bread and a lump of cheese, together with a couple of bottles of wine and some beer; humble fare, but exceedingly welcome. Virginia was not hungry, but she welcomed the wine, curving her hands around the glass to steady herself. At Virginia's request, the landlady also brought a basin of water and some cloths. She bobbed a curtsy and left.

Virginia took a healthy gulp of the rough red wine. Her trembling had largely stopped, but shock still reverberated in her mind. Such violence, some of it aimed at her, had shaken her to the core.

"I had my doubts about that Winston," Butler confessed. "If I may speak freely?"

Since she'd been reduced to ma'am, Virginia saw no reason to stand on ceremony. "Please do."

"I'm new to your household, ma'am, and while the London servants were like any other London servants, the ones you brought from home wouldn't mix with us. It was like they were their own private club." He shrugged. "It happens sometimes, but not as bad as that."

"I see. What about Winston?" The lady's maid had been engaged for her by her husband. She'd been waiting in Virginia's bedroom the first night in her new home. Virginia had never been encouraged to confide in the domestics, so she had not concerned herself with anything other than Winston's skill in her post. But the woman was local, from a family in the village that supplied many of the servants for the main Dulverton estate.

"She talked to us, but she was more comfortable with the staff from your home."

So her overprotective staff? They cared about her, or so she had thought. Were they watching her as well? Virginia's suspicions were hardening. Whatever was causing these attacks, it had its origins in Devonshire, not in London.

Francis returned, Hurst behind him. Francis appeared much too hale and hearty for a man who had been at death's door two days ago, but she was glad to see it. He poured a tankard of beer and handed it to the footman before pouring another brimming mug for himself. "I've hired a chaise. It's a little cramped and not of the best quality, but I want to get out of here as soon as possible."

"Oh. Where did you get the money?"

Francis shrugged. "They didn't get my purse." He dug his hand in his pocket and drew out a fat leather pouch. "And I found this one back at the Three Cranes." He dipped back in his pocket and produced another.

Virginia gasped. "Where did you get that?"

"It was just lying there underneath one of your footmen. I had just put him to sleep," the infuriating man said. "Compensation, I thought. We left a traveling carriage, luggage, and two excellent horses back there."

They did, but Virginia didn't see it like that. "Count the contents. We'll call it a loan and repay it in full, if we have the opportunity."

Hurst grumbled but drew a number of guineas from the purse and counted them back in. "Twenty," he said.

Virginia couldn't deny the money would come in useful. "Sit down," she told Francis. "Let me bathe your wound and rebind it."

Francis shook his head. "No. The wig was clean when I put it on, and it's acting as a seal. You might have to cut it off, and we don't have time for that. Just rinse off the visible blood, if you would be so kind."

She had to agree that such an operation wasn't possible if they were to leave this town quickly, but she would make him do it later. At least he let her clean the smears from his neck and as far as she could reach, but he was right. His wig was stuck to that gash. Lord knew what would happen once she loosened it.

When he'd drunk his beer, he stood up, scraping back his wooden chair against the slate floor. "Let's get out of this benighted town, and keep our fingers crossed that our luck holds and nobody recognizes us. Because whoever is after us will not give in so easily."

He led Virginia outside to where a battered traveling carriage awaited them, a small man holding the reins leading to four job horses. "Hurst and Butler will act as our footmen. We are Mr. and Miss Strathearn, brother and sister, visiting friends in Cornwall," he said. "We'll hire a different vehicle every day, and make pursuit as difficult as we can."

She had no clothes other than what she was wearing, didn't even have a hairbrush, but Virginia had never felt more free.

* * * *

The carriage was built for only two, and it was a snug fit at that. Francis wouldn't rest until they had put at least twenty miles between them and Staines. Much though he hated to admit it, he would appreciate a few hours' sleep.

If he died, he'd do it on his feet, fighting for the woman who meant so much to him. The strength of his rapidly growing need for her shocked him. No woman had ever affected him that way. Oh, he'd had lovers. What man hadn't? But when he'd realized that she was sharing her carriage with an assassin, he'd vomited as his stomach clenched in terror for her.

Although he'd passed off his reaction as the result of his injury, it was nothing of the kind. His head hurt, but he did not feel sick anymore. Just terrified that he'd be too late to save her.

"At least we don't have the poisonous lady's maid with us."

"Murderous, more like," Virginia muttered as she took her seat.

The landlady had kindly furnished them with a basket of provisions, so after Hurst loaded that in with them, he swung up behind, and they were off.

"Winston disappeared into thin air," she added.

"Probably with the rest of them," he commented. The maid's disappearance worried him. She could still be after them, and she would know what Virginia had planned. They had to change their plans completely. "Virginia, until we discover more about this, I want to keep you safe. You cannot go back to Hatherton Cross until we have cleared it of servants and replaced them all."

After her husband's death, Virginia had made Hatherton Cross her home. The main house had gone to Jamie.

"I know that," she said, her lovely mouth turned down at the corners.

Even dressed plainly, in stained and torn clothes, her hair pulled back plainly, wearing the kind of linen cap more often seen on maids and a plain, old straw hat, she was still the loveliest woman he had ever seen. Possessed of a natural grace, she bore herself like a queen.

He longed to pull her into his arms, but he might frighten her. God knew she'd been through more than enough for one day.

He had no right to claim her. Not yet.

They had four slugs pulling the chaise, and a hired coachman. They were lucky to have them.

"The landlord was in alt," Francis remarked, stretching his legs as much as he could. "He said the Three Cranes' business will return to him."

"Not if this is all he has to offer," Virginia grumped. She shifted, and then moved again. "This seat has been stuffed with cricket balls."

"Never mind, we'll hire a better vehicle tomorrow." Francis pulled his watch out of his coat pocket. He'd bought himself a cheap pinchbeck version of the gold half-hunter he usually carried. This one did not chime, and it did not have diamonds on its hands, but it told the time well enough. "We should reach Blackwater by nightfall."

"I usually try to reach Basingstoke," she said.

"We should avoid the major stops. We don't want to be recognized. After Staines we must take even more care." They would travel as quietly as possible. Fortunately at this time of year the roads were relatively busy.

She nodded. "I had already planned to stop at different towns, in inns that do not know me."

"Indeed." He turned to face her. She deserved the truth, but he hated to be the person to tell her. "You do understand that these people are desperate enough to kill us?" When he reached for her hand, she let him take it. "We're together in this adventure."

She bit her lip. "Yes, it seems so. But why would a perfectly respectable lady's maid do what Winston did? Why would she take money from someone else to watch me? I paid her well, and her perquisites were generous." Her voice rose in tone slightly. He couldn't bear to hear her distress.

He squeezed her hand. "We'll find out, I promise you. You said she was from Devonshire?"

"The village near Dulverton Court furnishes most of the staff for the house," she admitted. "There are several Winstons there. When I moved to Hatherton Cross, after I was widowed, a number of staff came with me from Dulverton." She put her finger to her lips, nibbled on the nail then pulled it away. She shared a wry smile with Francis. "Does that mean my house is not safe?"

He sighed. "I'm afraid it does. I will take you home with me to visit my mother."

"Not until I've been to Combe Manor."

"You cannot go to that house," he said bluntly, which considering Virginia's character was not his best ploy. But he was too tired and in too much pain to be tactful. Who knew what awaited her at Combe Manor? How could she stay there safely?

"I am going to the manor," she repeated firmly. "You should be thankful I am not immediately heading to Hatherton Cross."

Ice crawled down his spine. "Walk into the lion's den? If Winston is disloyal to you, who knows who else is?" Would common sense change her mind? "Let me take you to Wolverley Court. You'll be safe there, and I can investigate…"

She interrupted him. "No." Her blue eyes flashed fire. "I can trust Hurst and Butler; they've already proved their loyalty to me. I'll take them. The place is uninhabited, only a couple of caretakers living there. I mean only to stay a few days to look the place over. I had always meant to go."

He groaned. "Hence the unmarked carriage."

"Indeed." She folded her arms, despite her bedraggled appearance the epitome of haughtiness. The tiny lift of her chin did things to him that he'd better not think about now. "I will of course take care."

"I forbid it."

She had the effrontery to laugh. "Who are you to forbid me anything? I don't answer to you."

Francis regretted that mistake. She was right, but if he admitted it, he'd lose ground, and this was too important to him. He wouldn't willingly put her in any danger. "I could tie you up and keep you prisoner."

What he saw in her eyes then heated him to fever pitch. Enough to tell him he wasn't dealing with an innocent. Although, regrettably, that was not one of his fantasies, if he ever won her he'd be more than willing to experiment.

He couldn't think of any more arguments. Or anything else, come to that, but he would. Abruptly, he changed the subject. "You're not wearing your brooch." The distinctive gold coin pin pendant that she wore more than any other piece was missing.

"I put it on this morning, but it wasn't there after the altercation."

"Altercation," he mused. "That makes what happened sound positively civilized."

The carriage went over a rut, jolting him painfully. The suspension in this thing was nonexistent. This carriage must be ten years old or more, and hard-used. Francis resigned himself to a painful journey. At the next stage they would not be in quite so much of a hurry, and they could find a better vehicle.

"I still have my jewelry. The SSL pin and the pendant brooch." She drew them out of her pocket. "We might be able to sell them if we need to."

He took the pendant from her, turning it over in his hand. "It's an unusual piece."

She nodded. "The coin is an ancient and rare one. Ralph had two. He had one on his fob, and he had the other made into the brooch pendant for me. The coin is pure gold."

"I've never seen one like it before. What happened to the one on his fob?"

She pursed her lips, drawing his unwilling attention to them. "I don't know."

If that coin was real gold, she'd seen the last of it at the inn. She seemed to find solace in it, so he was sorry she'd lost it. But privately, he thought she looked better in pearls. He could certainly do something about that, if she'd let him.

He leaned against the lumpy squabs, trying to find a dent that fit the one in his head so he could rest more comfortably. Although wild horses couldn't get him to tell her, the wound hurt like the devil. And it throbbed, making him concerned that infection was setting in. They'd get to an inn long before that became critical, but getting the damned wig off his head would be hellishly difficult. If at all possible.

Ah! Finally he found a friendly dip in the worn leather, and he could wedge his head across it so that no pressure was put on the gash. That felt much better. Just a short rest, and he'd be as good as new....

Chapter 12

Virginia counted the breaths, watched Francis's chest rise and fall. He was still alive and in little distress from his wound. He remained asleep, hardly stirring, until they got to Blackwater.

As requested, the coachman drove past the main inn and stopped at a smaller place further along the road, on the edge of the village. At last they were out of Middlesex and into the part of the country where several counties met.

The Blackwater River marked the boundary between Berkshire and Hampshire. Blackwater was a pretty village and one she was delighted to see, since dusk had fallen and night would not be far behind it. They had traveled longer than usual, their adventure in Staines delaying them from attaining even the modest distance she'd planned for. The slower speed of the rickety little carriage would not allow them to go further. The horses were crawlers, too.

Virginia found such comfort in having Francis with her, far more than she should have. Even her concerns about his wound did not prevent her recalling the surge of relief and happiness when he'd joined her.

The journey gave her time to recover from the ordeal at the inn and the shock of the events in London. Virginia had never been faced with anything like the attack before, and the events of the past few days had shaken her badly.

Her concerns kept moving toward two factors. One, the most obvious, was Jamie. The attacks had begun after she refused his suit and Francis had come upon them. That had finished any chance he had of getting his property back by marrying her. If she died, Jamie would inherit her estate.

The key was Jamie. Who else would do this to her? And why?

As she watched the cottages, hovels, and inns by the side of the road disappear until everything was green fields and rivers, Virginia still pondered her dilemma. But by the time they reached the inn, she was no nearer to working out a solution to her problem. At least she was calmer.

Francis blinked awake. Watching him come to life was intimate, the kind of thing relatives did. Of course, they were supposed to be brother and sister, but she didn't feel like that, although she would try.

As he moved to the side, he winced.

"We need to get you inside," she murmured. "Get that wound seen to."

He grimaced. "I'm afraid the wig is done for. We'll have to pick one up somewhere or I won't be in the least respectable in the morning." That would suit her mood, then, because she wasn't feeling respectable at all.

Because of the potential danger of someone following them, Hurst had not ridden ahead to bespeak a room. Fortunately, they found one at the small inn they stopped at. But only one. "Sorry, but this isn't as big as the Swan up the road," the landlord told them, scratching the back of his neck. "If you want to go there…"

"No," she said quickly. She had stayed at the Swan before. She might be recognized there. "We'll take the room."

Hurst came out from the taproom, where he had gone to check the place. He sent them a terse nod. It was as safe as they could make it. But only one room? She couldn't let Francis sleep down in the taproom or the stables, not with his injury. But if she did so, she would cause a potential danger.

The landlord's broad face brightened. "Glad to hear it. It's a good room, Missus, and the mattress is new."

Missus. He thought they were married, not brother and sister at all. Probably for the best, because she wouldn't consider letting Francis sleep in the taproom, as a brother would. She could sleep in a chair.

Brushing a strand of hair back, she tried to regain her poise. "Mrs. Durham," she said when she could, choosing a name from the map book she'd left behind in Staines. She seemed to be fond of the letter *D* as far as aliases went. She should have ventured further from Dulverton, but it was too late now. She was surprised she wasn't struck down by lightning where she stood. Lies did not come naturally to her, made her feel uncomfortable in her own skin. But she received an approving smile from Butler. Even in his current guise as footman, Butler had a certain gravitas. She'd lost hers over twenty miles back.

"May I have a large basin of water, and a can of hot water sent up, please?"

The landlord nodded, keeping his face clear of expression. Clearly he thought they were being too particular.

"And a pair of scissors," she added.

The bedchamber was a low-ceilinged, wide room at the back of the house looking out over a small garden and rooftops. She'd have preferred a view of the yard, so she could keep an eye on the comings and goings, but this was the only room available and the inn did not appear overly blessed with bedchambers.

This one contained an old-fashioned four-poster, a little cramped to her jaundiced eye, a sturdy wooden washstand with cracked tiles on the top, and a small chest of drawers with a spotted mirror hung on the wall behind it. Apart from that it contained one battered, leather-upholstered chair. No screens to protect her modesty, no way of snatching any privacy.

Ah well, she could sleep in her ruined riding habit. When this journey was done, Virginia would have the thing burned. She never wanted to see it again.

"This will do very well." Francis looked around, smiling. "Eh, my dear?"

So she was reduced to a "my dear" now, was she? Ralph had used that term more than he'd used her name, as if she had given up her own identity when they married. Virginia had always disliked it, but in Francis's mouth the words were at least tolerable.

Butler accompanied them while Hurst went to oversee the treatment of the horses in the yard. As soon as the landlord had gone, Butler spoke. "There's a shop up the street, ma'am. Sells all kinds of things. If you wish, I could get a traveling trunk with a few bits and pieces. Make us look more respectable."

Taking out his purse, Francis handed him five guineas. "You know what to get. And buy me a wig and another hat, so I may look respectable."

Butler bowed and left.

She was alone with Francis. That had last happened a few days ago. A lifetime. Abruptly she turned to the window. "We should be comfortable here."

Turning back, she spied a tinder box on the mantelpiece. At least they could have light, since a few candle stumps sat in the sconces by the unlit fire. A couple of half-burned candles stood ready in pewter candlesticks on the table by the bed. She made good use of the box, recklessly setting light to all the candles. The room glowed with gentle light, the dark panels absorbing it.

"This looks almost cozy," she commented.

His harsh laugh made her turn around. He was gripping the back of the plain wooden chair set before the chest of drawers, his knuckles white.

"That depends on where you're standing," he said. "If I sit down, can you help me off with my hat and wig once the water has arrived?"

He'd gone pale. Was the wound worse now? If he'd taken an infection, it could kill him.

That would not happen. It must not. She wouldn't allow it.

A maid arrived with the promised basin and water. The small girl, no more than thirteen by Virginia's reckoning, the tip of her tongue sticking out of the corner of her mouth, placed the chipped pottery basin carefully on the washstand and placed the can next to it on the floor. Then she turned and bobbed a curtsy. "Would you like me to fetch you food, madam?" she piped.

"Yes please," Virginia said. "What do you have?"

"Stew and bread, if you please, ma'am, with a dish of potatoes and carrots."

"That will do nicely," Francis said. "Bring it up here, if you would, with a bottle of wine. In half an hour. Give our servants what they want and put it on our account."

The girl bobbed another curtsy and left.

At last, Francis released his grip on the chair, but only to drag it over to the washstand, as if he didn't have the strength to pick it up.

Something was wrong. He'd slept all the way from Staines. Virginia's heart rose to her throat, and she found breathing difficult. Infection could kill him. And it would be her fault. "I should have made the servants keep you in bed in London," she said.

A sharp, harsh laugh escaped him. "How could they do that when I knew you were in danger?"

"Indeed, I'm grateful, but I won't be if you're hurt worse."

Francis stripped his coat off and carelessly let it fall to the floor. "Don't be." With an absence of his usual grace, he slumped down into the chair. "Help me off with this wig, will you? It hurts like the devil."

That was the first time he'd admitted to any discomfort. Pausing only to strip off her coat and push the sleeves of her shirt out of the way, Virginia hurried to help him. She wrapped a towel around his shoulders, her hands shaking.

His cocked hat refused to budge at first. She took her time, easing it away, terrified of what she would find beneath. "I wish this room was better lit."

She brought the two candles closer, perching them on the nightstand. As she set to work again, she tried easing the hat around the sides, until only a patch was stuck.

Francis took a couple of sharp breaths. Blood was already oozing from under the hat. "Pull it," he said. "Just do it fast."

Putting all her strength into it, she jerked the hat.

Part of the wig came up, and he cried out, suppressing the sound by clamping his jaw. Air hissed between his teeth. Blood poured down his neck.

Virginia swallowed and picked up the scissors. "Hold still."

Francis clamped his lips together and gripped the arms of the chair.

His wig was saturated with dried blood. Steeling herself, Virginia took up the scissors and clipped at the edges of the wig, removing the curls rolled above the ears, and the edges, snipping gingerly until she found her way under it.

She chopped the wig away, bit by bit, the only sound in the room Francis's heavy breathing and the sharp snap of the scissors. When she had reduced the wig to a patch, where dried blood made the gray curls dark and stiff, she put the scissors down. "We'll have to soak the rest."

The chair and the washstand were at the wrong height for him to tilt his head back far enough. The gash was on the right side, at the back of his skull. Virginia swallowed her nausea and set to work, getting him to lean his head over the bowl while she repeatedly poured water over the remaining patch of wig, turning his dark brown hair into a black, bloody mess.

And still the scrap of wig refused to budge. She daren't pull it because of what it might bring with it. The hat had been bad enough. Her heart pounded, her tension palpable. But she said nothing and did everything she could to keep her hands steady.

A knock at the door made her shout, "Wait!"

Glancing at Francis, she hurried to the door and opened it, standing in the opening, preventing the little maid seeing him.

"Let me take that," she said, putting her hands under the large tray that contained a brown pot, plates, and a bottle of wine with glasses and flatware. A loaf of bread sent a welcome fragrance to her nostrils, giving her temporary respite from the heavy, metallic scent of blood.

She even managed a smile before she pushed the door closed with her foot. As if everything here was normal. But she was afraid. Her stomach had clenched like a fist, and despite the appetizing scents emanating from the tray, she wouldn't be able to eat a single morsel.

Balancing the heavy tray between her hands, her elbows resting on her hips to help with support, she nearly dropped the whole thing when Francis came to stand before her and firmly took the tray.

Fresh blood was pouring down the right side of his face and neck.

Virginia gasped and held her breath, lest she give herself away with a scream. He looked as if he'd come fresh from the battlefield. Ignoring her response, he nodded at a drop-leaf table set in a corner of the room. After she hurried to open it, he placed the tray carefully on the surface.

"Now," he said, turning back to the washstand. "Let's get this thing sorted out before our dinner gets cold."

"This thing" took another fifteen minutes and all the cloths the maid had brought. But eventually Virginia could see the gash, and to her relief, it wasn't as bad as when she'd first seen it. "There's no infection that I can see. Either there was none or the blood washed it away." No swelling at the edges of the wound, no heat around the site. "Does it throb?"

He swallowed a laugh on a snort. "Somewhat," he agreed mildly. "But better than when it had that wig stuck in it. I thought it would burst."

"It won't now. We'll leave it open for an hour or two, and then dress it." Amazingly, a clot was already forming. "I've never seen anyone quite so resilient."

"Not even your husband, the brave soldier?"

"No." Virginia bit her lip. She'd answered too quickly. "He had scars from before I knew him, and a bad one from the injury that put him out of active service. I never saw his wounds when they were freshly inflicted." Only the deep, angry scars and what his injuries had done to him. "He had a dent in his head he said was from where a bullet had parted his hair."

Francis huffed a half laugh as Virginia swabbed away the worst of the blood around the wound. She would leave the gash to heal itself. She had considered stitching the wound, but that would have been a last resort, as stitched wounds were hotbeds for infection. "It doesn't need packing."

If the gash had been worse, she'd have packed it to keep it open, so the wound could heal from the inside out. But this wasn't as bad as she'd feverishly imagined all day.

At some points she'd considered stopping the carriage and racking up wherever they found themselves so she could deal with this injury. Infection could take hold and kill a patient in a matter of days. Ralph had told her of men taken hale and hearty from the battlefield, dead from a minor wound by the end of the week. His stories had curdled her blood, but he'd needed someone to talk to, so she had let him talk.

That was when she'd decided that stoicism was her best strategy, so that nobody would ever know what had happened during her marriage. Or more precisely, not happened.

Carefully, she smoothed his short hair away from the wound. She'd washed all the old blood out. It only had to dry now. She rinsed the blood from his throat, spread his shirt open at his neck so she could do so. The intimacies would have made her blush had she been thinking about her actions, but she concentrated on the one thing.

"Do you think Jamie had my house watched?"

"Undoubtedly. I did not call on you by appointment. They were waiting for me."

"That makes my skin crawl." Because it did. To think someone was spying on her made her shiver.

"I can't tell you how much better that feels." He examined the pieces of wig littering the floor, a wry smile curving his lips. "Thank you." Scraping the chair back, he got to his feet, his shoulders drooping in weariness but his eyes more alert.

She smiled back, sharing her relief with him.

"Let's eat that food now. I'm ravenous."

Her stomach growled. It unfurled from its tense knot, reminding her how empty it was. A lot of time had passed since their adventure in Staines.

This time Francis took charge, ushering her to the table and carrying the chair over for her. He found a three-legged stool by the bed and settled on that, balancing easily. No swaying or dizziness greeted her perceptive gaze.

He doled out the stew onto the plain white plates and added a generous helping of vegetables before reaching for the loaf and firmly cutting a few slices from it. "Eat," he commanded.

Relief had given her back her appetite. The meal was plain but delicious. After hours of cooking on the fire, the meat melted in the mouth. When the first mouthful hit her taste buds, Virginia groaned. She plied her spoon faster until she caught Francis watching her. "What is it?"

"However hungry you are, you never forget your manners."

"Of course not."

He turned back to his food, smiling. "Don't talk, eat."

She was only too glad to follow his example. They didn't speak again until they had finished, and she leaned back with a most unladylike satisfied sigh.

A knock sounded on the door. After a glance at Francis, Virginia got up to answer it. Nobody must see Francis with that wound. People would remember it, and then their attempts at traveling quietly would be at an end.

She opened the door wider when she saw who it was.

Hurst and Butler came in, carrying a small, battered traveling trunk between them. "We got what we thought you might need, sir, ma'am. Told the landlord we was bringing it in from the carriage," Hurst said, before casting Virginia an apologetic smile. "I'm not familiar with what ladies need, so Butler saw to that part."

"Butler has experience with the ladies?" Francis drawled. He'd turned his chair so that it had its back to the window, making his wound less visible.

Butler bowed his head. "I had a wife once."

Virginia didn't want to ask what had happened to her, but he volunteered the information.

"Went off with a soldier, ma'am. Haven't seen her in years."

Goodness. In her world weddings were a contract as meaningful as any other. A marriage had ramifications far beyond the joining of a couple in wedlock. Butler behaved as if marriage was a temporary condition. No doubt if he met someone else, he would marry her without concerning himself too much with the details. Such as being married to somebody else.

"Have you eaten?" Francis asked.

"Yes, sir. When you told us to leave you alone for an hour, we took the opportunity to eat," Butler said.

"Good food here," Hurst added.

Had he done that, asked to be left by themselves? Virginia had been so busy she hadn't had time to wonder why the men had not reappeared. And Francis's position now, turning his wound away from scrutiny. The men knew he was hurt, so he need not hide it from them. Was he sensitive about it? Did the injury make him feel vulnerable?

Together with the knowledge came the understanding that he had let her into that world, into the inner circle. Francis was a difficult man to know, and he was allowing her close enough to get to know him. The veneer she'd hated in London because it prevented her getting close to him had gone.

Lord, that was something. Too late to wonder if she wanted it. Of course she did. His trust sank into her as if he'd stroked her from shoulder to toes, a warm, reassuring touch of support totally foreign to her. Nobody trusted her, nobody had treated her as an adult, until she'd taken control of her life and made them.

A brief recollection of her father's utter bewilderment when she'd refused to come home after Ralph's death crossed her mind, forcing her to suppress her smile.

"We ate well, too."

"Ma'am, the taproom goes front to back of the house, so we'll sleep there tonight. We'll spot anything unusual," Butler ventured. He seemed to be relishing this adventure. Her London butler had hidden depths. A treasure indeed.

After glancing around at the mess, he set to tidying the room, sweeping up the bloodied towels and rags, opening the window before carrying the basin over. With a shout of "*Gardez l'eau!*" he tipped its contents out of the window.

"Thank you. We'll leave as early as possible in the morning," she said.

Francis spoke. "Send today's coachman and carriage back. We'll hire new ones for tomorrow. If we do that every day, we'll have a better chance of deterring any pursuers."

Surprised, Virginia said, "I thought we'd already lost them."

Francis gazed at her, his expression as serious as she'd ever seen it. "Possibly. I'm taking no chances with you, my lady." His eyes held an unspoken message, one she chose to disregard. Too warm, too intimate.

"Your injury, my—sir," Butler said. "How is it?"

Francis waved the man's concern away. "It will do. It's bathed and clean, and it hasn't taken infection. Although it cost me my wig."

"As to that, sir, we bought you another, as you asked. We obtained razors, strops, soap, and a wig at the barber's at the end of the street. But the wig isn't like what you're used to."

Francis shrugged. "It's of no concern. I'm pleased you found one. The less we stand out and make ourselves memorable, the safer we will be." He counted out guineas from his severely depleted purse. "Take these to pay off the coachman from today and procure another carriage and driver for the morning, if you will. If you cannot, then we will have to keep the ones we have. Get the new one before you dismiss the old."

Butler took the money and bowed, his ingrained habits getting the better of him. Hurst nearly did the same, but caught Virginia's sharp gaze and changed his mind, giving a short bob of his head instead.

Hurst gathered up the remains of the meal, piled it on the tray, and took it with him, leaving the half-full pitcher. After a doubtful glance at Francis, which said more than words ever could, Butler followed in Hurst's wake. Virginia went to the door and closed it behind them.

Suddenly unaccountably shy, she took her time turning to face him. "I'll take the chair," she said hurriedly. "I'm sure it will be comfortable."

"I'm not." He got to his feet, the easy motion belying the way the lines bracketing his mouth deepened. He was still in pain. "I'd offer to sleep there, but I assume you won't allow that."

"Absolutely not."

"And you're not going down to the taproom," she said, equally firmly.

So there was the bed. As if drawn to it, they both looked. It was a perfectly ordinary inn bed: old-fashioned, perhaps discarded from a nearby manor. Virginia had slept in them many times, mostly with a maid or Emilia Dauntry for company. She steeled herself.

When she'd shared a bed with Ralph, especially in the latter half of their marriage, they could have been in different beds for all the contact they made. So why shouldn't she share with Francis? She knew him well, and he was not about to force anything on her that she did not want. She could remain mainly dressed.

But it mattered. So much that after coping with everything thrown at her today, she had to swallow her rising panic.

He watched her. Had he seen the disturbance churning up her insides?

Instead of confronting him, Virginia went to the trunk, knelt and flung open the top. The trunk had the remains of a leather cover on the wooden case, some of which flaked off to the floor.

The contents were neatly packed. A nightshirt, and a night rail, caps, a fresh linen shift and petticoat, even a warm cloak met her appreciative gaze. The pile of men's garments she left to Francis, but she pulled out what was laid reverently on top. Holding the bob-wig in both hands, she burst into laughter.

Country squires, merchants with no pretension to fashion, and comfortable vicars preferred the bob-wig. It had no curls, no tail, nothing to stop the squat object from making its owner anything but respectable. The idea of Francis wearing this sent her into gales of mirth.

Francis waited for her to finish. "Better than a snowy-white, fashionable queued wig," he commented, regarding the shreds on the floor. "Perhaps I'll be less recognizable in that."

She would know him anywhere. Her laughter died. "I suppose you are right." Though she doubted anything could still the traitorous desire that had only increased over the last few days.

She would fight it. The firm resolve that had got her this far in her life would aid her now.

He got to his feet. "Well, at least I can show my face downstairs now." Plucking the wig from her hands, he examined it critically. "It's lighter than my usual style, too. And it will help to disguise me. I never wear these." He dropped the wig on his head, letting it settle over the thick scab that now covered his wound. "How do I look?"

Even the ugly wig wouldn't conceal his sheer male beauty. If that didn't, nothing would. "I would abandon the wig altogether, but for this thing." He touched the site of the wound very lightly.

"I'll go downstairs and find out what I can," he said. "I'm Mr. Durham, is that not so?"

The Strathearn siblings had faded away as if they'd never existed.

She nodded. "Come back upstairs when you're done." Tempting though it was, she couldn't let him stay in the taproom. She wanted, no needed, to keep him under observation.

She meant it for him, but he took it another way. "I wouldn't leave you alone for long, my sweet. I'll be back in less than an hour." Giving her time for herself. "Should I ask for more hot water?"

"Yes, yes please." Finally she could have her strip wash.

Perhaps detecting her discomfiture, he said nothing, but left the room.

Finding a clean cloth, Virginia bundled the remains of the wig into it and folded it over, securing the bundle in a knot. That could go over a hedge tomorrow. For the rest, she would have to cope. Somehow.

Chapter 13

As always, Francis awoke all at once, awareness snapping into place.

Last night he'd come upstairs to find Virginia taking up as small a space in the bed as she could. She was enveloped in a voluminous night rail evidently meant for someone much larger, since she'd had to roll the sleeves up, and fabric was wrapped around her. She was sound asleep.

He'd hurried into the nightshirt left for him and climbed in next to her, taking care to rock the bed as little as possible. Since this was the kind of bed that had ropes slung under it to hold the mattress in place, it creaked alarmingly, but he had not woken her, and he'd been asleep in five minutes.

This morning she had somehow ended up in his arms, and he wasn't about to question how or when.

He lay very still, savoring the fulfillment of a dream. Naturally, he'd have preferred it to come true after a night's lovemaking, but a man couldn't have everything, and he was not about to cavil at that.

Her head rested on his shoulder. Virginia felt exactly as he'd imagined, but more so. Warmer, softer, more alive.

Her breath breezed over his throat, bathing it in pure Virginia. Her delectable breasts moved rhythmically under the linen of her night rail. The material was maddeningly thick, but even so he detected the flush of skin beneath the creamy ecru linen.

The tapes at the top that kept the night rail tightly fastened had come undone, giving him a tantalizing glimpse of her unfettered cleavage. No boned stays lay between his chest and her upper body, no hoops prevented him from feeling her thighs pressed against his. She'd lifted one leg and draped it across his upper thigh, perilously close to where his erection was showing distinct and inappropriate interest. If she moved, she'd touch him there.

If she did that, God knew where they would end up.

And her hair flowed loose. He would try to ensure that nobody found ribbons to fasten her hair into braids at night. They would be a sin. Dark and silky waves of it lay across her shoulders, straying onto his chest. He wanted so badly to feel them stroking his bare skin, teasing him while he caressed and persuaded her body to blossom.

For the first time he was seeing the true Virginia, the twenty-nine-year-old widow who had shunned him for so long.

He'd met her when she was a new bride, a month before he'd left for his Grand Tour. Even then an air of gravity had distinguished her. And her beauty had astonished him.

When he'd returned three years later, she had adopted her persona of dignified, haughty viscountess, and her husband forbade her to befriend him. Still he'd felt that pull, wanting her close and yet despising her for her treatment of his mother.

Except, from what she had told him, she'd been obeying her husband, not following her own inclinations. On the occasions they had met, she'd shown him her icy side, frozen him, so he'd moved away.

He'd been a fool. He was not staying away this time. Circumstance had brought them together, but it felt right, as if they would have always come to this, sooner or later. If not like this, then another way.

As he watched her, her eyes flickered, and she opened them, meeting his gaze. For a full five seconds she stared at him, then she jerked away, dragging the sheet and blanket, bundling it around her. "Why did you do that?"

"I woke up, and there you were." He smiled, reaching for her. "Come back."

"No!" She scrambled out of bed, looking more unconsciously seductive than any woman had the right to be, especially one who'd had a day like yesterday. Her skin was pearly, an inner glow giving it life. He already knew how warm she felt.

Grabbing the sheet, she dragged it out and wrapped it around herself, before turning her attention back to him.

Francis lay on his back, not bothering to disguise his state of arousal. The nightshirt covered him from shoulders to knees, but that was all he wore. His condition was no secret now.

Fascinated, he watched a blush creep from her throat to her forehead. "You can hardly expect me to remain immune to you," he said mildly. "You're far too lovely for that."

"I—I…"

He found her confusion adorable. Sitting up, he swung his legs over the edge of the bed. Her eyes widened, and she inhaled sharply as she stepped back.

"You know I will never force myself on you," he said, making no move to stand, because that might unnerve her even more.

Her husband had been a straightforward, blunt soldier, a high-ranking officer who'd communicated well with his troops. Francis could not imagine Ralph being less than straightforward with the woman he had married. His desire for her had been reported far and wide. Theirs had been a love match, or so people said. Like the one between his parents. His father had set eyes on his mother and instantly fallen in love.

Just as Francis had when he'd seen Virginia. He'd mistrusted his response to her, but nothing had dimmed it. He loved her still. He'd nearly lost her back at her house, when she'd told him her secret and immediately rejected him. This time he'd take much more care.

What he did on this journey could seal his fate for good. Holding his passion in check would nearly kill him, but he'd do it. He had to, because her safety was paramount. He'd waited four years, so he could wait longer.

Not that she fully realized how much he wanted her yet. If she'd been married, she'd known the phenomenon of the morning erection. She could put his state down to that, although in fact, it was all for her.

As he crossed to the trunk and threw up the lid to find the razor, he was careful to keep his distance. He stayed crouched on his haunches until her breathing became more regular. If the sight of his manhood had disturbed her that much, he must take care not to show her more until she was ready. The last thing he wanted to do was distress her.

Taking out what he needed, he got to his feet in one smooth movement, holding his clothes before him. "I can't let you go downstairs on your own," he said, "but I promise I'll be as discreet as possible getting ready. Then I'll go downstairs. Should I send a maid to you?"

She nodded, then shook her head. "I can manage."

"Very well. I'll have Butler bring breakfast up to you. I'll tell him to knock four times, two short, two long, so you'll know it's him. How long will you need?" While he spoke he made himself busy at the mirror, stropping the razor.

"I can be ready in half an hour."

"Three quarters of an hour will do," he murmured, examining himself in the spotted, faded mirror.

Changing his mind, he put the razor down. "If I'm not as clean-shaven as usual, that might help. I'll remain somewhat slovenly."

The sight of his incipient beard in the mirror made him realize that it made him look different. Butler had shaved him two days ago, so the dark fuzz was readily apparent now. But he couldn't leave it too long. It would drive him mad.

He poured cold water into the basin and set about washing his face and hands. "But only a little," he owned, drying his face. When he emerged from the towel, he was still facing the mirror. She was watching him.

Hunger, raw and unmistakable, leeched from her eyes, arcing from hers to his and back again. She wanted him. The connection between them, if visible, would have been fiery. But it was not, and with supreme effort, Francis looked away, back to the towel.

He managed to dress without revealing too much of himself, rather like a shy boy trying not to reveal his body, but all the time he was startlingly aware of her watching him. Tingles spread over his skin at the thought of revealing himself to her.

He put his breeches on first, under his nightshirt, then pulled the nightshirt over his head, and with a touch of wickedness, stayed half naked while he folded it carefully before he put it in the trunk. He'd give her a good look at his torso. He would preen if he didn't know better.

Dressing didn't take long, and after he'd loaded his pockets with money, his small knife, and his watch, he was on his way, pausing at the door to throw her a kiss.

She turned her back, but he didn't miss her reluctant grin.

* * * *

Of course Virginia had shared a bed with a man before, but not often and not for long. Ralph had frequently seen her in her night rail, but even though this one was as voluminous as a tent, she'd never felt so vulnerable before. Francis was so much more of a man. Would he believe her if she told him of her ironically virginal state?

Ralph had taunted her with it sometimes, when he'd said her name in company, emphasizing the first part for her ears only. Of course, his friends had taken the innuendo the wrong way, as he'd meant them to.

He'd never accepted his inability to perform and preferred to blame her. Knowing he had done so didn't help Virginia to cope with her feelings of inadequacy. Perhaps he was right. Perhaps she wasn't enough for any man.

Except, this morning…

Hastily, she moved her mind away from that. Men had that reaction. Ralph had sometimes, but it had slipped away from him.

It could have been anyone in bed with Francis this morning.

Virginia the virgin. As she slipped out of the night rail and found a shift to put over her nakedness, Virginia tried to shrug her distress away. But for the first time in her life she found the task difficult.

Of course she had noted handsome men before, but she'd admired them at a distance. Never tempted like this. She had not thought of the intimacy shared between husband and wife, man and mistress, for years, had considered that part of her life over before it had begun.

Francis made that dispassionate survey so hard to do. Before she'd come properly awake this morning, she'd relished the warmth, the security surrounding her. Then her awareness had kicked her awake and she pulled out of his arms. Francis was strong, protective, in the prime of life. And he was everything she wanted but should not, *could* not, have.

She had to use the trick her mother had taught her to lace her stays, and she couldn't do it as effectively as she wanted. Pulling the tapes simultaneously gave her the support she needed, but not the firmness she preferred.

The thought of him dealing with her nervous, fumbling innocence made her huff an ironic laugh. They had taken their attraction further than she had ever allowed before, and she was suffering the consequences of that. No, that was wrong. She'd yearned for him long before their first kiss.

The fault lay all on her side. She trusted him not to force her to anything, especially now she was so vulnerable to his advances. No, she was safe with him, however much she might wish she was not.

Recalling Francis's unshaven state, she smiled and conceded that a less than fashionable figure might serve to present her as the wife of a country gentleman better.

So did the clothes in drab colors that Butler and Hurst had supplied. She found a bum-roll to pad her hips rather than a hooped petticoat, a quilted petticoat to pad her hips further, then a skirt over the top in a particularly bilious shade of green.

The skirt was a shade too short for her, reaching just above her ankles, but it was respectable, especially when paired with the linsey-woolsey stockings, plain garters and sturdy shoes.

The thigh-length brown caraco jacket boasted a little frill at the back, and the fichu was the coarsest she'd ever used. All the better to hide her breasts with.

When she was dressed, she couldn't deny how comfortable the well-worn but soft clothing felt, even though she'd prefer a fine linen shift against her skin.

Her own shift and the remnants of her riding habit she put in the trunk, in case she should need it, though both garments were ready for the ragbag.

Tying the plain linen cap over her simply dressed hair, Virginia had to admit that nobody would recognize her now, not even her own mother.

The shoes, nailed to preserve the leather of the soles and heels, rapped satisfyingly against the uneven, dark floorboards when she crossed the room to answer the door. She only recalled her promise to take care at the last moment, but as expected, Butler had brought her some breakfast. His eyes widened a little, but he made no comment.

He laid the tray on the small table with the care of a born butler, nudging the flatware into place and standing back to judge the result. "Mr. Durham asks if you will be ready presently, ma'am." He gave a small bow as if he couldn't help himself.

"By and by. I'll eat a little of this and pack the rest."

There was a pot of tea. Heavenly. "Thank you so much for the tea."

"I'll do my best to ensure you have it in future, ma'am."

They might be in deepest peril, but at least she still had tea.

* * * *

The sun was peeping out from a heavy bank of clouds when they left the inn to get into the carriage Hurst had hired for them. The new coachman had swathed himself in an old greatcoat, even though the day would not be a cold one. His pipe stuck out of the folds of gray cloth that enclosed his face, a wisp of smoke spiraling up to join the other clouds.

Fresh horses had been put to the carriage. At least they appeared more lively than yesterday's slugs. Francis helped Virginia aboard, and she settled in a corner of the chaise, which was somewhat larger than yesterday's vehicle. He followed her up, and the coachman whipped up the horses. But as they left the small inn yard, an equipage whisked past, a grand berline complete with outriders and liveried footmen clinging to the back of it.

Before she could register the sight, Francis dragged Virginia into his arms and pushed her head against his chest. His curses rent the air.

The carriage rocked, but remained stable as the coachman guided them onto the main road.

Virginia pulled away.

"Look," Francis commanded.

As they turned onto the road, the carriage in front of them, a fine, glossy vehicle drawn by four frisky horses, turned a corner, giving her a glimpse of the crest emblazoned on the side. They were too far away for her to see the coat of arms properly, but the colors attracted her attention. "That looks familiar."

"They should. They're yours."

"What?" Indignantly, she turned to face him. "I sent my crested traveling carriage ahead to Hatherton Cross with my maid. Has someone…?" Her voice trailed away as realization hit her. "Jamie. That's Jamie's carriage."

Her crest was set inside the widow's lozenge. This one had none. The current Lord Dulverton was on the road.

Despite the moderate weather, she paled and her fingers went cold. "Jamie was supposed to be visiting a friend in Canterbury, then going to Lancashire. He shouldn't be on this road at all." She buried her face in her hands. "Oh, God, if he sees us…"

"He will not." Francis pulled her hands down and held them between his, chafing them. "His equipage is much better than ours, faster and with better horses. So we'll let him pull ahead. We'll linger over the next change and let them get even further ahead. By the end of the day, they could have ten miles on us. That's a safe distance." He murmured the words, talking softly until Virginia's panic subsided.

"This is so foolish." For the first time she recognized the peril in her actions. She'd longed for privacy and quiet, and had ignored several warning signs. But when Francis was injured, what should she have done? Left him behind, called his friends at the club? "We should have hired two carriages and traveled openly."

Francis shook his head. "I tell you now, Virginia, and you had best listen. You would not have left me behind or sat in a carriage that did not include me. If you had tried, I'd have abducted you. The people who wanted to harm me did it to leave you unprotected. I will not allow that."

She laughed shakily, the mood cautiously settling into wariness. "You would not. What would people think?"

"That I was mad with passion for you," he said promptly. "Like that dreadful melodrama at Drury Lane Theater last month. Appalling stuff. But don't you see the danger you're in? You rejected his suit. Now the only way he can get to you is with your death."

He didn't need to finish. "Jamie." She left her hands in his.

"Undoubtedly."

The swiftness of his reply irritated her. "How can you know that? Jamie might be pompous and eager to, as he put it, reunite the estate, but is he really capable of murder?"

Francis's mouth flattened. "Not in person, perhaps, but he could employ someone else to do it. Who has the most to gain from your death? And who has the most to lose if you remarry someone else?"

"Who said anything about remarrying?"

He smiled gently. "I have. I made sure society knew I was pursuing you, don't forget. I followed you around, appeared by your side. Perhaps Jamie thought I was getting too close."

She stared at him, her mind occupied by a notion that had not occurred to her before. "Did you only do that after the first time you were threatened? That time you did not tell me about?"

He dropped his gaze and did not immediately answer.

The anxiety and fear she'd experienced this last week boiled to a head of steam. "I'm right, aren't I? You appointed yourself my knight errant." Indignation made her snatch her hands away from his. She folded her arms, tucking her hands out of the way where he could not touch them. "What gave you the right to do that? And then someone nearly killed you outside my house."

He shrugged. "What did you expect me to do? Meekly back away, leaving you wide open to whoever wanted you? If I had not been at the ball that night, Dulverton would have compromised you into accepting his suit. If I had not been in the way, he could well have abducted you. Then you would have had to marry him."

"He would not have liked what he found." Not just her virginity but the heavy conditions attached to her inheritance.

She suppressed her shudder. Francis did not deserve to see any weakness she might feel. "I expect you to tell me when something affects me. I am not an object, or a thing to be protected."

In the years after her husband's death she'd learned she was stronger than she'd thought. With nobody to "guide" her thoughts, she'd thought for herself and discovered that she liked it.

Still agitated, she paused to force her indignation back under her control. Lord, what a mess!

"I should have told you about the earlier attack. I'm sorry I did not," he said.

His admission took her completely by surprise. Since when had the high and mighty Lord Wolverley admitted any fault? Not like that, in a voice so humble she could hardly credit what she was hearing. And what should she say to that? "Yes, you should be."

"We could have surrounded you with protectors."

She snorted. "That would deny me any freedom of movement."

"Only until we could identify who was doing this and put a stop to it."

Better, but still not perfect. "And if I refused?"

"Would you be so foolish?"

The idea of having her movements limited was intolerable, but she might have had no choice if the person was desperate enough to make attempts on the life of a peer of the realm. "Probably not," she was forced to admit. "But I cannot like being treated like a parcel."

He stared at his hands, then lifted his gaze to meet her eyes. "Truthfully I thought the first attack was all there would be. It was ill-thought-out and impulsive. If Jamie organized it, it would have been very fast, since it happened after the ball. He could have sent a couple of his footmen after me. Once I'd repelled them, I assumed whoever had ordered them would back away. Which was a mistake."

"Jamie wants to marry me, to reunite the estate," she asserted. "He has always wanted it, but only this season has he pushed for the match."

He raised his brows. "I remember the occasion vividly," he said dryly. "You refused him."

She nodded. "I did. But—" She broke off her words hastily. "I don't love him. I swore I would not marry again unless I was in love with my husband to be, or at the least, very fond of him."

"Then I'll have to try very hard," he murmured. "Won't I?"

In a jerky movement completely devoid of her usual studied grace, she turned her head to stare out of the window, watching the hedgerows and the rolling hills.

They traveled in silence for some time until they stopped to change the horses. Another second-rate inn, but as she was finding, the quality and size of these places varied considerably. Some were as good as her usual stopping places.

To Virginia's relief, Francis elected to alight to stretch his legs. Their conversation had reduced the already small space considerably. He did not stay away for long but returned to the carriage after a quick trip to the inn to follow the call of nature. She was almost asleep when he returned.

"Here." He slung a large basket into the confined space before leaping up. "I walked up to the Hart and bought us some decent food."

What else had he done? "Did you see Jamie?"

He shook his head. "If I had seen the carriage, I wouldn't have gone in. They're a couple of hours in front of us, I discovered when I asked. And don't worry, I acted like a rustic and asked if they'd seen any grand vehicles recently. If we stop after another ten miles for an equally extended period, that will give them a longer head start. Then we'll be unlikely to catch up with them."

He gave her a reassuring smile, which did not at all reassure her. "Don't worry." He threw his hat on the opposite seat, closely followed by his wig. "When we face Jamie Dulverton again, it will be on our own terms."

Seeing him like that, with his real hair on display, gave him an intimate appeal that Virginia refused to acknowledge. Utterly refused.

He unfastened the basket and produced a fragrant, cooked chicken, a loaf of fresh bread, and several other items, including plain white plates and mugs. Virginia cut the bread and found a pot of fresh butter. When a pound of cheese made its appearance, Virginia could imagine herself in heaven.

"Did you get anything for the men?"

He nodded. "They already have it. I told them to eat before we set off. That will give your cousin-in-law more time to get ahead of us."

She took a slice of bread and tore off a leg of chicken, surprised to discover how hungry she was. She'd eaten well last night, and now she was digging in with gusto.

Francis demolished half the chicken before he reached for the wine and uncorked it. He poured it into a glass and handed it to her, taking another for himself.

"Jamie will kick up such a fuss if he catches us like this," she said gloomily.

"I doubt it. Think about it. He wants to marry you to reunite the title and lands, does he not?"

She nodded and took a healthy gulp of the wine.

"Then he won't want you to marry me. And I will be duty bound to offer for you if he catches us."

"That sounds enticing."

He chuckled as the coachman whipped up their new steeds and they set off again. "I can make it more so. Be warned, my lady, for I'll not walk away now."

Her heart sank. She tried for levity. "Now you know how I appear without frills and furbelows, and in the mornings, I would have thought you would be disillusioned."

"On the contrary." His voice became low and intimate. "It has only made me more eager."

A flush rising to her face, Virginia turned away again. But the scenery was tedious, the same hedgerows and what appeared to be the same cows and sheep in the fields as she'd seen yesterday.

They ate in silence, until Virginia had finished. After wiping her hands on her napkin, she bundled up the waste from her meal, the chicken bones, apple peel and cores, and tossed them out of the window for the birds to pick over. Feeling much better for her impromptu meal, she turned back to the topic at hand. "You promised not to seduce me on this trip."

"I have not promised to hide my true feelings for you. What I have promised is not to take advantage of our current circumstances." He shrugged. "But I have not promised not to allow *you* to seduce *me*. I should warn you that the task won't be very arduous. Ask me, and I will oblige you. Touch me, and I'll respond." He sat very still, as if afraid of moving. "Virginia, we both know what runs between us. But if we take this step, be sure. I won't back away once we've reached our destination."

His words put a series of images into Virginia's mind that she could not dispel. Being naked with him, having the freedom to touch him, spread her hands over his bare chest, run her fingers along the powerful muscles in his arms and legs enthralled her. She wanted to claim him.

Sensations rioted through her when she came into his vicinity. They always had, but before now their meetings had not been as frequent as this. Truthfully, and she must be truthful with herself, she wanted it. Longed for it.

To test herself she imagined Jamie in bed with her. She went cold in a minute. Jamie was young and strong, and he undoubtedly wanted her, not just her fortune, but she did not care to imagine intimacy between them.

Closing her eyes, she allowed herself to consider other men in society who had reputations for their skills in bed. People were not as circumspect around widows as they were with unmarried maidens, so Virginia had heard plenty of stories. Some were divinely handsome, some powerful, or elegant, said to be exquisite, whatever that meant in this context. But none of them had the same effect on her as Francis.

That worried Virginia. Francis had a power over her that she must take care not to show him, but that was becoming increasingly difficult. The better she knew him, the more she liked him, and that was apart from the physical appeal he had for her. And now this desperate journey.

What was she to do? How could she ever forget this man? Or watch him marry someone else? Because she must not deviate from her course.

Her mind was still whirling when she fell asleep.

Chapter 14

"Virginia," he said softly.

She opened her eyes.

"We're at the inn where we'll rack up for the night. We're in Salisbury, well away from the finest inns."

"Won't someone recognize us?"

"Not here. Not dressed like this." He glanced out of the window. "We can disappear easily in a larger town. This place isn't on the usual route for any of the great roads."

Realization hit her hard. "If nobody knows us here, then we can travel as brother and sister now."

"If you wish." His voice was quiet and steady. "Do you?"

She stared at him as the sound of a busy inn yard went on around them. Horses whinnied, and men shouted instructions, but she ignored them all, for this was a turning point. If she confirmed that she wanted to travel as brother and sister, he would accede to her wishes. He wouldn't flirt with her or approach her in any way society would consider shocking.

But she could no longer deny that she wanted him badly.

They could be lovers.

And then there was the other problem.

Perhaps he would not notice her virginal state. He was mad for her as she was for him, so in the throes of passion, that small event could pass unnoticed. And she was tired of waiting, tired of being neither one thing nor the other. Not a proper wife and widow.

In six years she would be well past the age when a woman could consider marrying and bearing a child.

She would be alone, and although she had thought she'd reconciled herself to her fate, even looked forward to it, all she saw now was years of loneliness. Comfortable loneliness to be sure, but a solitary existence doing good works and becoming a matron, an established face in society as a widow.

Never to know married love, never to experience intimacy.

She wanted to do it at least once in her life, but she balked at doing it with a stranger, or an acquaintance. And she would not become the kind of widow who took frequent lovers. She did not have that in her.

If she was to do this, it would be with Francis, and it would be tonight. She shook her head.

"Say it, Virginia. Shall we travel as siblings from now on?"

"No." She choked the word out and could not say any more.

He didn't speak again until he was standing on the cobbles of the inn yard, reaching up to help her down. Instead of allowing her to use the steps, he clasped his hands around her waist and swung her down. "You are sure?"

He released her and took a step back.

"No." She swallowed. "But I don't want to close the door on the possibility. I..." She couldn't find the words.

"You don't want your life to be bereft of intimacy."

"No," she said, thankful that he knew what she meant.

"Here it is then, Virginia. If you accept me as a lover, you must know that I will not give you up. I want you in every way possible."

His eyes told her everything she needed to know. Unmistakable desire shone from them.

"But I won't have you dangling me by a string, and I will not accept the status of eternal lover. Not from you. My ambition has not changed since our first kiss. Since I first set eyes on you. I want to spend all the time I can with you, and we cannot do that without marriage. Not in our world."

She bit her tongue on the response that came immediately to mind, but then decided to say it anyway. "Yes. But not marriage. You're moving too fast."

If he continued to insist on that, then she would have to tell him the consequences. And if she did that and people discovered he knew, then she could lose everything.

He gave a brief nod. "I can't force you, Virginia."

As they turned to enter the inn, she said, "Your father felt the same way, did he not? And yet he condemned your mother to a life that was neither one thing nor the other."

He didn't take offense, although his muscles tightened under her hand. "They both considered the sacrifice worth the time they had together."

"What took your father off?" Francis's father had died six months before she'd arrived in Devonshire and first set eyes on the new Earl of Wolverley. He had never worn his heart on his sleeve. Only since she'd grown to know him had she realized how much he'd loved his father.

"A fever. Two days it took, that's all." He swallowed.

"I'm so sorry."

He squeezed her hand. "So am I. Thank you."

They went inside the inn. Night would not fall for another hour or two, but they had chosen to stay here and give Jamie more time to get ahead in the superior carriage.

The landlord, a tall man wearing a crisp, spotlessly white apron, bustled up to them. "Good evening my lord, my lady."

For a few breathless seconds Virginia thought the man had recognized them.

"Mr. and Mrs. Ferguson," Francis said.

"Ah. Very well, sir, madam. I have a good room available at the back of the house, should you wish to stay."

They took the room.

Feeling as nervous as a new bride, Virginia went upstairs while Francis announced his intention of exploring the taproom and investigating the lay of the house. She found a snug chamber containing a comfortable, clean bed and the rest of the furniture she expected. A maid came up with hot water, and a servant with their traveling trunk.

Virginia set about washing and making herself comfortable. A church clock struck the hour, the bells ringing out. They could hardly go to bed at five o'clock. In London she rarely got to bed until after midnight, and even in the country she lingered until later.

Strangely at a loss, excitement and apprehension bubbling inside her, Virginia went to a chair by the window and sat watching the activity outside. She had no embroidery to do, no letters to write, no books to read. No activities to hide behind.

People seemed to have a purpose. The sounds of activity came from below. All had something to do. But Virginia had at least three more days of this before she could start her normal life again.

If she ever did. The thought came to her unbidden, but she dismissed it. This journey was out of time, a different existence where she barely knew herself. Even her clothes were wrong. The fabrics were soft and worn, but not because of her. Because they'd been worn by somebody else first.

When the door opened, she jolted and grabbed the curtain. A cloud of dust went up, making her choke, and before she could recover, a pair of arms went around her, steadying her. She didn't have to look to know who it was.

"I think we'd better leave those alone and just pull the shutters closed tonight," he murmured, his voice rumbling softly in her ear.

So much for romance. Virginia took advantage of his closeness to rest her forehead on his shoulder while she recovered. "Thank you."

"I have something else for you to be thankful for."

She said nothing, but having recovered from her coughing fit, she lifted her head and regarded him balefully. "Are you another of those men?"

"What men?"

"The kind that think they are God's gift to humanity because they have a…"

Fortunately she didn't have to continue. A knowing smile spread over his face. "Ah. No, although I haven't had any complaints." He let go of her and dipped his hand into his pocket. He came out with a pack of cards.

Sheer delight surged through her. "Oh, I see! How thoughtful!"

"Not entirely. We have at least three days yet, and I'm aware that neither of us have our usual entertainment to hand." He smiled. "Yes, we have each other, and I can't tell you how—wonderful that is, but cooped up in a small, rickety carriage together with nothing to do might not be entirely advisable." He left her in no doubt of the other way they could entertain each other.

Virginia had not credited Francis with any measure of tact before, but he'd proved her wrong. And she was so stupidly pleased about the cards that she would have forgiven him any amount of lascivious talk. Well, maybe not forgiven him, but she had to admit that between the bouts of anxiety, stretches of pure boredom had set in.

When she lifted her head, naturally, she kissed him. Anxiety dissolved, anticipation remained.

Yes, she would enjoy herself and give no thought to past or future.

The kiss was short, sweet, and enjoyable, but then he released her. "I ordered dinner sent up. This is a small but efficient establishment, so you can hire a maid if you want to."

To have a maid again, someone to unlace her and brush her hair, would be…

Useless. Virginia could easily manage, and so she told him, "I'll be completely different for the next few days. The kind of person I might have been, had Ralph not met me."

She crossed to the trunk and opened the lid, looking for the brush Butler had bought for her. As Lady Dulverton, she had a polished mahogany dressing case banded with silver, filled with crystal and monogrammed bottles, containers and brushes, everything a lady could wish for. It even had a secret drawer for love letters. She had never used the drawer, never needed to. That had gone before her in the crested carriage.

As Mrs. Ferguson, she owned a brush, a pot of hair powder, which she had yet to use, and a small case of hairpins. That was all. Simple and easy.

They ate in their room again.

"What will we do if someone sees us?" she said over a generous helping of meat and potato pie.

"Use our acting skills?" he suggested. "We look most unlike our usual selves, that unless we come face-to-face with someone who knows us well, I doubt that will happen." He spoke soothingly, as if reassuring her.

She was not reassured. "We should consider the possibility."

He shook his head. "As long as we maintain a good distance between ourselves and your cousin, I can't see it happening. I have a few ideas. Most of them include this." Wryly he lightly touched his wig, below which the healing gash lurked. "We can say I was out of my mind, delirious with a fever, so you were good enough to care for me."

She regarded him, her eyes narrowed. Would that work? It might. But his words reminded her of a duty she had yet to do. "I have to look at that."

"It feels fine."

"Nevertheless…"

Perhaps the leap she had taken today would not happen. She would refuse him if she saw any trace of infection. Anxiety rose once more. Francis would be unlikely to tell her unless he was in so much pain he could not bear it. Even then, he would not tell her. But she'd seen no trace of fever, nor felt it.

"Eat this excellent food, then I'll call the maid to take the plates away."

They finished the meal in harmony, chatting to one another about matters outside this room and their immediate dilemma. Such as her parents. "You rarely speak of them," he said.

She shrugged, feigning an insouciance she did not feel. "We live separate lives, and we have for some time. I had my season, a short one, when I was presented at court. I took fairly well, but I had no serious suitors."

She had told the story before and practiced hiding her pain. A young girl's brutal disillusionment.

"You took, yet you found no takers?" He leaned back in his chair, his attention riveted on her.

Virginia tried not to squirm under his perceptive gaze. "The year of my presentation contained many beauties. They sparkled more than I did, and there were a good number of heiresses presented that season, too." She shrugged and glanced down at the remnants of their meal. "Everything worked out well eventually. I married Ralph, and I became Lady Dulverton."

He glared at her. "If I had met you during your first season, you would not have married him."

Heat flared between them, but neither moved. He nodded. "I take it his wound did not help his mood?"

She sucked in a breath at that reminder of Ralph's nature. "It did not. He was injured abroad and was shipped home as soon as he had recovered enough to do so." As far as anyone knew. "His wound pained him at times, but he bore it bravely."

"In which battle was he wounded? I forget."

No he didn't. Francis never forgot anything. "A skirmish in the colonies," she said lightly. "He was so angry that he missed the Austrian war because of his wounds, but he had attained the rank of general by the time he retired from active service. He met me after my season, when he came to Nottinghamshire to visit my parents."

From the moment Ralph had arrived he'd watched Virginia. Everything she did and said, everywhere she went, there he was. But she had admired him, and Ralph had a kind of rugged handsomeness.

Flattered by his attentions and wounded by her mother's comments after her lack of success in London, she'd been easy prey. "When my parents told me who I was to marry, I was flattered. I imagined myself in love with him." She bit her lip. Too late to amend what she'd said. And of course, Francis picked up on what she'd said immediately.

"*Imagined* yourself in love?"

She laughed, but it sounded false even to her own ears. "Imagined, yes. I was barely eighteen."

"And by the time I met you?"

"I'd been married six months. I loved my husband," she affirmed, more to herself than to him. After all, while their relationship had been unconventional, she'd had a fondness for Ralph. He'd taken her away from her parents and introduced stability into her life.

"Naturally."

He snapped that word off so quickly, she wondered at it. "You lingered on your Grand Tour."

"I did." Again that sharpness. "Fortunately, I discovered some lucrative investment opportunities on my travels."

Which had forced society to acknowledge him. Wealth had triumphed over his mother's low birth. An earl of moderate means with a low-born mother had turned into a wealthy peer with influential friends. More than that, he'd become—Francis.

She recalled the gossip. "You were in Paris, but people talked about you. I heard about you long before I met you after you returned."

"I'm sure you did."

She remembered the moment. "That ballroom…"

A smile teased the corners of his lips. "I remember. I had just arrived back in Devonshire from Paris. I was an oddity, and people did not know what to do with me. The son of a peasant, someone called me." The smile disappeared. "Nobody did that again."

He was too wealthy to ignore, but that was not the reason. When Francis entered a room, everybody looked, including her. Her first sight of him at twenty-one, diamond earring and all, had fascinated her more than the first, if that was possible. Enthralled her, and at that moment, she'd understood what she had lost by marrying Ralph. Not that she'd had much choice.

Her first sight of him in Devonshire she had put down to an immature passion, one that would pass. And indeed it had seemed that way until he'd returned from the Grand Tour, polished and wealthy, and a man. Then she knew her feelings for him hadn't changed.

Until tonight, wild horses would not have dragged that truth out of her. She'd denied it even to herself.

She'd been a new bride when she'd first met the Earl of Wolverley. After her one dance with Francis, Ralph had ordered her to ignore him. She did not do so, and when Ralph taxed her with it, she told him that was all that society needed to point at them all. Ralph was forced to agree, seeing the truth of her words, but he only ever treated Francis with distant politeness.

"The Duke of Richmond still refuses to receive me," he continued. "Pompous oaf."

Most of society shared that opinion about the duke, but few were quite so honest, even in private. She smiled. "He nods distantly to me."

His laugh warmed her as a knock sounded on the door. Before she could give her automatic "Come!" Francis got to his feet and crossed the room to let the maid in.

The woman cleared up the remains of their meal, leaving the wine behind, and carried the heavy tray piled with dishes and cutlery as if it weighed nothing. Francis opened the door for her and latched it behind her. Then he picked up his chair and took it to the door, wedging it under the top rail, tilting it so that nobody could come in. The door had no lock.

"You can move this any time you like," he said, coming back across the room to her, his tread heavy on the floorboards. "But only you."

Standing before her, he held out his hands. Without hesitation, she took them and let him draw her to her feet. "You're shaking," he murmured. "There is nothing but pleasure ahead for you. For both of us."

Breathing deeply, she tried to calm her pounding heart, her tightening throat. One more thing remained. "Your head. A few days ago you were at death's door. Promise me, Francis, that it doesn't pain you."

Francis smiled down at her. "If it did, I would not notice. I want you so much, Virginia. From the first moment I saw you. Learning that you were married was a blow. Then we were on distant terms for so long. That time is over, but say the word and I will treat you like my sister, rather than the lover I long for you to become. Say it now, Virginia. Tell me no."

Keeping her gaze locked with his, Virginia said nothing.

"So be it," he said, softly, like a prayer, before he drew her into his arms.

Slowly, as if savoring every moment, he curled his arms about her, held her firmly, though not with the overwhelming, unthinking passion she had expected. When she'd imagined this, she thought they would be overcome by passion, that everything would unfold without thought, a surge that would guide them both.

Francis did nothing of the kind. He lowered his head slowly, his gray eyes shining with an inner light. When he pressed his lips to hers, it was with a reverence she had never known, a steady claiming she welcomed.

Hooking her arm around his neck, she held on and did her best to respond. He'd taught her how, even though he was probably unaware of it. No, not probably. If he suspected for a second that this was her first time, he would be on the other side of the room, leaving her to guard her virtue.

She would not allow that to happen. She must be bold and confident, responding as a woman should. That should come reasonably easily because of the way she felt about the man holding her so tightly.

Truthfully, she couldn't stand not having him. She'd held him off as long as she could, but given this opportunity, the chance of knowing, of holding him, and being able to walk away afterward—she couldn't resist that.

She wanted Francis so much, she couldn't bear it if he left her now. Climbing the hurdle to surrender had taxed her, but she was over her self-imposed barrier now.

Francis kept his movements soft and sweet, even when she opened her mouth under his. He took her invitation, swept his tongue into her mouth, and made a small sound that reverberated through every inch of her body.

He roamed the length of her back, his strong hands encompassing her, claiming her, and she responded, pressing close to him. When he finished the kiss, he lifted his head and gazed at her as if he'd never seen her before. "Then, sweetheart, allow me to help you to disrobe."

His first tug loosened the fichu she wore over her breasts. She had not secured it with pins, merely tucked it in, so it came away easily, pulling free of the low neckline of the jacket. Francis lifted his hand and traced the swell with one finger. Her breathing grew shaky, and he smiled. "I love knowing that I affect you so much. You do the same to me, Virginia."

Pushing his finger into the opening of the jacket, he found the first hook and slipped it free. He passed on to the second, dispensing her of it just as easily, and the one after that.

Virginia held still, watching the small frown between his brows as he concentrated on freeing her from the garment. "This has served you well," he said, "but now it's time to give up your secrets. I intend to see every inch of your delectable body."

Her throat caught on her next breath, but she let him continue. Once he had the front undone, all he had to do was to slide it off her shoulders and pull it down her arms. The linen ruffles were attached to the elbows, so it fell away, leaving her in stays and shift.

He smiled at the sight of her brocaded silk stays, obviously a costly garment, all she had left of her usual finery. "Like a pearl revealed at the heart of the oyster. But it stands in my way now. Turn around."

Obediently, she did as he asked. His fingers unlaced her stays, the sound of the cord whipping through the holes loud in the stillness of their room. "You don't have to do that," she said, "just loosen it."

He chuckled. "Don't worry, I know how stays are laced. I want you out of this thing." He stopped pulling the cords free. "Arms up."

Like the best lady's maid, he eased her stays up and pulled them free, over her head. The cord caught in her hair, and he stopped to untangle it patiently, as if they had all the time in the world. Apparently he meant to keep his promise about only giving her pleasure.

After tossing the stays over the nearest chair, he finished unfastening her hair, pulling out pin after pin until it fell free, cascading over her shoulder blades. And with it went all her misgivings.

Francis let out his breath in one long sigh. "You can't know how often I've wanted to do that, to see your hair down, and to do this." He threaded his fingers through the locks, sliding them gently through. "Pure silk."

When he walked away, she turned around to see him take a few steps to the chest of drawers pushed against the wall by the window. Carefully he placed the pins there, then came back to her, slipping off his coat on the way and letting it fall to the floor. "Explain to me why we wear so many clothes," he said, unbuttoning his waistcoat.

She laughed. "Speak for yourself. I seem to have considerably less." She had to work to keep her mood as insouciant as his. But she was supposed to be used to this kind of thing, so she'd better put on a show to hide the sensations rioting inside her, as if she'd swallowed a gallon of bubbles.

"Let's correct that, shall we?"

He kept watching her as he unfastened the buckles at his knees and the fall of his breeches, kicking out of his shoes, and dragging breeches and stockings off in one impatient motion. His shirt hung down nearly to his knees. Virginia braced herself.

His erection made the fall of his shirt awkward but ripe with promise. The muscles of his arms and chest proved he needed little padding in his coats. She narrowed her eyes. He looked bigger out of his clothes than in them. "You have a magnificent tailor."

Bursting into delighted laughter, he closed the distance between them and pulled her into his arms. "Now who is overdressed?" he growled before claiming another kiss.

Virginia gave herself up to him with pure pleasure running through her veins. When the cord of her quilted skirt loosened, she merely stepped back a little to allow the garment to fall. Francis dealt with her pockets and her petticoats the same way. Virginia only felt freed. The fewer clothes, the nearer she got to her ultimate objective. And now she was this far in, she didn't want to go back. Ever.

Once she'd rid herself of this idiotic virginity she'd been carrying far too long, she could free herself from the years of secrecy. This man was in her head, constantly in her thoughts, even when she was not sharing a cramped carriage with him. Perhaps this would help. Either that or make the fever worse, and at this point, she didn't care which way it went.

Did every man kiss so divinely? Francis certainly did. He explored her mouth with his tongue, sometimes delicately, then with a passion that burned her from the inside out. Virginia did her best to respond, clutching those powerful shoulders and tasting him, twirling her tongue around his, gaining in confidence as he accepted her caresses and returned them.

When he drew away, she gazed at his reddened lips and half-closed eyes. She'd done that, made him look like that. Totally enthralled, which would be even better if she didn't feel the same way. Virginia preferred to remain in control, but she was losing it fast and not regretting it like she should.

She had no choice but to give herself to him and trust him to return her at the end of their time together, more or less intact.

"Time for bed," he murmured, so softly that even if the room had been filled with people, only she would have heard him.

Before she could turn he scooped her up and, smiling, carried her there. After depositing her gently on the floor, he swept back the bed covers, revealing pristine linen sheets.

He picked her up again, his muscles flexing deliciously, and placed her down. Virginia stroked the bulging muscle in his upper arm while he bent and lifted her shift above her knees, disposing of her garters with two quick flicks of skilled fingers.

Her stockings went the same way. Without being prompted, Virginia sat up, her hands going to her shift. Before she could outthink herself, she pulled it up and over her head, emerging breathless with her hair in her eyes.

Pushing it back, she laughed, and watched the change in his expression as she revealed her body.

Awe shaded his gaze. "My God, Virginia. You're beautiful."

That she could cope with. "So I've been told." Not by her husband, but he did not have to know that. Only by her maid.

Mustering all her self-control, she assumed the pose of a society lady waiting for her lover, one she'd seen in a so-called classical painting.

Raising a knee, she rested her wrist on it and gave him a bored stare through half-closed eyes. Her thigh grazed her nipple as she leaned forward, making her suck in a breath. She was so sensitive. Seeing him fix her with such an intense scrutiny only made her nipples tighten more, and the place between her thighs dampen.

He didn't laugh this time but paused to unfasten the buttons at his cuffs and get rid of his neckcloth and shirt. They fell—somewhere, she wasn't watching.

So much man stood before her. What seemed like acres of him to her dazed senses. She took inventory. A broad, hair-sprinkled chest, wide shoulders and strong arms, all beautifully sculpted with smooth muscle. Narrow hips and long legs. What reared between them—passed her understanding. Long, thick, slightly curved, and for tonight at least, all hers.

"When you've finished your study, do let me know," he said in a fashionable drawl, laughter in his voice.

Her attention flew to his face. He was smiling, but he had not lost that sultry, fiery glow in his eyes. Leaning forward, he urged her back to lie against the banked pillows. Slowly he climbed onto the bed, his movements smooth but determined, until he straddled her. Dipping his head, he touched his lips to her forehead, her nose, and her lips almost reverently.

"I won't ask you if you're sure," he said, "but I would like you to know that if you tell me to stop now, you'll kill me stone dead."

That made her laugh. She was still laughing when he kissed her.

He plunged her into passion. Virginia returned his kiss, more confident now, lifting her hands to grip his shoulders, holding on for her life. He finished the kiss, only to drop small, feathery kisses either side of her mouth, down her neck, pausing to lick the hollow at the base of her throat, where he'd caressed her before. He must already know she was sensitive there.

But not her breasts. He made up for that lack now, cupping the plump mounds, rubbing the tips with his thumbs before lowering his head and taking her right nipple into his mouth.

Sensation shot from her nipple to her groin. If she'd thought she was aroused before, she was doubly so now. Moaning, she turned, so he had to chase his quarry, but she didn't resist. He kissed the nipple and switched to the other one, delivering the same delicious torture, making her sigh and moan.

Kissing underneath her breast, he nuzzled the soft skin and continued down, laying a trail of soft, damp kisses down her rib cage, lingering at her navel before continuing down.

Where was he going? What was he doing? Did men do this? As he urged her to spread her legs wider, he pushed his arms under her knees. "Open for me, sweetheart. Let me in."

After a second's resistance, she did as he bade her. He rewarded her with a lick.

Virginia came off the bed, and if he hadn't pushed her down, his hands on her hips, she would have vaulted right off. The sensation was as if he'd sent lightning flashing through her. She'd touched that place before, but she had only brought herself comfort, not this wild, uncontrollable feeling.

Shuddering, she uttered small wordless sounds. If she'd thought his treatment of her breasts was intense, she was wrong. *This* was intensity personified, tingles pouring through her whole body, turning her into a creature of desire, with one aim, one desire. "Francis…?"

"Lie back, let me do it all," he murmured. "Don't be afraid, don't worry. I'll make this good for you."

After kissing her, tasting her, and rendering her completely helpless, he returned the way he'd come, only this time something much thicker and longer than his finger nudged her entrance. He pushed slightly, just enough to lodge himself at her entrance.

He gazed down at her, smiling reassuringly. "Hold on to me, sweetheart."

She gripped his shoulders as he reared up over her. He gave a few short, exploratory jabs, pushing his hips in and down. Then, before she could catch her breath, he plunged deep, piercing her maidenhead in one hard thrust. She had expected a pinch. Sharp pain arced through her body. "Ah!"

She hadn't meant to cry out, hadn't intended to indicate this was something she'd never done before. Then he was with her, holding her, kissing her lips with a soft tenderness she'd never experienced before in anyone, not even him.

"All done," he murmured against her lips.

Virginia opened her eyes wide, met his, so close she saw the darker rings around the gray centers. "You knew?"

"Not for sure, but I suspected you weren't as experienced as I'd thought when I kissed you that first time. You did not kiss as if you were used to it." His voice shook. "Virginia, sweetheart, I have wanted to make love to you for so long."

He was inside her now, his shaft disturbingly different, filling her to the brim. Not sure she was comfortable with this new sensation, she shifted, only for him to groan. "That's it. Move. Get used to the way I feel inside you."

"Oh. How did you know?" She tried another move, wriggling her hips.

He closed his eyes and groaned. "Can we talk about it later?"

She saw his point, especially when he responded to her next tentative shift. "Is that right?"

"Everything is right. Everything. What we do here is for us and nobody else."

That suited her. When he kissed her this time, he was not gentle. He swept his tongue into her mouth, stroking her tongue, teasing her and delivering a succession of jabs, as if mimicking what was happening below. For he did not remain still any longer. He moved up and down, gently at first as if testing her, each thrust increasing in power.

By the time he lifted his mouth from hers, he was moving in earnest, driving in and then out, varying his strokes, moving his hips until she cried out. This whole experience was intense, but this was above everything else.

"Ah, there it is."

Whatever he had been searching for, he'd found. Keeping the angle, he pushed, withdrew, thrust, pulled back, repeated the action until a spot inside her burned, sprang a flood of sensation, growing and deepening until it encompassed her whole world. She knew nothing else, wanted nothing else.

As her body convulsed around him in a series of spasms that delivered exquisite sensation to every inch of her body, Virginia cried out, calling his name.

In response, he pressed his forehead to hers and groaned low as he, too, reached his pinnacle.

Chapter 15

To Virginia's consternation, Francis insisted on cleaning her with a cloth dipped into cold water. He enjoyed her confusion and that he could persuade her to trust him. He didn't want her to suffer any discomfort. And he had every intention of indulging his powerful urge to look after her.

Despite her weak protests, he nudged her legs apart and placed a cold, wet cloth over her sex. She snapped her legs shut, an adorable pink flush spreading over her breasts and neck, but then gave a wry smile and opened them again. She sighed happily.

"See?" he said. "That feels good, doesn't it? I don't want you to be sore."

"I didn't think you'd notice," she said.

"What? That you were innocent?"

"I was not innocent!" she fired back. "I knew what was about to happen, and I wanted it. I made my choice freely, Francis."

And he would be ever grateful that she did. He loved her fiery response. She was right, she was not innocent. "I know that. But why were you still a virgin?"

Emphasis on the past tense, because she wasn't one now. He wanted this part of the evening over with, together with her uncertainty. It was so unlike Virginia, who had conquered society with a quiet, gracious confidence. Until that first kiss, he'd thought her experienced, if only in a physical way. Despite his age, Ralph Dulverton had given every impression of a man in charge of his world.

"Yes." She paused. "How did you know?"

"Your kiss was wonderfully fresh, untutored. I enjoyed you learning with me. After that I thought your marriage might have been one of those where making love was a swift, clinical business. Some couples regard it as a necessary task, rather than the joy it can be."

She said nothing for a moment, then, "It wasn't like that. I will tell you. Let me find the words."

He gave her the time, until he removed the cloth.

Tossing the cloth in the bowl, he returned to her. "Not much blood, a mere trace, so you need not worry that the chambermaid will know that there was anything amiss." He pressed a kiss to her forehead and drew her into his arms before drawing the sheet over them.

"Good." Virginia rested her head on his shoulder. He relished the way their bodies entwined as one, when she nestled her leg between his.

"Do you want to tell me what happened? Or to be more precise, what did not happen?" he asked her.

"I did not, that is, I was willing, but…"

He stroked her back, trying to soothe her. "It's all right. Take your time. I'm content if you choose not to tell me at all." She was as skittish as a kitten.

"No. I will tell you. If I cannot trust you, I can't trust anyone. And Ralph is gone now, past his pain."

"Yes, he is."

She pulled in a deep breath. "You know Ralph was injured. He made no secret of it. But nobody knew how badly, except his doctor and me."

After a short pause, she carried on. "He was serving in the colonies when he took a bullet. In fact, he took two bullets, but he insisted on staying in the field where he rode out the worst of his pain, only leaving when he was sure his men were safe. He was shot in the leg, and further up in his groin."

Here came the important part. "Because of the groin injury, amputation would not have helped him. For a few days the doctors thought he would not live. News that he'd inherited the title arrived while he was sick, and when he heard that, he determined to survive. He was very brave."

Francis grunted, an essentially masculine sound intended merely to tell her that he was listening. The groin injury was news to him. Why had Ralph kept it quiet, when everyone knew he'd been hit in the leg? When Francis had met him on his return from France, the general always used a cane.

"My father had served under him, and they had become friends when my father sold out."

Francis had never noticed before, but Virginia never used a fond name like Papa when she referred to her father.

"By then I was out, and a failure, as I told you before, so I was reconciling myself to a single life."

Before he was done, he'd ensure she never saw herself as a failure again. "Had you met him before?"

"Only a few times, as a child. I barely remembered him. At first Ralph talked to me as a friend and confided in me. I accompanied him on his daily exercise. He was determined to walk without a cane, so he took a gentle tour around the gardens every day. He was then General Lord Dulverton, learning his new life. The title had passed indirectly for the past few generations, so Ralph was the nephew of the previous viscount." She sighed. "He was much older than me, but he was a strong man who treated me well. My life with my family was not happy."

He swung up on one elbow, alarmed by her last words. "How? Tell me. I want to know everything."

"Everything?"

He dropped a kiss on her lips, because he wanted to. "All of it."

"Then you must tell me your story in return."

What there was of it society knew already. There was no secret, but he would tell her when she needed a rest from pouring her heart out.

Her story might be the key he was looking for, the reason why she married a man so much older than herself. He knew what a bride much younger than her groom looked like when love truly passed between them.

Although Virginia and Ralph gave every impression of a devoted couple, the few times he had met them, or seen them together, had revealed none of the telling touches, the small smiles passing between them that were the common currency of his own parents.

"Are you an only child?"

"Their only daughter. I have a brother ten years younger than me. He was the miracle. My parents had not expected to have another child." She paused. "For my first few years, I was pampered and indulged. My mother in particular doted on me. But when my brother arrived, everything changed. The only notice they paid to me was to criticize me. I was never good enough for her, never learned my lessons properly. My brother was now the favored child."

Francis sucked in a breath, angry for her parents' treatment of her. "Did they hurt you?"

Her shrug lacked conviction. "Sometimes. But they never marked me. They were careful not to do that."

If only he had met her then! So young, so untutored, and so beautiful.

"I was glad when Ralph courted me. Glad to get away."

Abandoned and ignored by her parents, Virginia had fallen on the visitor who had paid her attention. For her sake Francis quelled the anger rising like a tide inside him. Virginia deserved tender care tonight, and he would give it to her. "I see. Now tell me why you were still a virgin after marriage to such a vital man."

"I feel as if I'm betraying Ralph by telling you."

He touched her lips with the tip of his forefinger. "You know I will tell no one. And as you said, he is gone now, past his pain."

She nodded. "Ralph was strong and steadfast, a man to rely on. Also three times my age when we married, but I did not let that concern me. Apart from his injuries, he had the body of a man half his age. But during our bride-trip from my home in Nottinghamshire to Devonshire, he did not touch me, did not come to me at night. He said he wanted to save it until we were in his home. Then, when we were finally at Dulverton Hall, he came to me."

She paused for so long Francis thought her confidences were at an end. But then she spoke again.

"He—he was abrupt. He did not kiss me. And we did not remove our nightclothes. He said it was to spare my blushes, but I suspect he did not wish to remind me of his scars." She swallowed. "I saw them another time. But he did not—could not…"

Francis nodded. He did not need the gory details. Ralph's groin injury had rendered him impotent.

"He said I was at fault."

How could this exquisite woman believe she was to blame for her husband's failure? How could Ralph have done this to her?

"He said I did not do things right. I did the best I could." She met his eyes boldly, but Francis read distress there.

He was pushing her too far, but he desperately needed to understand. "Did he hurt you?"

"No. He kept trying, but the result was the same. To protect his reputation, he told people I was barren." She bit her lip. "I might not be."

He would not tell her the shock that realization had brought to him. He had prepared to accept her, barrenness and all, but perhaps he did not have to. "Did he strike you?"

"No!" Fire returned to her eyes, and he untensed. This was the Virginia he knew, not the frightened child he'd briefly glimpsed. Dulverton had been her escape, but she'd found a different horror with him. Frying pans and fires came to mind.

And yet here she was, facing him with defiance and fire, telling her story as if it was a normal series of events. While her husband had been a fearsome warrior in full public view, Virginia had fought a secret battle.

And come out of it triumphantly. He would never forget that, or her honesty with him tonight.

He brought the discussion to an end by the simple expedient of kissing her. "Are you tired?"

She shook her head. He got out of bed and unashamedly moved about the room, lighting candles and closing the shutters. He felt her eyes on him and gloried in it.

When he returned to bed after giving her the respite she needed, she moved to him and let him take her in his arms.

They would not be making love again tonight, even though the temptation of her body sliding against his was almost too much to bear. She was everything he had ever wanted in a woman, and more besides. But even now, winning her would prove difficult. Virginia was fiercely independent, and she had won her status dearly. She would not give it up easily.

* * * *

Francis lay awake long after Virginia had fallen asleep. Should he tell her that he remembered what she had told him the day of his injury? That she had asked him to wait six years? She might insist on it, and that he would not bear.

Presumably the property would revert to Jamie when they married, where it should have been in the first place. What did that matter? He didn't care if she came to him with nothing. Clearly, he had work to do.

Ralph had hurt her. Virginia was a strong woman, but his accusations that she was responsible for his failure as a husband had burrowed into her skin. And his will had done the rest. He could not have her, so nobody would. In six years society would have slotted her into her allotted role: benefactor, philanthropist, widow.

She deserved more than that. If she was entirely content in her role, he would have left her alone. No, he amended, he would probably have waited for her.

He would have to wait until she confided in him and told him her secret again. Or should he tell her that he already knew? Damned if he knew.

And he wanted her so badly, to have her by his side, to introduce her as his wife.

Virginia should not have to give up her dreams. He would not force her to bear children, but after what they had just done, conception might have happened already. And the thought of a child—their child—filled him with excitement.

God help him. What a fool he was, to want all those things when he could not even persuade her to marry him. But if he was foolish, so be it.

He drifted off, holding her close, her soft breath warming his chest.

* * * *

In the morning they had breakfast in their room before climbing into the carriage Hurst had acquired.

Francis was so careful of Virginia, determined to keep her this time. He hadn't made the mistakes he'd committed before. She accepted him as a lover. But he wanted more.

This one was worse than yesterday's, smaller, the bodywork dull with age. Another hired coachman sat on high, bundled up despite the heat of the day. Hurst and Butler climbed up behind, and they were off.

The day was tedious, but Francis was glad of it, giving him a rest day and time to think. His head was still tender but healing well. His arm was a mass of bruises, but they were turning yellow now. And he was with the woman he wanted above all others.

Francis sat next to Virginia, amusing her, playing cards for kisses, and wanting her more every day. That night they shared a bed again, and while he was gentle and only made love to her once, the experience only made him long for more.

He wanted her, and he refused to wait six long years to claim her. Mistress was not enough. Not that she had offered that to him, but she would. He knew her too well. Marriage was what she deserved and what she could have, but he wanted her to come to him with a whole heart. He laid his plans, certain he could persuade her to marry him before too much longer.

They were a day away from Exeter. With the countryside passing the window, combined with an occasional glimpse of the sea and the sails of the ships populating it, he said lazily, "I think we are out of trouble now. Your cousin must be a long way ahead of us."

"And nobody has tried to attack us," she said, beaming.

Which was one point he meant to address. "I don't intend to leave you alone. Obviously, I can't come and stay at Combe Manor with you in case word gets out, but I will find somewhere close by."

"You don't have to," she said quickly, glancing out the window.

"Oh, but I do." He watched her closely. "The manor is near Newton Abbott, is it not?"

She nodded. "It overlooks the most beautiful bay. Or so I have been told. I've never been there. It is not uninhabited though; a caretaking couple lives there, so it will be ready for us."

She'd said "us."

Virginia was intelligent, she was beautiful, she was everything he wanted. But she was not as cynical as he was, and sometimes a man had to listen to the devil on his left shoulder instead of the angel on his right. A succession of showing her how he could make her feel and backing away to allow her to accept it should work. Not pouncing on her like a starving wolf all the time and forcing her to do something she hadn't fully accepted.

She would be his.

They traveled to the next inn, where they would change horses in comfortable silence. This place was larger than they preferred, but they didn't have much choice.

This village boasted a mere two inns. The yard of the first one had more private, luxurious vehicles in the yard than less well-appointed ones. They moved on.

Fortunately neither Francis nor Virginia had visited before, but he only learned when she gave him a terse, "No," to his query. She was tense. Perhaps getting near to their home county was affecting her.

He alighted first and held out his hand to get her down. She ignored it, but stumbled, so he had to catch her to prevent her tumbling onto the none-too-clean cobbles beneath their feet.

"Steady, sweetheart," he murmured, eliciting a smile from her.

Francis snatched a quick kiss, outrageously brazen. Worse that she responded, giving him a quick smile before she pulled away.

Relief swept through him. That was, until a voice boomed out. "Lady Dulverton! We were not expecting to meet you here!"

Oh no, oh Lord, what were they going to do now?

Sir Bertram had found them. They had been so concentrated on her cousin-in-law that they had entirely forgotten another person who could be on the road.

If he did not think quickly, Virginia's reputation and standing would be utterly destroyed. Unless they took him for a servant.

Only one response came to mind. She might hate him for it, but he could see no other way.

Chapter 16

They had just alighted from the same small, enclosed carriage, and they had no companions. That was bad enough, but they were obviously traveling hugger-mugger, with the minimum of servants. Scandal or his way.

Francis remained facing her. "Courage," he murmured, and turned back to Sir Bertram, who unfortunately stood in the yard with his wife and three daughters. Keeping his head down, he waited for a miracle. Perhaps they would not recognize him in a bob-wig and plain, unadorned clothes. He could pass for a servant. As long as they had not seen that playful kiss.

The miracle failed to appear.

"Lord Wolverley!" Lady Dean exclaimed. She fanned her face with her hand, as if overwhelmed by shock. "Did I see you—*embracing* Lady Dulverton?"

No help for it. Virginia would kill him, but he couldn't see another way. He glanced at Butler, who was standing quietly by, while Hurst helped the coachman with the horses. He took a step forward, bringing a reluctant Virginia with him.

"You mistake, Sir Bertram." He pasted on a broad smile. "I have the ineffable pleasure of presenting Lady Wolverley."

Her hand tightened over his. Francis did not flinch, even though he suspected the feeling wouldn't come back to his fingers for a while.

The Deans did not speak for a whole minute. The busy yard seemed miles away as they waited. The three girls gaped, and Lady Dean's expression hardened, as if she'd made an effort to freeze it, lest it slip into something more unseemly. Sir Bertram glared, a deep frown creasing the small space between his bushy brows.

Francis was content to wait. The pause gave Virginia time to catch up with him.

The masquerade was necessary, but it had jettisoned all his plans out the window. Not rushing her into anything was gone now. Only a small chance remained that she would ever talk to him again.

Damn and blast.

Eventually Lady Dean curtsyed, and her girls followed suit.

Sir Bertram gave a reluctant bow. "When did this happen?"

"In our own time." Francis owed him nothing, and he would give nothing, in case they needed to change their story later. "We felt that too much fuss was somewhat—vulgar, don't you agree?"

"Oh, yes," Lady Dean said eagerly.

Lady Dean seemed to have recovered herself, for she swept a hand down, indicating their appearances. "Have you decided to change your style, now you are married?"

"Hardly."

Francis was relieved to hear Virginia speak. She was coming out of her stupor. He had best make sure there were no weapons nearby when they finally reached their room, because she was like to kill him.

Her voice could cut glass. "Our luggage was purloined. Stolen," she kindly explained for Lady Dean.

"Those jewels?"

Virginia half closed her eyes. Despite her simple, worn clothing she was every inch the lady. "Naturally not. They went ahead. We decided to travel quietly, not wanting any attention. The thieves must have been sorely disappointed with what they found."

Virginia had turned from tired but adorable to haughtiness personified.

When Lady Dean tried to scan their appearance, Virginia raised her chin and gave the lady a querying stare. "You will join us for dinner, my dear?" Lady Dean asked her.

Francis watched, fascinated.

"I'm afraid we have to refuse your kind offer." Virginia glanced at Francis. Her hand was steady now, and her gaze cool. Oh Lord, what would she do to him when she got him alone? "We are traveling on until dark. I am keen to reach home as soon as I may. But we will take a little refreshment while the horses are changed."

Lady Dean smiled and gestured for her daughters to follow. "We have already bespoken a parlor. Please join us, even if only for a short time."

Sir Bertram regarded them carefully. Like Francis, he had remained silent while the ladies jousted, but he shot Francis an alarmingly astute nod. He drifted away, after a murmured, "Will you ladies excuse me?" as if planning to use the necessary.

Taking the hint, Francis followed him, satisfied Virginia could more than hold her own with Lady Dean and her daughters. Finding himself in the rough building behind the inn that contained a number of chamber pots, he moved to stand in front of one and unfastened his breeches. Since he was here, he might as well take advantage of them.

"Do I congratulate you?" Sir Bertram asked.

"If you wish," Francis said cautiously. "My wife would not accept me for months, even though I have been courting her all season. Virginia is a lady of high standards."

"Glad to hear it. But you should have waited."

"What for? Snow in July?" He had waited long enough. In any case, who was Sir Bertram to question his actions?

Sir Bertram concentrated on buttoning the fall of his breeches. "For Lady Dulverton to conclude establishing her orphanages."

What the devil? Where had that come from? "I will not prevent her from doing that, should she wish to continue. Do you have an interest in her philanthropy?"

Sir Bertram sent him a considering glance. He didn't answer immediately, but after a significant pause, he said, "No, but I admire it. I would be sorry to see her stop."

"There is no reason she should not continue."

"True enough."

When they'd done, they strolled together toward the main building, dodging past a couple of skittish horses being led into the yard. Sir Bertram put his hand on the latch of the door into the inn and paused, as if struck by a sudden thought.

Francis was not fooled. This was no impulsive remark. Sir Bertram had something on his mind. He might as well hear it.

"You know, this is all very sudden, your marriage." He touched his wig, which unlike Francis's was new and well kept, crisply neat. "This, for instance. One might almost think you did not want to be recognized."

"One might," Francis said smoothly, "when one wished for privacy."

"Or an adventure."

"That as well." What was the man getting at?

Sir Bertram gave him an indulgent smile, the crow's feet at the corners of his eyes crinkling, reducing his already small eyes to slits in his generous flesh. "You are not truly married, are you?"

Francis stared but said nothing, waiting to see what Sir Bertram was saying. What he wanted. He suspected the three daughters had something to do with this start.

"If you wish, I can prevail on my good lady to say nothing of meeting you here. I suspect you wanted to reach Hatherton Cross unnoticed. Adventures take many forms, and I don't pretend to understand the ways of the aristocracy, but you, sir, are entitled to any privacy you wish for."

"Aren't you afraid we might corrupt your daughters?" Francis asked.

"No, sir. My daughters are aware of the way the world works. Although if anyone were to treat them as you have treated Lady Dulverton, I would call him out. Unfortunately, Lady Dulverton's parents take little notice of her these days, do they…?" He raised a brow.

He was calling Virginia a whore, accusing her of immoral behavior. "So let me understand," Francis said. Anyone who knew him would have taken his cool, slow drawl as a warning tone, but Sir Bertram did not know him well enough to take the warning. "You believe I am having an affair with the lady, and you are willing to overlook our indiscretion. In return for what?"

"Why, nothing, sir. But I suspected as much the moment I saw you. I dare say I could think of a small favor…" He winked. "Never fear, I will not tell anyone."

Francis stepped back, prepared to walk around the man. "I'm sorry to disabuse you, Sir Bertram, but I need to get back to my wife. She will become concerned if she does not see me soon."

He walked away, fully aware he had burned his boats. He would have to warn Virginia that Sir Bertram suspected their story. Once she had finished ripping him to pieces.

* * * *

Virginia listened to Lady Dean's chatter with only half an ear. She nodded at what appeared like the right moments, but vouchsafed nothing new. Nothing Lady Dean could gossip about. When the oldest daughter, Mary, commented that her presentation at court had gone well, Virginia launched into a long story about her own presentation, sprinkling in more anecdotes than crumbs in a cake, spinning out the tale while she watched the family. Halfway through her account, Francis and Sir Bertram came in, but Francis motioned her to continue and watched her, seemingly fascinated, while she spun out the most boring story in her repertoire.

But sometimes tedium proved useful, giving them a chance to observe and avoid awkward questions.

Like, when did they marry? Why did they leave it until the end of the season? Why had they not held a ball to celebrate their union? Why did none of their friends know?

Questions she would have asked in Lady Dean's situation.

Eventually, after several dishes of tea and a quantity of bread and butter and good farmhouse cake had been consumed, Sir Bertram pulled out his watch. His fob glinted gold in the daylight as he flicked open the lid of the elaborately chased hunter and checked the time.

Taking the hint, Virginia brought her story to a close as Francis got to his feet. "We must be going if we are to make Exeter by nightfall." He bowed and made their farewells.

Sir Bertram shook Francis's hand. "I would call on you soon, sir. I have a proposition for you that could benefit us both."

Francis raised a brow. "Oh?"

"A favor, which should lead to an excellent investment."

Francis exchanged a glance with Virginia. She glared back. This was what it was like to be married, to have to stand by and watch men make all her decisions for her.

Memories of events she thought she would never experience again crowded in her mind. All the times Ralph had undercut her, or spoken for her, telling hostesses what she liked to eat and drink, expressing opinions for both of them, instead of consulting her. Now here she was again, with another man riding roughshod over her.

This was a nightmare. Surely they could work a way out of this.

"I confess, sir, the marriage is so recent I have not considered anything except my good fortune in gaining a wife. But we agreed that she would continue to administer her late husband's lands."

Sir Bertram smirked, a particularly unpleasant expression on his homely features. "If you say so, sir."

What a coil!

Virginia did not speak until Francis handed her into the carriage, and they were once more on their way.

"He will tell everyone," she said gloomily. "What possessed you, Francis?" Although she tried hard to keep her voice and temperament under control, tears stained her voice, and she was trembling. Distress and anger had their effect, and she would have to work hard to keep her wits about her.

She disposed her skirts and sat bolt upright, freezing him out.

He did not remain frozen. "What would you have me do?" he demanded. "They recognized us both as soon as they clapped eyes on us. What else could we have done?"

He leaned back, his expansive gesture of exasperation illustrating his words effectively.

She had to concede that. Although she had been prepared to brazen it out, she had seen recognition in the eyes of the squire and his lady. "We could have come up with something. Like my carriage had broken down and you were taking me to the nearest inn. I was ready to come up with that when you said we were married. We could have thought of no end of reasons!"

"Reasons why we are dressed like this, and in the same closed carriage? Why we kissed in the inn yard?" He gave a derisive snort. "Whatever the reason, Virginia, that situation alone is enough to ruin you. You have kept yourself aloof for years. You would never have willingly climbed into a closed carriage with a man. You've made a name for your virtue and correct behavior. The Deans would not have believed your story for one minute."

It was true. If she had not made a point of behaving correctly, of keeping herself completely apart, she might have escaped with an excuse. But not this. And that kiss! If she had not kissed him, intending to punish him in the way lovers knew best, they could have escaped. She could not blame him for that particular indiscretion. "What do you suggest we do to get out of this pickle?"

"Why, my dear, we must marry. Nothing else will suffice." He sighed and tilted his head back. "If you must know, Sir Bertram only half believes our story, and offered to stop his wife and daughters talking about us."

"He wants you for his daughters."

He grunted. "I am aware. But I don't trust them not to gossip anyway."

"Neither do I."

Tears sprang to her eyes. What was worse was that she had brought this on herself. She'd taken too many risks, allowed Francis to be seen to court her, and then agreed to travel with him.

Not to mention what had happened last night and the night before.

"Did you intend this all along? To trap me into marriage, since I would not marry you another way?" Bitterness infused her.

She was ruined. If she married him, any independence she might have won was lost. If she did not, all the rakes in the West Country would come knocking on her door.

Her fears returned, the terror of returning to her parents, or being trapped in another situation just as bad. Francis was a charming, attentive lover, but sometimes they made the worst husbands. And she was too weakened toward him now. If she did not love him, she was close, try though she might to pull away.

Ralph had promised her independence, but when he'd given it to her, it had come with severe penalties for failure. So severe, she would be left penniless if she disobeyed his dying wishes. Her parents would not concern themselves with her once she'd failed to add to the family prestige. She would be on her own.

"No, I did not." He leaned toward her but did not close the final six inches that lay between his lips and hers. "Virginia, I wanted to court you properly. I swear I had no intention for this to happen. I was and am genuinely concerned for your safety, but I don't want your wealth. You must know that."

"Do I?"

He had the temerity to laugh. "I have plenty of my own. More than enough. You have a section of what was never an expansive estate. You are rich by some people's reckoning, but not by mine." His mouth flattened, the lines either side deepening. "I meant what I said at the inn. I do not wish for your property, and you are free to manage it any way you choose. Continue with your orphanages, if you wish."

Except, the minute they married, it would pass out of her hands forever. Surely he wouldn't want her if she had nothing. Her parents' cruel treatment of her returned now, the constant repetition of "nobody wants you, nobody cares about you" hammering through her mind.

She had to tell him, but she did not know how. The humiliating terms of Ralph's will would become known, since there would no longer be a way to conceal it. She would have nothing, worse than when she'd left her parents' house.

Was there a way out of this mess?

An idea struck her. Perhaps there was a way out of this after all.

"Francis, I cannot marry you."

* * * *

Dropped into the silence, her words caught and held. The information sank under his skin like needles.

"Virginia, Sir Bertram Dean knows we traveled as man and wife. His wife knows. So do his children. By the time we reach Combe Manor, the whole county will know, even if Sir Bertram tries to deny it. London will know. There. Is. No. Escaping. This." He emphasized every word of the final sentence, just in case she had missed his point.

There wasn't a scrap of color left on her face.

Exasperation forced him to punch into his open palm, because if he hadn't used that futile gesture he might have put his fist through the carriage window. "For God's sake, talk to me, Virginia."

Tell him what he knew already, what he wasn't supposed to know. If she did not, he couldn't counter it.

She bit her lip, and tears sprang to her eyes. One trickled down the side of her face. Although he longed to sweep her into his arms and offer all the comfort he could, Francis held back. She needed to do this herself.

"Very well." She sighed, her shoulders slumping.

That single tear shamed him. He should not make free with his temper, however maddening she became. But hell, he couldn't deny it. He seized her hands, clasped his own around them, and lifted them to form a joint balled fist between them.

"I am going nowhere, Virginia. And I will continue asking you until you tell me the truth. If you still refuse to marry me, if you want to slip into the solitary existence of the social outcast, I will come with you. Ruin yourself, and you take me along with you."

She gave a heavy, shaky sigh. "You won't accept my decision not to marry you?"

"No." He wanted marriage.

Although they hadn't spoken of it, what they had done could have circumstances beyond their control. Any child of his would be born in the sanctity of marriage. And he desperately wanted the right to protect and cherish Virginia.

"I swear I will not seek to control you in any way. I will not voice your opinions for you or decide on your social calendar."

A small, wavering smile touched her lips. "You noticed Ralph doing that?"

"I noticed. Everyone did. We thought you'd agreed to it."

She swallowed, staring at a spot above his head rather than meeting his eyes. "I promised."

Francis hated the tiny voice, the fear in every word, but he had to make her tell him. Again. And he was so afraid of a repeat of what they'd done before when she'd sent him away. He clasped her hands firmly, drawing them up between them. "If you tell me, I swear I will keep your confidence, whatever it costs me. Virginia, you will find such relief in telling someone."

He glanced out of the window. The road followed the coast. They would arrive at Newton Abbott soon, and then she could well slam this door shut again. "Tell me now and lance this poison."

Her sigh came from the bottom of her heart. "Yes."

He felt the fight go from her, and he was sorry for it. He regretted bringing her to this, but whatever was forcing her to make impossible demands needed to come to light, if only between them.

"My inheritance is bound up with the orphanages. The project was dear to Ralph's heart, but he died before he could fulfill his plans. They were most detailed."

Ah, a general and his plans. "I see," he said carefully, although he didn't. Why would orphanages prevent them from marrying? This part was new to him.

"He left me a list of the houses he wanted to make into orphanages."

"And Combe Manor is one of them."

She nodded. "That is why I can't sell it to you. He was most specific. He left provision for each orphanage, and what I needed to invest in the trusts attached to each. I could sell some properties to fund that. What is left is mine to keep and will be signed over to me ten years after his death."

In six years.

She glanced up at him, then down at her hands. "I have ten years after his death to fulfill his legacy. If I remarry before the ten years are up, then the property passes to Jamie, with the same provisions for the orphanages. If I die before the ten years are up, the same thing happens."

He put his hand over hers and gave it a reassuring squeeze. She had told him. He could deal with this. "I swear I will tell nobody. Whatever happens next, your secret is safe with me."

"Thank you."

"I will marry you with your dowry, which is probably modest. I don't care, Virginia."

She shook her head. "The forfeiture is severe. I lose *everything*. My inheritance from Ralph, my own portion, my settlement—everything."

Shock arced through him. He hadn't known that part. No wonder she was so concerned. That was unconscionable.

"Surely that can be avoided?"

She shook her head. "If I tell anyone, or if I marry anyone else before the ten years are up, I lose everything. Everything, Francis. My home, my possessions, even the clothes on my back. And my dowry." Her voice lifted in pitch, her distress obvious.

Despite the warmth of the day, he went so cold that he shivered. How could anyone do that to her? He'd thought Ralph had loved her, but nobody would do this to a loved one.

He would take her with nothing. His task now was to persuade her of that.

She lowered her chin. "It is my fault. We had an argument not long after we married. You know what it was about."

His inability to perform in bed, of course.

She went on. "I told him I did not want to marry anyone ever again. So he wrote that into his will. And he wanted me to concentrate on his project. The orphanages meant a great deal to him."

Oh no, that was not the reason at all. A suspicion took hold in his mind and grew into an unhealthy plant. He knew he was right. Ralph had never cared for orphanages or destitute children. Only about Virginia.

A streak of sunlight shone through the carriage windows, lighting glints of red in her hair, skimming across her fair skin like a lover. Then it was gone.

When Ralph had married Virginia, he'd sported her around town like a prize, something he'd won, a possession. He'd dressed her in fine clothes, repeatedly asked people if they did not think she was lovely, boasted about his prowess with his new bride. Although Francis had not been there for her first season as a married woman, he'd heard about it. And when he returned, Ralph was still doing it.

All false, all rotten. When Ralph had realized he was impotent, had the seeds of his revenge sprouted then? Had he made up his mind that if he could not have her, then nobody would? In six years, Virginia would be well past the age of marriage and childbearing, at least in the eyes of society.

Instead of a philanthropic gesture, Ralph's last task had turned Virginia's work into drudgery.

Damn her parents for not cherishing the treasure they'd had in Virginia, for destroying her confidence in herself. Damn her late husband for cherishing her to the point of possession.

Francis loved her. Of course he did. At first he had put it down to her beauty, to his desire for her, but that was foolish. She was the only woman for him.

"Francis, if you wait until the ten years are up, I will gladly marry you."

"In six years?" He shook his head. They had gone this far. He must press the point. Giving her time meant six months, not six years. "No. Ralph will not keep you as his wife in death. We will marry. Reconcile yourself to that. But I will force nothing else on you."

He lifted their hands and kissed her knuckles. "You will be free in our marriage, sweetheart. You will have enough to live independently of me, if you wish it. I will give you everything you stand to lose and more. But I cannot let you walk away from this. From us. Let Jamie have it all. Everything but you."

She was trembling, and Francis had to force himself to keep his voice low, to treat her gently. She deserved none of his temper. Her late husband had earned it all. If he were still alive, Francis would have tracked him down and beaten him to a bloody pulp. The wickedness of the scheme appalled him, using charity and good works to cover up a selfish, craven-dog-in-the-manger act.

He reached out and, before she could snatch it away, took her hand in his. "I'll settle on you whatever you want, whatever makes you feel safe."

When she was strong enough, he'd tell her his final secret: that he loved her. But not yet. He would show her instead.

Ralph had told her he loved her. Frequently and in public. In her mind that must be part of the possession, the need. Yes, he, Francis, loved her, but that did not stop him seeing the woman. And she would only be his if she said she was.

She swallowed.

"Can we not defer it for a while?"

Not now they couldn't. "And what if you get with child? What then?"

She closed her eyes. "Let me think, Francis. Please."

He had to tell her what the man had said. Not to do so would be cruel. And dangerous if she ever found out he'd kept it from her. "Sir Bertram offered to keep our secret. He said he suspected we were lovers and not married at all."

"Which is the truth."

He nodded. "It is."

She opened her eyes and met his gaze. "Thank you for telling me. I will tell you before we reach Combe Manor, I promise."

That was the best he could expect. Any more and she'd break.

Chapter 17

They reached Exeter that evening. In many ways the center of the West Country, the seat of the bishop, the place people gathered for social occasions and to shop, there was more chance of Francis and Virginia meeting their peers here than anywhere they had stopped before. But their reasons for speed and secrecy had effectively gone. According to the world, they were married.

They traveled in near silence, Francis only telling Virginia what he had planned. "We'll go to the George. I want you to sleep in comfort. But I need to make another call. I should visit my godfather, the Bishop of Exeter. He'd take it amiss if I did not call on him. I would take you, but I fear you would not enjoy it. He can be somewhat—severe."

"Will you tell him?"

He nodded. "If he asks, I have to. I can't lie to a man of the cloth."

Virginia, whose mood was the lowest it had ever been on this trip, watched the familiar streets pass by, barely seeing the sights. They had so nearly reached their objective, and yet they'd failed. And she was painfully aware that she only had herself to blame. Too many chances, too much excitement.

She could have employed a companion, or insisted that Mrs. Dauntry came back to town, but no, she was so sure she could live on her own. But she had taken too many risks, and here she was.

If she married Francis, she could bring him nothing. How could she bear the humiliation? Once she'd broken the terms of the will, she could give him nothing. Be his pensioner, dependent on him for everything. Belonging to him.

After her father and Ralph, she had sworn she would never put herself in that position again. And yet here she was.

One chance remained. "Before we leave tomorrow, I will visit my Exeter lawyer. Tell him what I plan, see if anything can be salvaged from the will."

"An excellent idea," he said warmly. "I will call on mine, too. And collect more funds."

If her lawyer could find a way to break the will, even to help her to keep her dowry, then she would have something. But she would have to give up that precious independence she had enjoyed so much. Was it enough?

What kind of husband would Francis make? Oh, he was an attentive lover, but would he abandon her for other entertainments once he had her safe?

Oh, why had she rushed into intimacy?

* * * *

The brief delay in order to visit their respective lawyers had been a good idea.

Butler had purchased another gown for Virginia, one somewhat less worn than the one she'd been wearing since Blackwater. Instead of petticoat and jacket, Virginia could dress properly in a decent gown over a small hooped petticoat, and even a single ruffle of Nottingham lace at her elbows. A new hat, too, a crisp, tightly woven straw with a jaunty green ribbon around the crown.

For a finishing touch, she had the SSL pin and the gold coin pin placed on either side of her bodice. Not bad at all.

Mr. Henderson's office was situated in a narrow street near to the river, a respectable area containing businesses and some private houses, all crammed close together in an old-fashioned style. Virginia got out of the hackney she had hired, Hurst close behind her, and glanced at the highly polished brass plaque by the door, proclaiming Henderson's business. She stepped inside.

She had sent word to expect her the previous day and received a gracious request to visit at eleven in return, just as if she were the plaintiff and he the master.

The clerk showed her into the office her solicitor occupied. She spared barely a glance for the familiar surroundings of bookcases and a large partner's desk. The furnishings, solid but elegant, proclaimed the owner of the office a man of substance in this part of the world.

Henderson rose as she swept into the room and bowed punctiliously. He was a man of medium height and build. He wore an excellent suit of clothes of deep red velvet, coat, breeches, and waistcoat all the same. A show of wealth.

"My lady," he said, "I trust you are well?"

Virginia murmured the expected response, although a sick feeling churned in her stomach.

A tray of tea things stood on a side table. While Henderson poured them a dish each, Virginia took stock of his smug, controlling attitude. His smile was supercilious, his pose that of her master. Why had she never noticed that before?

This man knew the contents of the will and the conditions like he knew his own hand. To a great extent he had dictated how she lived, what she did, and he was empowered to check her work whenever he wished. He had been in many ways her master.

He behaved like it now, shooting her sharp glances as he poured the tea and brought it over to the desk. She clasped her hands, resting them on the desk. He took his seat behind it, and he had two stacks of papers before him. He perched a pair of gold-framed spectacles on his nose. "How may I help you today, my lady?"

"What would happen if I remarried?" she demanded.

He regarded her in silence for half a minute. "Are you?"

"Not yet." Surely he would keep her counsel if word got out about her tryst with Francis.

"Yet? My lady, I must strongly advise you not to take such a reckless step. If you remarry, you will lose everything."

"What about my dowry?" She had brought that to the marriage; surely, despite Ralph's threats, that could not be withheld. If she had that, she could go to Francis with, if not a clear conscience, then with something to contribute.

"That is now part of the estate. If you can find a man to take you with nothing but the clothes you stand up in, then you are a lucky woman indeed." He swept his gaze over her, once, twice, as if her modest garb was all she would have.

"What about the orphanages?" After all, small children were part of this bargain. How could she abandon them?

"Lord Dulverton would have to take over the project as a condition of his inheritance."

She had planned to tell him about the danger they were both in, but abruptly she changed her mind.

What if this man were part of the attempts? She couldn't trust anybody outside her small party, not even this man.

One detail had always irked her. She might as well ask now. "Do you have the names of the members of the trust which administers the estate?"

Being a woman, she couldn't be trusted to handle her own monetary affairs, she thought bitterly. At least, that was what the law thought.

Henderson's pale gaze showed nothing but contempt. "I cannot, my lady. Mine is the only name you need to know."

Removing his spectacles, he tapped them on his palm. "If that is all, my lady?"

Fuming, she left his office.

Butler, standing outside, followed her silently.

* * * *

Francis's visit to his godfather had been successful. He had the bishop's license safe in his coat pocket. On visiting his lawyer, he made his instructions clear. He wanted to make more than ample provision for his wife-to-be, however matters turned out. He left instructions for a complex trust, which would leave the settlement he intended to make on her completely separate from the main estate. He would leave her in control of it.

His lawyer thought he was mad, and was not shy in saying so, but Francis rode over his objections and insisted on the settlement being drawn up exactly as he'd promised Virginia.

And he'd learned more. Combe Manor was run-down, isolated, and possibly dangerous, much closer to the cliff than he'd assumed. Too isolated for his liking. Despite the impropriety, if it became known, he wouldn't stay at Newton Abbott and allow her to go forward to the manor on her own.

Her sparkling eyes when he met her outside her lawyer's offices gave him pause. Virginia was in a temper. But he said nothing until they had climbed into the infinitely more comfortable traveling carriage he had bespoken from the George, and seen her settled.

The first thing he wanted, once they were clear of the town and out of the sight of curious eyes, was to haul her close and claim the kiss he'd been looking forward to for hours.

She melted under him and lifted her hand to his cheek, cupping it. He could kiss this woman for hours, and once he had his ring on her finger, he intended to do just that.

When their lips finally separated, she pulled away, although he wanted to draw her close and carry on. She sat up straight, her hands folded in her lap in the approved pose of the gentlewoman.

He glanced out of the window. "We're approaching Newton Abbott. We'll be at Combe Manor before nightfall."

"I could do nothing," she said, anger rumbling low in her voice. But not for him. "Henderson would only clarify the terms of the will. I lose it all."

She closed her eyes. He hated seeing her defeated, so pushed down. "I wanted to establish the orphanages. I found the work truly rewarding. The ones I have set up are working now, the children heading for respectability instead of life on the streets, living in fear. I don't discuss it much because I don't want to be known as a Lady Bountiful. I don't want to be thanked. I just want to do it. The orphanages are in Ralph's name, and they were his idea, after all."

"Then you shall continue with the work if you consent to marry me," he said softly. "Come. For the hour left of our journey, rest."

She laid her head on his shoulder. For now, he was content, although the new information left thoughts rioting through his head.

* * * *

Virginia couldn't think properly. Telling Francis her secret had released a flood of tension she'd been holding since Ralph died.

Twice. The second time he'd accepted it much better than he had at first. Perhaps he would wait for her, after all.

When they arrived at the best inn in the pretty town of Newton Abbott, they paused only to change the horses and send a message ahead, warning the couple who lived in Combe Manor to prepare for their arrival. Virginia watched them numbly. "Will you stay here?"

His mouth flattened. "No." He rested his hand gently on her shoulder. "Let's call this our time."

Turning her head, she regarded him with a jaded expression, her mouth flat. "Our time?"

"We have a few days in an out-of-the-way house. We can give ourselves that." And give her time to make her decision, instead of making it for her.

The carriage jolted over a rut in the road as their path narrowed and grew more rustic. Virginia sat up and leaned back. "The sea," she murmured.

"We've been following it for a while."

This was not a stretch of tranquil ocean. Instead, the gray, white-tipped waves supported a collection of vessels of all kinds, from large sailing ships that had come from halfway across the world, to small fishing vessels that set out every morning and came back before noon.

She was tempted to sink back into his arms, where she knew she would be welcome, but she still didn't know what to think or how to have what she longed for.

While Virginia was not a native of the West Country, nowhere else had felt more like home. Driving along the coastline through the town, she felt a spring inside her unwind, a relaxation as if she was finally on home ground.

The carriage pulled off the road and drove up an overgrown drive. She had expected nothing less, since she only employed a gardener once a week to cut down the worst of it. "The couple who look after it are Mr. and Mrs. Yarnock," she said as they jolted over yet another rut.

Virginia's mind was in too much turmoil for her to think rationally about the issue now. But they would be sharing a bed tonight, and she could not be sorry about that. Nobody had held her as he did. Nobody had held her at all since she'd quit the nursery for the schoolroom. She had not known how much she was missing before now.

He took her hand, and she curled her fingers around his. Warm and reassuring, he gave her the strength to do what had to be done. "I was proud of the orphanages," she said in a quiet voice.

"I know. There is no reason why you should stop your philanthropy. In fact, I would like it to continue. But instead of having it imposed on you, I would rather you found out your true areas of concern and worked on those. And take proper credit for them."

She liked the orphanages, but perhaps if she established them on her own she would not restrict them to the children of soldiers. And she would have more than fifteen to a house. Ralph had laid that down, but some of the houses could carry more, she was sure of it.

Combe Manor was a six-bedroom manor house rather than a great mansion, once the home of a prosperous yeoman farmer. But it could hold more than fifteen youngsters in relative comfort.

"I'm sorry I couldn't let you have the house," she said. But at least he knew why now.

His hand tightened on hers. "If it came to a choice, I choose you."

The carriage had climbed most of the way to get to the house, which sat on the top of a hill. It stopped at the front door, allowing them to take stock of the house.

They stared at it in silence.

"Traditional materials," she said. "Flint and granite."

Tall windows with stone mullions, a boxy frontage, and an arched front door met their gazes. As Butler and Hurst collected their meager luggage off the carriage, they stared at it. Nobody came out of the house to greet them.

Caught by sudden doubts, Virginia turned to Francis. "I've never met the couple who live here." She picked at a fold of her skirt, held it up and dropped it. "Will they believe me when I tell them who I am?"

"They will," Francis said firmly. Although he now had his usual style of wig back and still wore plain country clothes, he nevertheless stood out. Virginia saw what he was doing. Standing tall, she straightened her spine and stuck her chin in the air.

"All right, missus?" the carriage driver said. "I'll be on my way then."

He drove along the front of the house and turned the carriage. Virginia wondered if they should keep him, then decided against it. They would have some kind of vehicle here, even if it was only a gig. Enough to get them to Newton Abbott or the village of Combe, a short distance back on the road, if they needed to.

He'd already been paid, so they let him go, bowling back up the uneven drive they'd arrived from.

"I'm glad we've done with that," Francis said. "I'll send to my house for a proper carriage, one suitable for my bride."

She heard him with mixed emotions. She could not deny that she wanted him, but in order to have him, her whole world was crumbling around her. Falling to pieces. That part terrified her. All her childhood memories emerged to strangle her, until her throat tightened and she had to force herself to take a breath.

Francis slipped his arm around her waist. "I know," he murmured, although he didn't.

Chapter 18

The front door was open, so they walked through, the men bringing the luggage, such as it was. "Ho, there!"

Francis's call echoed around the hall and up past the stairs to the top of the house. Nobody responded. Francis exchanged a glance with the men.

The hall was clean, that was, it was dusted and the wooden stairs were polished, though not very enthusiastically. The surface was dust-free but dull, and the bare wooden floor was swept.

So far, so good. After glancing at Francis, Virginia moved forward. For now at least, she was mistress here. The downstairs rooms, a snug parlor, a study, a breakfast room and a couple of others, seemed in order, even if the shutters were closed. At this time of year sunset would not come for at least four hours, but perhaps the caretakers were protecting the furniture and fabrics from the sunlight.

The furniture, while old, was in good order, and the cushions and curtains were fresh, if plain.

Virginia turned to Francis. "I like this house."

He nodded. "I have never visited before, but I agree."

This too would be lost to her if she married Francis. She had spent the last ten years, from the time her parents had told her she was to be married to now, building her shield, ensuring she would never be dependent on another human being ever again. Only to see the whole structure torn away, leaving her with nothing.

Not that she did not trust Francis, but…

"What is it?" Francis drew her aside as the two men went ahead, back into the hall.

Virginia cleared her expression. "What do you mean?"

"You're distressed. Don't deny it. While I can't see it in your face, it's in your eyes and the way you're holding yourself."

So even her usual defenses were useless where Francis was concerned. By now he knew her too well.

"Where is everybody? There should be someone here at all times. Or the door should have been locked. If they took their time securing the shutters, why did they leave the door open?"

He gave her face a searching look before he nodded. "That had occurred to me, too. Let's see the rest of the house, and then decide."

She held her sigh of relief until he'd turned his back to open the door. By the time he turned back to her, she had schooled her features better, with the help of a mirror hung on the opposite wall.

They went upstairs as Hurst came up from the servants' quarters. "Nobody down there. The kitchen fire is warm but banked down. Maybe they were called away."

"Yes, that has to be the reason. The couple I employed are from the village, so perhaps something happened there." That sounded like a rational reason. And they left in a hurry, so did not secure the doors properly.

Upstairs they found more reception rooms and six well-appointed bedrooms. The largest held an old four-poster, but it was as different to the one at the inn where Virginia and Francis had first made love as it could possibly be.

This one had barley-sugar supports and a coat of arms engraved on the bedhead. The mattress was a thick feather bed on top of a horsehair one, to give it support. The sheets were the finest linen, as she discovered when she pulled the embroidered coverlet back to check.

Francis exchanged a heated look with her. He made his intention clear; tonight they would share this bed.

Hastily, Virginia moved to the window. This one had casement openings, rather than the more fashionable sash ones, and the stone mullions spoke to their age, but after a cursory glance, her attention went to the view. "This is astonishing."

Francis came up on her other side. "Yes, it is."

The room looked out over the sea. Smooth, gray waves rippled beyond the greensward leading to the cliff edge. There was no fence to prevent anyone tipping over the edge. "I shall have to build a wall," she said, her mind going over the ways this comfortable house could be transformed into an orphanage for fifteen children. The task would not be difficult, but that cliff edge worried her.

She caught herself up. "This doesn't seem to be the best place for an orphanage."

"It would be inadvisable," he answered calmly.

This place agitated her. "The house is old. Do you think it has ghosts?"

"Undoubtedly."

Her brow creased, but before she could turn away, he pulled her into his arms. "Don't worry, we're alone, and the floorboards will let us know. They creak if you so much as breathe on them."

With her face buried against his chest, she laughed shakily. "Where did the men go?"

"To explore the rest of the place and bring up our trunk, presumably. The house is habitable. We'll stay here at least tonight."

In a snap, Virginia made her decision. How could she turn this man away? She loved him. And if she sent him away, this time she was certain he wouldn't return. To see him marry anyone else would cause her such agony she didn't think she could bear it.

"I wanted to see it." She lifted her face and gazed up at him. "I'm not sure why now, because I won't be doing anything with it. I'll continue until I am officially informed to desist."

He gazed at her, one brow raised.

"Yes, Francis. Yes, I'll marry you."

"Thank you." Warmth flooded his gaze, and a sense of relief she had no idea he'd been carrying.

He dropped a light kiss on her forehead and nudged her with his nose, persuading her without words to tilt her head back further so he could kiss her lips.

With pleasure, she acceded to his unspoken request and returned his kiss. She was used to his way of kissing now and anticipated his kisses eagerly. Touching his lips with her tongue, now-familiar thrills of pleasure rippled through her. When she pressed her body against his, she found reassurance, as she always did in his arms.

She let go, released all her preconceptions. Began anew.

She was worth something to somebody, more than her dowry, or her behavior, or the connections she had made in the years of her widowhood. All those had been cited by suitors in the past, and she had sent them all away.

He caressed her tongue with his, then withdrew, finishing the kiss and lifting his head, his eyes warm. "Before we get too carried away, we should eat," he murmured. "If there is any food in the house, that is."

They separated, but not far. He kept his arm around her shoulders as they turned to leave the room.

"Here you are, ma'am," Hurst said cheerfully as he carried their traveling case into the bedroom.

Francis did not remove his arm from her, nor did he let her pull away. "Thank you," he said easily. "Is there anything for us to eat?"

"Plenty of food in the kitchen, sir. No staff, though. Mr. Butler says he can make a simple meal, but says he can't create food as fancy as your cook."

"I wouldn't expect him to," Francis said calmly. "I'm grateful that he can cook at all, which is more than I can. Did he say how long the food would be? I'm sharp set, and so must you be."

Hurst glanced at Virginia before he returned his attention to Francis. Was he checking with her, or did he recognize the identity of the person giving the orders? Because by accepting Francis, Virginia had lost authority. When Francis was by, he was the natural master.

She knew what she was about to lose. But that was the way of the world, and she could do little about it now. A series of choices had brought her to this place. She had merely taken the final step.

Hurst bowed and left. Instead of following him, Francis led her to the couch at the bottom of the bed and sat her down. He took his place next to her. "Now before we take this final step, tell me what is troubling you," he said. "I don't believe it's about the house, or the ghosts, or even being discovered *in flagrante delicto*, or very nearly so."

"Of course it is! That is, yes, of course." How could she tell him? Perhaps she should just come out with it. "Being totally dependent on another person terrifies me."

"It is the state of all women, unless they remain unmarried. Do you know why?"

She shrugged. "An accumulation of things. My parents, mostly my father. The way they changed after my brother was born." She smiled wryly. "I remember that night so clearly, the excitement I felt when I was told, and the breathtaking sight of the baby. But that night signaled the change in my life. I was no longer indulged. I was shown no favor, and instructed in everything a lady would be expected to know.

"One day I was the pampered, special child, and the next, the very next, I was nobody. I determined to be sufficient to myself, to ensure one person cared about me. After my one season, my mother told me I was a failure, and she washed her hands of me. I would not get another season, and I could not expect to live on their charity forever. She would look for a husband for me locally. That was what she said. Shortly after that Ralph arrived, and I all but fell on his neck."

His silence told her that her lighthearted tone had not fooled him. "That explains a great deal. Ralph doted on you, did he not?"

She nodded. "In his way. Ralph did not love me as a man loves his wife. I was his pet, his possession. When I behaved well, he loved me. I should be grateful, he said, and I was. He'd taken me away from an intolerable situation and treated me with what I thought was kindness, taken notice of me."

But she was not grateful, and that made her ashamed. Hastily, she continued. "After Ralph, and after my father, I turned my back on marriage, or lovers, or anything to do with men. I never expected—never thought I would marry again." She hurried to explain herself. "I've been shot into this. I expected my life to continue on the course I set for myself. We avoided each other for years."

"Because of this," he said, touching his lips to her forehead again. "Feel that? Every time I touch you, that connection is refreshed and renewed. I want that for both of us, Virginia. God knows we deserve it."

"I didn't shun your mother because I wanted to." Where that had come from she had no idea.

He smiled, the warmth in his eyes showing no doubts. "I know it now. And you didn't approach her after you were widowed because you did not wish to get closer to me. Admit it."

She couldn't deny it. "I thought it for the best. You pushed, though, didn't you?"

"I did. After Ralph died, I watched you. You were not the kind of person to despise a person because of her birth. I saw the pleasure you took in giving destitute children a home. That was not all obligation."

He took her hands, held them between his big ones. "You are so strong, Virginia. I don't want to leech that from you. When I thought about a wife, I did not expect to find everything I've found in you. I don't want you ever to be less than you are, less than you were when I first kissed you."

Tears sprang to her eyes, and she had to swallow to get rid of them. "You should not say that. You might get a reputation as a henpecked husband."

He didn't speak at first, not until she realized what she'd said. *Husband.* But what else could she do? "You?" She forced a shaky laugh. "Nobody would ever think that of you."

"I sense that losing your independence makes you uneasy. I will do everything I can to make sure you have everything you always had, and more."

* * * *

Francis did not sleep. After making love to Virginia and feeling guilty about it because she was so tired, he tucked her by his side and watched her sleep. They had gone to bed naked, and remained so, but he'd made sure clothes were laid ready for them.

He hadn't yet told her he loved her, only showed her.

This house made him edgy. The caretakers had still not arrived. Where were they? There could be an innocuous reason, but they should not have left the house unsecured. This place was much better cared for than he'd expected, especially after Virginia told him that she had never visited.

How would Combe Manor compare to the other orphanages she had set up over the last four years? Eight, was it? Two a year since Ralph had died. Dulverton had left her a list of the houses he wanted to become orphanages. How had he selected them?

Francis had stationed Hurst and Butler in rooms either side of them, at each end of the corridor, effectively bracketing them and making Virginia as secure as possible. They were all armed, with the pistols they'd brought with them and with six more Hurst had found in the house. This was the most vulnerable they had been, stuck in this isolated place, but he didn't know if Virginia knew it.

Profoundly grateful that she had not realized their peril, he let her sleep. He would stay awake all night and insist they leave in the morning. At first light, if necessary. Something was wrong here; he just knew it. Felt it deep in his bones.

He'd already instructed Hurst to go to the village and hire horses to pull the gig they'd found at the back of the house. That would take them to Newton Abbott. Then, by God, Virginia would travel in style. With outriders, and she would stay protected until they tracked Jamie Dulverton down and made him pay for his attacks on her.

He stood to gain much by Virginia's death, or her marriage. That part puzzled him, but Virginia had told him that Jamie didn't know the property would go to him, and not Francis, on her marriage. Her lawyer had not informed him. Jamie probably assumed he would lose all the wealth he should have inherited. That would give him cause to kill Virginia or warn off potential suitors.

Francis took some pleasure planning what he would do to Dulverton and to Virginia's perfidious servants, including the devious lady's maid. Better than sleeping.

He glanced out of the window, having chosen to leave the shutters open in this room. The overcast night showed a star or two, but little else, since this was the dark of the moon.

A floorboard creaked. Every hair on his body stood on end. Lying perfectly still, he waited. Perhaps Butler or Hurst had forgotten something.

But no. That was a booted footstep.

Another creak, nearer to his room. And then a shout, which made him sit bolt upright and clamp a hand over Virginia's mouth. He brought his lips close to her ear. "Quiet, for God's sake."

That shout did not sound like Hurst or Butler. And the responding shout, which came from downstairs, sounded like neither of them, either.

"Sir!"

"Yes?"

"Somebody's been in here."

A raucous laugh exploded outside their room. Francis reached for the loaded pistol on the nightstand. The small grating sound as he lifted it clear made him wince. Virginia, now fully awake, lay next to him, perfectly still.

They listened.

"Go through the rooms."

Damn.

He did not recognize the two voices, but that didn't mean Dulverton wasn't nearby.

Perhaps this was the real reason for the attempts on his life.

On the sea, a ship floated into view. A two-masted brigantine, sails out, barely noticeable in the dark of the moonless night.

At the end of the corridor, nearest to the stairs, someone opened the door, the latch rattling against the wood. Francis caught his breath. Motioning to Virginia, he rolled out of bed, hissing softly between his teeth when the sheets rustled as he drew them back.

Why hadn't he memorized which boards creaked the most?

Virginia did the same, sat on the edge of the bed.

"Nobody," a male voice said.

Another door, nearer, was opened. A shout went up. "Somebody's been in 'ere!"

Footsteps, more than two pairs of feet, ran past their room. Covered by the noise, Francis took the two steps to the chair and picked up his breeches, then tossed Virginia's shift and petticoat to her.

Then he picked up the second pistol, the one he'd left in the pocket of his coat. The spot he stood on did not creak, so he pulled on his breeches. He needed the pockets. And the knife in his pocket.

The noise from the room where Butler had been sleeping increased, wordless shouts of alarm. The sound of men talking came closer. Virginia had thrown her shift over her head, but she hadn't yet pulled on her petticoat. She was standing closest to the door when it opened.

Francis fired the first pistol. The air filled with the stinging, choking stink. Billows of smoke obscured their vision.

When it cleared, Francis discovered that he'd found his target. A man lay on the floor, doubled up and groaning. Blood poured from a wound on his shoulder. Another man entered the room and shoved his colleague aside with his foot. Francis did not take his attention away from the newcomer.

The man who faced them was nobody he knew. Dressed in a collection of clothes that looked as if they belonged to other people, some big, some small, stood a man of about Virginia's height, half a foot shorter than Francis. His wig was tattered and askew, his hat jammed over his forehead. His thick leather belt was bristling with pistols. The man behind him held a rifle, a Brown Bess if Francis wasn't mistaken.

"Drop them," the man ordered.

Francis didn't move but kept his pistol pointing square at the man's chest. He didn't look away when another man forced his way into the room. Four in all, counting the one groaning on the floor, all heavily armed.

His opponent swung his weapon around, pointing it at Virginia. "I said drop it," he said to Francis.

Jagged fear made Francis obey him. "Hurt her and I'll kill you." Not a threat, but a promise.

Virginia stood absolutely still, chin up, glaring defiantly at their attacker. "Who are you?" she demanded.

Silently Francis begged her not to tell him who she was. If they knew that, they'd capture her and ransom her. And what were the odds that Dulverton would reject the chance, when Virginia's death would suit him so well?

"You can call me Crace," the man said. "So what are you doing in my house?"

Chapter 19

Virginia bit back her instant response. What did he mean, *his* house? She didn't need Francis to tell her the trouble they could be in if Crace found out who they were.

For the first time on this journey she was glad of her plain garments and apparent lack of wealth. The only thing of value she had on her was the silver pin, which she'd kept fastened to her shift, and the gold brooch pendant in her pocket.

She felt horribly exposed, and for once glad that the shift was a thicker, cheaper version of the gossamer-fine lawn she usually wore. At least they couldn't see through it easily. But without her armor of stays and petticoats, she felt as bare as if she was naked.

Crace stepped forward and plucked the silver SSL pin free. He turned it over in his hand. "This your name?"

"Sarah Lansbury," Virginia said, pulling the name out of thin air. But it went with the pin. "My husband and I were stranded here when our carriage lost a wheel."

"Where is it?"

She shrugged. "The coachman went to the village to hire a horse to get to Newton Abbott. We needed a place to stay. If you want, we can pay, Mr. Crace." Lord, that excuse was full of holes. Would Crace spot them?

The minute she'd seen that ship silently slip into view, she'd known. These men were up to no good.

In a flash she understood. They were smugglers. Their kind were endemic in Devonshire and Cornwall. Some people claimed that without it the counties would be in abject poverty. As it was, smugglers ruled whole villages, ran organizations more efficient than anything seen in

Westminster. And smugglers would behave with this kind of arrogance. Of course that was what they were.

Everything fell into place. The bay was private and secluded; the house was isolated on the cliff. No doubt there was a way down to the bay, so the men could come and go without causing comment.

The clock on the mantel struck three, the chimes falling into the air. Crace regarded them stoically. "That ain't going to work, now is it?"

The chill creeping up her spine had nothing to do with the weather.

A shout came from outside, and a ruffian shoved Butler into the room. He brought light with him, a lantern that cast a golden glow over the room. Butler was in shirt and breeches. A bruise was forming on the side of his face, and he cradled his arm. "Found this one," his captor said.

"That explains the used bedroom," Crace said.

He gave Butler a push, and if Francis hadn't moved aside, he would have crashed right into him. Francis caught Butler's shoulder to steady him, but said nothing. Butler winced and turned to face the men crowding the room. Five of them now.

Hurst was nowhere to be seen. Had he escaped? If so, they could expect help. But not from the village. Nobody there would be trustworthy. But if Hurst could find a horse, he could get into Newton Abbott and to the excise men.

The trouble was, in this part of the world many excise men, and the occupants of the villages and towns on the coast, were in thrall to the smugglers. Gangs ruled this part of the coast. But as far as she knew, Virginia didn't know of any large gangs operating nearby, the ones that caused the officials in London to scream in horror, but that just meant they hadn't raised a dust.

"Lansbury," Crace said, turning the pin over in his hand. He was standing so close to her that she could smell the tobacco and wine on his breath, although she tried not to.

If Crace decided to kill them, they might never be found. No sign of Hurst, but in this part of the country he did not stand much chance of getting help back to them fast enough. If he had managed to get away at all.

Their vaunted status would not help them now. Only compliance, and perhaps even not then since they'd seen all the smugglers' faces.

"Where are you from?"

"Brampton," said Francis, naming a town on the north coast of the county.

"And you decided to make yourselves at home here." Crace grunted and slid the pin onto his coat.

Virginia wanted to snatch it away, but she stayed where she was, only clenching her hands into fists to stop herself rushing forward and grabbing it. That pin was precious to her, more than diamonds. It represented friendship.

The man on the floor groaned, drawing Crace's attention. Leaving his men holding Virginia and Francis captive, pistols pointed directly at their hearts, Crace bent down. "Told yer that yer shouldn't be in a hurry," he said, the long drawl of the West Country strong in his voice. "People in a rush never get there first. You'll live."

Straightening, he addressed the man with the army rifle. "Get 'im out of here. Put him in one of the carts and get him 'ome. We'll manage without 'im."

The man hoisted the injured smuggler to his feet and slung his good arm around his shoulders. He half lifted, half dragged the man out, ignoring his colleague's shouts of pain. They echoed down the hall.

Another man came in to take the other's place. He had the rifle.

Crace eyed Francis, giving him a close scrutiny, up and down and back again. "You look like you could do some work. How do you fancy earning a golden guinea?"

Francis shook his head. "No. I won't help you ship contraband ashore."

"Pity." Crace turned his attention back to Virginia. "Not even to 'elp 'er?"

"I told you," Francis said patiently, as if he was talking to a child. "Hurt her and I'll kill you."

The men burst into raucous laughter when Crace looked around at them, but it sounded a bit forced to Virginia. "Get them downstairs," he said. "We don't want any loose ends. And we've got enough mess 'ere. We don't want more when we do these two."

He was going to kill them. Francis glanced at Virginia. He would fight, no doubt about it, and he would die. Not much doubt about that, too. But better to go out fighting.

Despair racked her. Nobody would know where they'd gone until it was too late. The patch of blood on the floor belonging to the man Francis had shot would be cleaned up, and nobody would be the wiser. Where were the caretakers here? Had they already been killed? Or was this man one of them?

Crace stepped back, a pistol in each hand, as the other men nudged her into moving. Francis growled but made no move. He would, though.

And she hadn't even told him that she loved him. Their only chance now was Hurst, and who was to say he wasn't dead already?

As they passed the chair, Virginia made a grab for her clothes. The man behind her wrapped his arm about her waist, dragging her away.

"Take them," said Crace, nodding to the clothes. "We don't want to leave anything behind."

One of the ruffians picked up the pile of clothes, throwing them over his arm. Something fell to the floor with a *clunk*, and Crace bent to sweep it up. Virginia swallowed, praying Francis did not make his move yet. There had to be a way out of this. There *must* be.

Crace dug into the first pocket, coming out with her handkerchief. Damn, the monogram. But it was embroidered white-on-white, and something else caught his attention first. He picked out the brooch pendant and turned it over, studying the gold coin carefully.

He pulled at his watch chain, and there, at the end, was a gold coin identical to the one on her pendant brooch.

"Where did you get this?" He looked up, fixing Virginia with a glare.

She thought rapidly. Why not tell the truth, or some of it anyway? "My first husband. He was from Newton Abbott, and he told me it would keep me safe."

Crace narrowed his eyes. "What was 'is name?"

If she told him she was Ralph's widow, she'd tell him her worth. Although these men were smugglers, they wouldn't hesitate to ransom her. That would at least keep her alive. But what about Francis?

Belatedly she recalled the name of a servant from Newton Abbott who worked at Dulverton. "Sam Satterley."

He regarded her through narrowed eyes. "The soldier?"

Trying not to be too eager, she nodded.

"He was a deal older than you."

She shrugged. "He was a husband."

"You should've gone to the village," Crace said. "Stayed with them there. Then you wouldn't be in this mess." He tossed the gold brooch in his hand and caught it. "I wouldn't say this will keep you safe, and Sam shouldn't have had it. But I won't kill you."

She let him see her relief. Her shoulders sagged.

He handed the pockets to the man who held the rest of the clothes, and pocketed the coin.

She'd told the truth, except for the name. That pendant brooch had been their salvation, but they weren't free yet.

They followed Crace, fully aware that two men were bringing up the rear, both fully armed. They kept enough distance to stop Francis grabbing their weapons, although Virginia caught him looking, assessing. She shook her head slightly. He reached for her hand, clasped his around it, and reassurance flowed through her. They could survive this.

They went down to the kitchen, the big fireplace dominating the space, flooding them with welcome warmth. The rough tiles were chilly under her bare feet, though.

Crace opened a door next to the fireplace and pushed at the empty shelves inside. It swung open, revealing a set of stairs leading down.

Her heart in her throat, Virginia followed him, Francis close behind her. The flickering light of the lantern held by the man at the back followed them down.

The second flight was cut into rock. Virginia counted. A hundred steep stairs led down, as a damp chill surrounded them like a living thing and the tang of salt in the air told them how close they were to the sea.

They were in a cave, and the sound of the sea was close by.

Crace nodded to some hooks driven into the gray rock. "Tie 'em up."

Butler screamed when a smuggler roughly dragged his hands behind his back. Virginia had never heard such a sound from a human. Jerking forward, Francis tried to reach him, but he was pulled back, arms banded around him.

"You've already broken his arm!" Virginia yelled above the din. "Stop torturing him!"

She had nothing to offer them, nothing she could do would make any difference. If she'd thought the gold coin did anything but spare her from immediate death, she would have been severely disappointed. Frustration and distress tore her up.

Francis was white with anger, his mouth pulled tight, his eyes promising murder.

Crace smiled, the gaps in his teeth doing nothing to improve his appearance. He nodded at the man. "Carry on."

Ignoring Butler's cries of anguish, they tied him up. By the time they'd finished, Butler was unconscious. Virginia's tears did nothing but obscure her vision.

They propped Butler against the wall. He slumped down as far as he could, then woke, screaming, and passed out again.

As the men lashed ropes around Virginia's and Francis's wrists, Crace spoke to them. "Now stay there until we get back. Clear? After that we can deal with you. This"—he dangled his coin at the end of its chain—"keeps me from killing you, but that's all the favors you get. After that we'll see. I don't believe you, you see. Sam Satterley isn't dead, as far as I know, but you got that token from somewhere, and I'm going to find out where."

Calling on all her training, Virginia kept her expression clear.

Crace glanced out of the cave opening. "I might just let the sea take care of you."

He nodded to the man holding the clothes. The man dropped them on the wet floor of the cave, out of their reach. Virginia tried not to shiver but failed. The air was sharp, and she was all but naked. The ropes chafed her wrists when she tried to move them.

"Just when my bruises were going," Francis murmured, "I get more." In complete contrast to his expression, he sounded amused, resigned, even.

Crace shot him a questioning look. The man might appear craggy, and his clothes wouldn't pass muster at court, but he was their master for the foreseeable future, and intelligence shone in his dark eyes. He was not a man they could win over.

Though that would not stop her trying. "You didn't have to do that," she said.

"Which part?" he demanded, and then the damned man smiled.

"All of it," she snapped. "What can we do?"

"Wait for us until we return," he answered. "And enjoy the show." He gestured to the opening of the cave. "You can see some of it from here. If it goes well, we'll be back before the tide's in. If not..." His wide shoulders rolled in a careless shrug.

He strolled—*strolled*—to the entrance of the cave, followed by his men, one with the rifle slung over his shoulder, the other swaggering like a pirate. They crunched over the pebbles and shards of shells, and then silence, as they hit the sand of the beach. Beyond, the ship was moored far enough into the bay to catch the gentler swells, far enough away to catch the tide as it went out.

Small boats rowed toward the shore, three of them at least. Men stood ready to collect what they offloaded. None of the scene was easy to see, but by concentrating she could make out most of it. And the men scurrying from boat to shore, and pushing the empty ones off.

An efficient operation.

"They're going to kill us, aren't they?" she asked, fighting back more tears.

"They don't have to. The sea will do that." Francis jerked his chin, indicating the walls of the cave. "You see that line about eight feet up? That's where the tide will reach when it comes in."

The floor under them was wet, the walls were wet, but only up to that line. Virginia swallowed. "So they'll leave us to drown?"

"They'll threaten us with it." He cursed. "Damn!" He jerked at the rope. "I have a knife in my coat. They took the other one." He glared at the offending object, perched on top of the pile of clothes ten feet away from them.

"They'll take the contraband and make it safe before they come back for us. If we're dead, then they'll untie us and let nature take its course." He gave the rope a vicious tug. "It's easier than killing us. If anyone finds us, it will appear to be an accident."

Virginia choked back her shock. "Thank you for telling me."

"Don't mention it." Turning his head, he watched her, but she couldn't see his expression in the dark of the cave. They'd taken the lamp with them. "I knew we were vulnerable. I should have insisted we move to the inn in Newton Abbott."

Heedless of the state of the green slime-streaked cave walls, Virginia leaned back, the cold freezing her bones. Just when she thought she couldn't get any colder, she did. The rope grazed the walls, but they were softened by the constant buffeting of the sea and she could not find a sharp edge. The rope was pulled tight, and she feared for her hands.

Standing up, something caught her shift and pulled a tear. She stopped moving. "The hook!"

His fraught gaze met hers. "Yes. The hook."

If she lifted her arms, she could snag the rope on the hook. It wasn't too sharp, but it was enough. Her arms hurt, ached, but she didn't give up. This was the only chance she had.

She pulled and teased and tugged until water swirled around her ankles and she couldn't feel her feet anymore. Still she worked. Three feet away from her, at the location of the next hook, Francis did the same, but with more power and less subtlety. Where Virginia worked carefully, he pulled. The rope was strong, and the sea was coming in faster, up to their knees. Their clothes floated around them, pushing and teasing.

The boats had gone, but the ship was still there. They were past speaking now. If Virginia tried, her teeth chattered.

Her pockets floated past.

Leaning forward, straining so the rope bit into her wrists, she grabbed the string with her teeth. She reared back, slamming against the wall. She would have shouted her triumph, except she'd have lost the string.

"What is it?"

His attention went from her to the pockets. He froze for a fraction of a second, then his gaze went to her face and he nodded. "Swing it," he said.

She shook her head, setting up a motion that swung the pockets toward him. He caught them, but she didn't let go until he'd pressed the pouch against his chest and secured the handle of her small fruit knife in his teeth. He was tall enough to bend over.

Virginia held very still as he stretched down and brought the blade to her bonds. The knife was not a particularly special one, nor was it very sharp, but it was enough. Eventually.

Water surged over them, each wave splashing up, filling her mouth and eyes with seawater. At least he couldn't see her despairing tears.

Butler woke up, moved, and screamed.

"No, no, don't," she begged, but she had no idea if he heard her.

Then she pulled, and her left hand came free, her right soon after.

She needed both hands to hold the knife. She took it from his mouth, first wrapping one hand around the hilt.

Holding the knife like a child might, forcing her body under control, she leaned over, letting the waves surge up, snatching breaths between each surge of cold water. Her shift clung to her body, and her teeth chattered, but she kept at her task, the knife slipping and skidding over the tight knots.

Blood threaded up to the surface, pulled into the waves, but not much, not like when he'd fallen from his carriage.

"Yes!" His sharp cry hit the roof of the cave and bounced back at them. He swept her up and pressed a quick kiss to her lips, cold and slimy; the best kiss she'd ever had.

Then he took the knife to Butler and efficiently cut him free.

Butler groaned, and then gave a wordless shout. He was conscious now.

"Can you swim?" he shouted to her.

Virginia shook her head. Most sailors couldn't swim, so why should she? The waves were deeper now, bearing them up. She went under and spluttered. Butler muttered something, and Francis shook his head. "Come here," he told her. "I had thought to swim out of the cave, but we'll try this instead."

She waded across to him. He wrapped his free arm around her waist. "I will hold you both up until we can reach those." He indicated further up the wall. Then she saw them, old rusty hooks, like the ones they'd been tied to. The steps they'd walked down were on the other side of the cave.

He saw her glance. "We'll be swept off them. There's nothing to hold on to, and the door is locked."

Only a latch, no handle. He was right. They couldn't get out that way.

It seemed impossible, but that was their only chance. She couldn't stop her teeth chattering, and lassitude was descending on her, pushing her toward blissful sleep. Perhaps when she woke up everything would be fine. Perhaps—

He nudged her hard with his chin. "Don't sleep. Don't ever sleep," he growled.

Butler wasn't screaming any longer.

With a squeal of hinges, the door above them opened, and the last voice they wanted to hear shouted Francis's name.

"Dear God, Wolverley! Over here, man!"

Lord Dulverton had found them.

Now they were dead for sure.

Chapter 20

Virginia opened her eyes. The events of the previous day flooded back, together with vague memories of her rescue, the smell of horses, the rocking of a carriage, and being carried and stowed into another rocking vehicle. After that she had a vague memory of being tucked between clean sheets.

She was alone in a pleasant bedroom she did not know. Sunlight filtered through the shutters, and elaborate silk drapes in a pleasant shade of light green were carefully arranged around them. The furniture was modern and not too ostentatious, but elegant and pretty. Gazing up at the canopy, she smiled.

She was alive. That was all that mattered this morning.

In a dizzying sequence of events, Jamie had pulled them out of certain death and forced them to climb the stairs, back to the main body of the house. With exhaustion swamping her, unable to make sense of what was happening, Virginia had been dumped into a carriage and driven away.

At that stage she had given up and sunk into a deep slumber. More like unconsciousness.

The clock chimed the three-quarter hour, a delicate chime, but she was not sure what hour it was. Planting her hands on the feather mattress, she heaved herself up, wincing as her sore wrists made their presence known.

A quarter to two? Surely not!

Someone sitting by the window stood when she moved, and came over to the bed. "Good afternoon, my lady."

Virginia had last seen the owner of that voice in Staines at the beginning of the week. Winston.

Pulling the sheet up in a protective gesture, Virginia called out. "To me! Help!"

Winston stood back as the door flew open and Francis raced into the room. He took one look at the maid and Virginia and came to her. "It's all right, sweetheart. Winston was set to protect you, not to attack you." He sat on the bed and took her hands. "She's here to look after you."

"I'll get a tray, my lord," the maid said and hastily left the room.

Francis kissed her hands, first one, then the other. "How are you feeling?"

Virginia shifted. "A little sore, but better than I have any right to. Where are we? How did we get here? How is Butler? Who saved us?"

"One question at a time." Francis had shaved. He wore his usual garb, fine cloth breeches in dark blue and a cream waistcoat, in shirtsleeves with no coat. His neckcloth was looped around his neck in a familiar style that brought tears to Virginia's eyes. She blinked them away.

"Butler has a broken arm, and he is exhausted. He's in bed, being well cared for. We're at Waltham Hall, about ten miles from Combe Manor."

She frowned. "Jamie's house?"

Waltham was part of the estate Jamie had inherited from his father before he'd become Viscount Dulverton. It was a pleasant manor house, blessedly inland from the coast. She had visited with Ralph, once.

Virginia never wanted to see the sea again. Or not for some time, anyway.

"The same."

With a jolt she recalled that voice at the top of the stairs. She'd been sure they were finished. After making all that effort to get out of their bonds, only to meet the man who wanted her dead. Perhaps he'd arranged the whole thing.

But Francis was relaxed and smiling. He wouldn't be that way if they were still in danger, surely.

"What happened? Why are we here?" Weren't they in danger, here at Jamie's house? "Doesn't Jamie have connections with smugglers?"

Francis shook his head. "None at all. He's below in the drawing room, waiting for us. I promise we will talk. I insisted on staying with you last night, which has created somewhat of a fuss, but I'm past caring about that now. Just that I needed to know you're well. When you're ready, come downstairs and we'll tell you everything. There's a Bow Street Runner down there, as well."

"Why is he here in Devonshire? What does he want?"

"He has business here."

"What business?"

Leaning forward, he kissed her gently, drawing away when she would have pulled him closer. "Eat, dress, and come downstairs. I swear we're safe, you're safe with Winston, and everything will be explained."

"Winston?"

"She is loyal to you. She was paid to look after you, not to spy on you. She has certain skills ladies' maids don't usually possess. Despite that, she lost you at Staines. She was knocked unconscious, and when she couldn't find any trace of you, she caught a stagecoach back here, to report to Jamie."

"He paid her?"

He nodded.

Virginia tried insisting that he tell her, threatening to send him away immediately, even pouting, but he would not tell her any more than that.

And the food came, and Virginia found that, after all, she was hungry.

* * * *

"My lady."

Winston, as neat and competent as always, came up after Virginia's breakfast tray was taken away.

Virginia resisted the urge to pull the covers up in an instinctively protective gesture. "Where have you been?"

"After Staines, I looked for you, my lady, and found no trace. Nothing. So I reported back to his lordship. He cares for you, madam, as he would a sister. And he worried about you, so he set me to ensure your safety. I failed." She hung her head. "I will understand if you wish to send me away, but please allow me to help you this one last time."

Assured by her maid, and more importantly Francis, that she was in no danger, Virginia consented.

Winston could work fast when she needed to. Little more than an hour later, Virginia was arrayed in a borrowed gown of apple-green and white, the petticoat embroidered around the hem with spring flowers. Winston worked in near silence, but she provided the skilled touches Virginia was used to and found comforting.

She fingered the embroidery before she put it on, admired the handiwork. With lace ruffles at her elbows, a fine shift, and a satin pair of stays, she felt more like herself than she had in days, although it felt longer than that.

And in that time her life had changed forever.

As the maid was dressing her hair, Virginia ventured the question that burned in her mind. "Why did you do it, Winston?"

The maid carefully inserted a hairpin into the style she was creating. "I was paid to take care of you and report any unusual occurrences. I swear I never informed anyone of anything else."

Virginia was too confused to demand more information. Her world had spun around several times, until she was dizzy with it. So she relaxed into the silence, gathering her strength for whatever awaited her below.

She was alive, and lucky. Her wrists were bruised and red where the rough hempen ropes had cut into them, and without asking, Winston tied wide ribbons around them to match the color of her gown. Virginia was no martyr, and she had no intention of wearing the evidence of her ordeal like stigmata.

When she entered the library, Francis came to meet her and kissed her hands, the expression on his face telling her he would have kissed her lips if he could do it without embarrassing her.

Two other people sat there.

If Virginia had thought she was beyond shocking, she was very much mistaken. Jamie stood protectively behind the chair of a woman she knew. "Miss Mountford?"

Maria smiled sunnily. She was dressed plainer than Virginia had ever seen her, and she beamed with happiness. "We share a name, I believe, but not for much longer."

Virginia's attention went from Maria to Jamie and back. Had he, then, snared the heiress? But more than that was displayed here. Both Maria and Jamie radiated joy. This was more than a dynastic arrangement. "You're Lady Dulverton?"

Maria rose and curtsyed, the precise dip she would give to one slightly senior in rank. Both women had been trained to the utmost degree. "Lady Dulverton."

From behind her, Francis took her elbow and gently steered her to a sofa by the unlit fire.

The windows were open, letting the scent of late spring, roses, and freshly cut grass permeate the room. The room was elegant, the furniture light, with blue cushions and curtains. The kind of room Virginia would have liked to spend time in, a far cry from the simple, chunky style of the house they had been in just yesterday.

Another world.

"Did you have anything to do with our abduction at Staines?"

Jamie met her gaze. "Of course not. Why would I do that?"

She had no answer. Or she had many. But slowly, matters were becoming clear to her. Of course she would suspect Jamie after years of Ralph's antipathy toward him. But she no longer saw things through her late husband's eyes.

Maria lifted her hand, and Jamie took it in a seamless motion that spoke of mutual harmony. He stood behind her chair, while Francis took his seat next to Virginia and stretched out his long legs.

Maria spoke. "Jamie and I met when I was eighteen, on my come-out. Our connection was instant, but my parents denied us." Her voice, soft and regretful, filled the air.

"I wasn't a rich enough prize for them," Jamie said. "At the time, I did not know if I was to inherit the Dulverton estate. You could still have produced an heir for Ralph."

Virginia's hand tightened, but she forced herself to relax. "So they would not allow you to marry."

Jamie grimaced. "They wouldn't allow me anywhere near her. We set ourselves to wait, but after Ralph died, you got half the estate, if not more." When Virginia would have protested, he held up his hand. "It was not your fault. I admit, I resented you at the time, but I had just seen all my dreams turn to dust, because the entailed lands were not enough for Maria's parents. They rejected me again."

His hand tightened its hold on his wife's. "It was a dark time. I did everything I could to increase my wealth, and I did succeed, but not enough for them. They had set their sights on a duke at least, or so Maria told me."

Maria made a dismissive sound between her teeth. "What did I care for that? But they put people around me to keep us apart, and in time I thought he would find someone else. Then they told me I was to marry the Duke of Colston Magna."

"He's a good fellow," Francis offered. "He is a friend of mine, you know, so I heard of the match." He sighed. "His heart has never been engaged, I fear. Even Angela Childers, who he says he is desperately in love with, knows better. They flirt."

"I like him well enough." Maria's teeth touched her lower lip. "If I could not have Jamie, then he was as good as any, but I had never wavered. I still wanted my first love."

"Why did you not tell us at the SSL?" Virginia demanded.

"I couldn't." She glanced at Jamie again, as if for reassurance. "I couldn't risk them discovering that we were still in contact, or they would have put me somewhere Jamie could never find me, and I could never escape."

That sounded ominous. "Aren't you an heiress despite your parents?" Virginia asked. "Could you not marry where you pleased?"

Maria shook her head. "My parents have to approve of my husband, or the estate will not pass to him. My grandmother put the clause in place to protect me from fortune hunters. Not that it helped much. They still came."

"But you're here," Virginia pointed out.

"Yes, I am. I have you to thank for that."

Jamie laughed roughly and went to the sideboard, where he poured himself a glass of wine and held it up. Francis nodded, but Virginia shook her head in polite refusal. Jamie brought the glasses over and handed one to Francis, returning to his self-appointed station behind Maria's chair.

He rested his free hand on the back in a protective gesture that melted Virginia's heart. "When I heard she was to marry Colston Magna, I thought all was lost. I confess, proposing to you was not my finest hour. I did it partly out of revenge, to show Maria I had moved on with my life, and partly out of despair. I wanted to put an end to that miserable period of my life. But instead, your savior arrived." He gave Francis a mock toast before taking a sip from his glass.

"Jamie found me on the way out of the Conyngham ball," Maria said, beaming. "When I heard he was courting you, I knew I could not marry anyone else. There and then we arranged to elope. I did not care about my fortune anymore."

"Neither did I," Jamie said. "Everything I did was for Maria, always." He shrugged. "I don't pretend to understand Ralph's reasoning, but I don't care anymore. I have what I always wanted. Maria reached the age of majority a week ago. I went to Doctor's Commons the day after that and obtained a special license. We married last week and set out immediately for home. Maria was afraid her parents might kill me."

"They still might," his wife said, her face tensing.

"No they will not," Jamie said softly. "I informed all the newspapers and set up gossip in all the clubs. Society will know by now that we are married. This is no longer a secret, my sweet. They may cast you off, but they cannot claim you."

"Clever." Virginia had to admire his tactics. If Jamie died mysteriously now, society would turn to Maria's parents.

"But I am penniless," she pointed out. "I have nothing."

"You have everything I have ever wanted."

Time for Virginia to make her confession. "I have nothing, either, or I will not once I marry Francis."

There. Both of her secrets in one sentence. She was breaking the terms of the will once more, but Jamie deserved to know.

As they listened to her account, horror, amusement, and shock reflected on their faces, but Virginia did not stop until she had come to the end. "So Francis and I are not yet married, but when we are, the property is yours, with extreme restrictions."

Jamie made a sound of disgust. "Such a waste. I have sent for my lawyer from Exeter to arrange a marriage settlement, so we may have the whole thing made final then. Have done with it all." He touched his wife's shoulder as if he couldn't bear to go a minute without making contact. "I do not care. I have enough to support Maria. I have all I want here. All I've ever wanted." He shot a glare at Francis. "And we will arrange for your marriage, as well as providing a settlement for Virginia."

Francis smiled mildly. "I have already made arrangements." Virginia turned in a flurry of silk to regard him with surprise. "When I visited the bishop, I confessed everything. He gave me a bishop's license and made me swear to use it. Which I intend to do the minute I have you safe. Before the month is out, we will marry."

Jamie hadn't been responsible for any of the things that had happened to her. He was entirely innocent. At the thought, relief swept through her. She had not wanted to believe it, and now she didn't have to.

"But if you did not send these people after us, who did?" she demanded. "The attacks on Francis, the attempts to isolate me from my friends?"

Francis shook his head. "I have no idea." He gave Jamie a speaking glare. "How about you? Do you know?"

"Smugglers," Jamie said. "They have a small empire. If the plans were threatened, they would not hesitate to kill to further their ends. With this plan, they would have created a web of secure places for their ships to land."

"I doubt Crace could have set this up," Francis said.

"So do I," Virginia answered. "And my late husband did not live in this area, despite being a native. He would not have known where to set the safe houses without advice."

"Whoever it is, they will have no way of getting to you again, except through me," Francis said grimly. "We will be man and wife, and until then, I will not leave her side."

Francis gave Virginia no option. But she did not want any. Nearly losing him had told her that. She would take Francis any way she could have him, and if that included losing her wealth and with it her security, then so be it.

Even marriage. There was only one reason for the change. She loved him. Just loved him, so dearly she was ready to throw everything she had away and go to him.

Not only loved him but trusted him. His word meant something. He would never abandon her or change the way he treated her. And she loved him. The more she repeated it in her mind, the closer she came to saying it aloud.

While she agreed with Jamie, that the estate would probably go to waste, exploited by the trustees and not cared for as it should be, it was none of her concern now. Time to let it go.

* * * *

A convivial dinner was served early enough for them to enjoy it. Truly, it was as if his body had marked a safe place to sleep and was now making the most of it, Francis acknowledged. He lifted a glass of excellent burgundy to his lips and took an appreciative sip.

The table was cleared and dessert set out. Nobody seemed inclined to leave the room, and Francis was disinclined to allow Virginia out of his sight. Not that he would not trust her with his life, but he needed to know that she was safe and happy. To call their recent experience at the manor a fright would be to underestimate how he'd felt to the point of irony.

He would not lose her. No doubts remained. This was the woman he needed to spend the rest of his days with.

"So Hurst came to the rescue," Francis said. He owed that man a stupendous bonus.

"He ran all the way here. I sent a man to inform the excisemen, and I rode back with more men to find you."

"He did well. I will certainly reward him."

Jamie nodded. "He deserves it. The smugglers have threatened me in the past."

"And me," Francis acknowledged. "Although never so much as recently." He took another sip.

"What about the couple who were supposed to be looking after the house?"

Jamie gave a sound of disgust. "Paid off by the smugglers to leave the house empty but open. They are local villagers. Used to their ways."

Virginia toyed with a piece of apple. "My husband was not against them. He said much as you have, Francis, but with fewer scruples. He said once that the smugglers could be an army if they were better organized."

"A navy, more like," Francis murmured. "And ruffians like that do find their way into the King's service. Perhaps we should have them all pressed."

They all laughed, but Francis did have a point. "So you did not know we were there when you raided the place?" he asked.

"No." Jamie's expression turned grave. "By the time we had returned here and discovered Hurst, you could well have been dead. They had cleaned up all traces of your presence. There was nothing left to indicate anyone else had been there."

"And Butler was captured with us."

"Yes. But there was this." Plucking a small item from his pocket, he tossed it over the table.

Francis caught it reflexively and burst out laughing. He handed the SSL pin to Virginia. "Crace took this from you."

"He had it pinned to his coat when we captured him," Jamie said. "I recognized it because Maria has one."

Of course she did. He might have known Maria was a member. And no man should be wearing that pin.

"At first he claimed he didn't know what we were talking about, that you must be hiding somewhere in the house, but the pin gave the lie to that." He grinned. "We persuaded him to change his mind and tell us where to find you."

Virginia turned the pin over in her hand. "And this saved us."

"It did," Jamie said. "If not for Crace wearing that, I wouldn't have known where to look for you. I'd have wasted time searching the manor house."

"And then you found us," Virginia said.

"I did. These houses have cellars. We found more than the silver pin." Dipping his hand into his pocket, Jamie came out with three golden coins. "Have you seen these before?"

Virginia gasped in shock. "I had a brooch pendant. I thought it was an antique coin."

"They're tokens," Jamie said. "I've seen them before in the magistrate's court. Safe passes for smugglers and their clients."

Francis growled low. "Her husband had one, and he gave one to her. Are they solid gold?"

"Yes. I doubt everyone gets a gold one. Crace had one, but the other men had the same design rendered in tin."

Virginia swallowed. "So Ralph was in league with them?" She had to face the truth before she could go forward with her life. Perhaps this was another reason for her hesitation. She needed to finish with the past before she could make a future.

Jamie shook his head. "I wouldn't say that. Merely that he received their goods and safe passage. Many people see smuggling as a way for poorer people to make a living. He could have been one of those."

Considering his other behavior, Virginia did not think that was likely. But the withdrawal of his protection might have caused the gang to attack her, fearful that she knew too much, that Ralph had told her more than he actually had.

Chapter 21

To her self-disgust, Virginia could hardly stay awake. Giving up, she retired to bed early, to the pretty room her cousin had assigned her. She slept alone, waking alone and feeling as if she was missing something. Francis, to be precise.

At their hosts' insistence they spent the rest of the day resting, thinking of nothing. Francis stayed with her and finally confessed he was bone tired. "I meant to come to you last night, but I fell asleep. It's hardly a romantic gesture, is it?"

"You fell off your carriage, raced breakneck to my side at Staines, fought off villains, traveled in the most uncomfortable carriages it has ever been my misfortune to encounter, nearly drowned—and you're apologizing for falling asleep?" She laughed, lifting her head and letting the joyous sound free.

"I did not," he said in a stiff voice, *"fall off my carriage.* I have never had an accident yet. I am accounted a tolerable whip. Someone fired a stone at me."

Her laughter increased, his tone of injured pride was so good.

A week ago, she would not have known him so well. A week ago, she had not fully appreciated how much she—

Was loving him so bad?

"Sweetheart, let it go." His voice gentled, became caressing. "For once, don't think. Just be, for a few days."

It was too late. The same old fear gripped her, that she had nothing, was nothing. Her title was an empty one. "I can bring you nothing," she said.

"You heard what your cousin-in-law said about his wife. You bring me your own sweet self. That is all I want, all I have ever wanted. Why is it so difficult for you to understand that?"

She shook her head. "I don't know. Truly I don't. But the feeling comes over me, and I feel useless and without purpose."

"You're tired. I want to take you home," he said. "To my home. I want us to be married there. We'll wait for our wedding day, rest and recover."

She stared out of the window at the garden. "At least I won't make him homeless," she said. "This is an elegant house."

"Indeed. I have every expectation of Miss—Lady Dulverton's parents giving in. After all, the deed is done." He lifted his hand, indicating the pretty room and the rest of the house. "Meanwhile, this is hardly purgatory."

Virginia agreed. "Does that make me a dowager?"

"For the shortest possible time." He took her hand, lifted it to his lips, and kissed her knuckles. Her melancholy passed; she actually felt it lifting. Perhaps that was the answer. It would not come all at once. He was right. They needed to rest. Her exhaustion was probably adding to her feelings of inadequacy.

"May I come to you tonight?"

She gave him all her attention. "You need permission?"

"I would rather have it. If you wish for another night alone, then you shall have it."

"No. I missed you this morning." That was the nearest she could get to telling him how much she wanted him. The revelation, that after all these years she had finally found that elusive creature, love, was still settling into her mind. And to find it with Francis.

* * * *

Francis and Virginia had been given rooms next to each other. As far as anyone knew, they were married. But Virginia still had a frisson of illicit excitement when the door to her room opened and he came in. He wore a robe of dark blue that was somewhat too short for him, since he was depending on their host to dress him suitably. Virginia rather liked it.

She wore a nightgown of fine lawn, and as she sat up, he groaned. "That is a deeply seductive garment." He threw off the robe, revealing his lack of nightwear.

Virginia drank in his strong body, from the thick dark hair on his head, down his chest with the patch of dark hair at its center, to the dark trail of hair leading to an impressive erection, and the long legs, banded with powerful muscle.

This man was hers. Every wonderful bit of him.

When she would have removed her night rail, he held up a hand. "No, don't. Let me." Crossing the room in three strides, he tossed back the covers and stared down at her. She loved that he had no shame, that he was allowing her to gaze at his powerful body. He leaned over, planting his hands on the mattress, and bared his sharp, white teeth. "Are you ready for the *wolf,* madam?"

Her smile came unbidden, broad and joyous. "More than ready."

"Let's see, shall we?"

He let his gaze roam over her. Virginia arched her back, displaying her body for him, no longer afraid of what he could bring her, or that he took such pleasure in her body. Her reward was a growl, a rumble low in his throat that she could feel when she flattened her hand against his chest. His heart beat against her palm, and she lifted her gaze to meet his eyes in blatant invitation.

"What have I unleashed?" he murmured with a sultry smile only she ever saw.

"We should find out, don't you think?"

She sat up and let him help her off with her night rail. "On our first night together, I was so very unsure," she said.

"Last week you mean?"

With a light laugh, she nodded. "Yes. Last week."

"Although," he continued as he slid into bed next to her, "we have known each other for much longer. This was our inevitable conclusion. I knew you first, wanted you always, and now you're mine."

His tone was altogether too self-satisfied for her liking. "Not yet," she reminded him.

"But soon. I will hold you to your promise, Virginia. You are not changing your mind now."

"No," she answered. She was not. Making love with him had been everything and more, but at the back of her mind, even now, as her body readied itself for him, she had misgivings.

But as he moved over her and took her mouth in a deep, passionate kiss, she gave herself up to him. Because she could do nothing else.

Francis's mastery over her body had only increased since their first night together. He knew her now, the way she enjoyed him tweaking her nipples before licking around them and taking them into his mouth, one by one, firing her up, sending heightened awareness soaring through her body.

When he settled between her legs, he hooked his arms under her knees and drew them up, opening them wide, and she adored the way he kissed down her body until he touched the heart of her passion, licking, kissing, caressing, and finally taking her up to ecstasy.

Virginia came off the bed, an orgasm rocketing through her. He'd taught her the words, too, the wicked words nobody ever uttered in her presence before. As he came back up the bed, she pulled him close, kissed him lavishly and tasted herself on him.

Francis guided himself home and plunged deep.

Virginia gasped, lifted up, responding to his thrusts, holding her body up, keeping it rigid, taking all of him. They kissed, murmured, and she brought her mouth to his ear, telling him graphically what she wanted him to do to her.

Taking her off balance, he rolled them, so now she was on top. His eyes had softened and deepened in color, the pupils wide. Was it wishful thinking that made her believe he had dropped a barrier between them? She had thought they were all gone, but no, there were some yet, a few they still had to overcome.

Not tonight. Tonight they moved as one. Sitting up, she rested her hands, palms down, either side of him and brought her knees up to hug his waist.

"I'm all yours," he said. "Do everything you want, everything you just told me."

Her laugh made him shift inside her. She did it again, enjoying what it did to her. Shivering, she sat up. Francis guided her hands to his chest, and she moved, taking control.

The joy of doing what she wanted, bringing the fulfillment to herself, instead of letting him do it, made her peak sharper, more intense. He held her waist, moving up into her with sure strokes. "Keep your eyes open," he ordered, his voice commanding.

She met his gaze, drowned in him as he cried out and dragged her away, letting his seed pulse out onto the sheets. Pulling a corner free, he roughly cleaned them and pulled her close.

They stayed like that, breathing, kissing, enjoying what they had shared.

"Will you marry me?"

Virginia gazed up at Francis. He was leaning up on one elbow, watching her with a softened, sated expression. She had to assume she was watching him the same way.

"You already asked me."

"The choice is yours, and only yours. Forget what waits for us outside this room. Forget everything except this and us."

"Why?" She placed her palm on his chest. His heart beat, slow and sure. "Why are you asking me now? You must know that I'm yours." She shifted, reminding them both of what they had just done.

"Because I want you to come to me of your own free will. Only because you want me." His gaze sharpened and held hers. "Come to me because you want to."

"What if I can't answer now?"

"Then I will ask you every time we make love, every time we kiss, until you answer me." He smiled, turning his words into a verbal caress.

"Is that not…" She paused, searching for the right word. "Badgering? Aren't you afraid I'll tire of you and send you away?"

"No to both. I love you, Virginia."

His heart gave one steady thump under her hand before returning to its regular rhythm. Hers did the same. She felt the union, sensed the life surging between them both. She loved him too, but she couldn't say it. Disappointment shaded his eyes, but he did not remark on her failure to respond.

"I have loved you since I first laid eyes on you, although at first I put it down to lust. When I saw you ignore my mother's offers of friendship, I grew angry, but that was because you followed Ralph's instructions, was it not? But I didn't know that then. It was easier for me to believe that I despised you. I never did, Virginia. I will love no other woman."

Nobody loved her, ever. Despite what they had let society think, to Ralph she had been a prize. While he might have been fond of her, their wedding night had destroyed any normal relations between them.

"Before I answer you, may I tell you more about my marriage?"

"Yes. Then we may have done with it."

She swallowed, forcing the memories back, the ones she'd submerged for years. "He made me do things, said they were usual for married couples."

His expression hardened, his eyes lightening to the color of polished steel. "What things?"

"Some of the things I have done with you with pleasure, he made me do, and I found no joy there." All her illusions had vanished then. "I was not sure what I was supposed to do, but whatever I did made no difference. Other things, too, until he blamed me. He called me cold and unfeeling, said I had the appeal of a dead cat."

Francis gathered her up, then, and rolled onto his back so she was curled up against him.

"Out of bed he was polite in public, but he ruled the house with a control that was inviolable. If anyone made the least little transgression, he would gather us all together and tell us how disappointed he was in us. But he never dismissed a servant, never left us alone. In private he told me that he should not have married me, that I was a complete loss to him. He criticized my clothes, the way I did my hair. I was young, and I believed him. After the way my parents had treated me, I thought I was as useless as he said. The more I tried to please him, the more he treated me like his servant. In public he doted on me, told everyone he loved me."

Francis said nothing, only watched her, but his eyes kindled, and his mouth flattened. Still, he held her gently.

Giving in to her weakness, she leaned into him. A weight left her shoulders, the burden she had been carrying for so long. That of the barren widow, a dual curse. No man wanting an heir and honorable marriage would approach her before this, but Francis accepted her for what she was, not what she could never be.

"Yes," she said.

He raised a dark brow. "Yes?"

"Yes, I'll marry you. As soon as you like."

He froze, his expression changing. A glow warmed his eyes, and the lines bracketing his mouth lightened. "You mean it?"

She nodded. "I love you, Francis. That is what makes this so different."

Only then did he let his feelings out. "My love, you make me happier than a man has any right to be."

He drew her close with the reverence of a man overwhelmed by his good fortune. She curled into his arms, slid her hands under his coat and encircled his waist, lifting her face for his kiss.

She didn't understand why he wanted her when she was bringing him nothing, but she wouldn't question it any longer. Despite all her misgivings, he was right, the man she wanted.

He loved her. That made everything right. And her love made their union perfect.

* * * *

Francis listened to Virginia's words with outrage, anger simmering through him. He had to fight to stop himself reacting as he wished, shocking her into pushing him away. She must not do that. She would not.

If he could, he'd have beaten Ralph to within an inch of his life for doing that to Virginia. Even if she had been any other woman, one he was not involved with, her story would have infuriated him. That he had done that to Virginia made him incandescent with rage.

Ralph had taken a young, lovely woman from her unhappy family situation, ensnared her by making her his bride, and then methodically destroyed her, before setting her up to become his creature, his possession, even after his death. Not a wife, not the woman she should be, but someone who needed him for reassurance and approval. All because he was impotent and couldn't give her the most intimate pleasure. The cause of his wound was not her fault, but she had suffered for it.

He had already condemned the dog-in-the-manger attitude, but not this.

Who was he to snare her again? He made a decision, one he might live to regret. He would do everything in his power to prove to her that if she married him, she would not be diving into another restrictive, controlling relationship.

He took her hand loosely in his. "Sweetheart, I won't trap you. Ever. You will have everything you need. Half of everything I am free to give you."

Her mouth rounded to an O.

Smiling at her response, he continued. "We will be man and wife, because we've already burned our boats on that. But you and I, we will know. We will be equals in everything. I will settle an amount on you in any case. Let society believe what it will, but I will not force you into doing anything you do not wish to."

"You mean it?"

He nodded.

Her smile warmed him. "And I can continue with the orphanages."

"Be assured of that."

"I had a lot of pleasure out of doing that. Being of use to someone."

He suspected that setting up the orphanages had gone a long way toward restoring her self-respect after first her parents and then her husband had destroyed it. He would not add to their efforts. Instead, he would do his best to restore it. So by setting her that task, Ralph had done her a service. He would have regretted it.

Drawing her close, he felt sleep creeping over his sated body. "When we're recovered, we will travel to Wolverley Court as man and wife. The ceremony will take place there, but we'll keep it private. Agreed?"

"You must wish to see your mother. You are close to her, are you not?"

"Mmm."

Not as close as he was to Virginia, Lady Dulverton.

Chapter 22

Wolverley Court was only a day's travel from Jamie's house, but Virginia and Francis took their time leaving for the journey. A week passed before they arrived there, prepared to face the life awaiting them. Jamie and Maria elected to accompany them, but this time they would travel in state. Virginia sent for her luggage and jewelry from Hatherton Cross and asked her Exeter solicitor to attend her at Wolverley.

As Francis's wife, she would have larger establishments to care for, more social events to attend. That meant she would need to appoint managers.

They traveled to Wolverley Court in style. She did not feel at all a fraud, climbing into his luxuriously equipped berline with the Wolverley arms emblazoned on the doors, even though they were not yet married. They would be soon. He had put her mind at ease, assured her she would never have to depend on a man ever again.

And of course told her he loved her.

The day was fine. In fact after that fateful moonless night on the coast, the sun had been reminded of the season and was making a daily appearance. In her apricot gown and new bergère hat, a double ruffle of lace at her elbows, Virginia felt more herself. And yet renewed.

Jamie and Maria followed in their vehicle, and another brought up the rear, carrying servants and jewelry. Virginia wore a double string of fine white pearls and matching earrings that Ralph had given her on their marriage. Later, he'd told her that pearls meant tears.

But they were lovely, and she wore them anyway. The first of many decisions that did not depend on what Ralph thought or what her parents told her. Her decision had liberated her, given her something she had never had before. So had her confession of love to Francis. The moment she'd said it, she felt the truth of it.

They settled in the carriage. Francis looked himself again, with a rich suit of dark red cloth and a new waistcoat of palest gold lustring. His wig was a fashionable confection of pure white, but once they were on their way, he pulled it off and tossed it onto the opposite seat. "While it's good to have something that fits, I confess I'm tired of wigs," he said.

"I love you with or without them." Following his example, she untied the ribbons of her hat and tossed it to join his wig, mute witnesses to their intimacy. "You know that if we call ourselves married for long enough, a court may rule it valid," she said lightly, surprised at how little she cared.

"I do, but I want us wed in truth. I have sent a message to my godfather, asking him to come to Wolverley." Reaching out, he took her hand, winding their fingers together. "It means something to me. What matters more is sharing my life with you."

"Oh." Tears of happiness threatened, but she blinked them away. She wasn't sure what to say.

They arrived at Wolverley Court in a few hours, well in time for dinner. Since Francis had sent a rider to advise them of their imminent arrival, the staff was ready for them. And so was his mother.

Wolverley had been remodeled by Francis's father into the elegant house she saw when she got out of the carriage. The elegant front in cream stone was pleasantly balanced, with small wings on either side. Large, modern windows let in plenty of light. This was the opposite of a house like Combe Manor, with its narrow windows and dark interiors. Virginia loved it.

Lady Wolverley met them in the main hall. While it wasn't the most imposing hall she had ever entered, the proportions were elegant, and it had a sense of the open air that appealed to Virginia. The walls were pale blue, the woodwork gleaming white. A portrait of the old earl hung at the first landing, before the main stairs split into two and climbed up to the floor above.

And it was crowded with neat lines of servants.

A quick tally told Virginia there were about forty servants ranked here. They waited, standing, presumably ranked most important to least.

When she married Ralph she had gone through this ritual, which was common when a new master or mistress entered the house. However, she was no cowed eighteen-year-old today. Nearly twelve years and a world of experience lay between Virginia and that girl.

When she would have curtsyed to Lady Wolverley, the lady prevented her by embracing her warmly.

"Welcome," she said. "This will be the final time I say that to you, as you will be welcoming people from now on. I can only extend my best wishes that when your time comes, you will do it as happily as I do now."

Goodness. Of course Virginia had met her ladyship before, but only briefly, since her husband had not approved of the countess. "A common dairymaid!" he had exclaimed to her. "I cannot have you hobnobbing with her. I forbid it."

Virginia had curtsyed and murmured her acceptance, as she always had with Ralph. The twin burdens of obligation and expected obedience had kept her to that resolve. But not now. Then she had behaved coldly to her ladyship. She was deeply sorry for that now.

Her ladyship smelled of spring flowers, and her fine blue silk gown was entirely appropriate to the heat of the day and the occasion. She spoke with no discernible accent and smiled with real friendliness.

"I am truly happy to be here," Virginia replied.

The countess glanced around at the silent, serried ranks behind her. "You may not be by the time we have finished here. Do not try to memorize all their names. I have instructed them all to introduce themselves as required."

With an equally warm embrace for her son, and a few murmured words of affection, she moved on to speak to Jamie and Maria.

Despite what the countess had said, Virginia did her best to remember all the names. Some ladies never even tried but used generic names for all their members of staff. But she was not of that ilk. The butler here was one McIver, a dour, tall man with a startlingly sweet smile.

"I have brought my butler from my house in town. He has been injured in my service, and I wish you to take special care of him." They had loaded Butler into the servants' carriage, well wrapped up and coddled. "My maid is Winston, and my footman is Hurst. The others are yours." She wanted Hurst retained, and she would find a place for Butler. Perhaps in his home city, in charge of her London establishment. He would never lack.

Nobody objected. She would ensure Butler was put in a comfortable room and had everything he needed. However busy she was, she would do that. She moved on, meeting the housekeeper, then moving on to the housemaids, the chefs, two of them, the kitchen maids, scullery maids, footmen, pageboys, and then some of the outdoor staff, the head gardeners, the grooms, including one who would be assigned for her use, and others.

Lady Wolverley waited with Jamie and Maria, who had declined refreshment in favor of a tour of the house.

And so Francis showed Virginia his house and welcomed her into his life. So different to what she had left behind! Dulverton Court was not so lovely, nor so modern.

Her husband's predilection was to fill the grand Jacobean house with armor. A great display of swords, shields, daggers, and rifles had graced the hall of her previous home—no, residence, because she had never felt at home there. Hatherton Cross, which Jamie had promised to bestow on her as a wedding present, was much more modest.

They ended in the drawing room, a state room with human dimensions. Virginia did not feel overwhelmed in this warm room with its windows flung open to catch the breeze. Lady Wolverley poured tea, and the maid brought them over. "I am expecting guests hourly," her ladyship told them, "so I might have to excuse myself to greet them."

"Who are you expecting, Mama?" Francis asked, his brow arched in query.

"Guests for the ball. I have arranged a ball to celebrate your marriage and invited half the county."

Taking exaggerated care, Francis put his tea dish back in the saucer and replaced them on the table. "How did you find time to do that?"

His mother smiled. "You sent me news a week ago, but I saw the way the wind was blowing in London. I've had plenty of time, my boy. Invitations went out a few days ago. I've arranged the ball for Monday. A comfortable affair, with dancing and supper. And a dinner to celebrate your nuptials."

Francis shot Virginia an "I told you so" look. He had said his mother would arrange a celebration, but the lady's efficiency impressed Virginia, who had never arranged a ball with less than two weeks' notice. She had a reputation for efficiency, but Virginia had never personally witnessed it before.

"I will introduce you to the county as Lady Wolverley, then I will take myself to Arkerley," she said.

"Arkerley is a pleasant house, and of course you are more than welcome to live there," Francis said, "but I tried to buy you Combe Manor, the house of your childhood. I do not think it's possible, though." He glanced at Virginia and grimaced. "I'm sure Virginia would have sold it to me, if she could, but her late husband requested her to retain it." Ordered her, more like.

And all the others. But as Virginia opened her mouth to corroborate what he'd said, her ladyship cut in.

"Oh, that would never do!" She gave a slight shudder, her tea dish rattling in its saucer. "It was always cold and drafty, and so close to the sea that it was always damp. My father chose to live there because it was good for nothing else, as he put it."

She paused, tracing the rim of her tea dish with one polished fingernail. "My childhood was hard, my dear. I've never made a secret of my origins, so that should not be a shock to you."

"You never spoke of it much," Francis said softly. Virginia watched the way his expression stiffened, as if preparing himself for bad news.

Jamie and Maria occupied the twin sofa to the one Francis and Virginia sat on, bracketing the countess's chair, so they could comfortably converse. The tea table stood to the right of the countess, and a small table was tucked at each end of the sofas.

Her ladyship looked around the company, taking her time, her shrewd eyes, so much like her son's, missing nothing. The clock ticked, and birdsong came from the garden.

Having the complete attention of everyone, Lady Wolverley gave a sunny smile. "Why should I speak of it, when I had escaped to this?"

She indicated the room. "My father barely spoke, because he never got out of the habit of working from dawn until dusk. He followed the hours of the sun, going to bed when polite society was only just beginning the night's entertainments. My mother could not read, and she made sure that I went to the village school every Sunday to learn my letters. But my father was never a humble farmer, and I was never a simple dairymaid. I helped in the dairy, that was all. Not that I would be ashamed of that, but the times I've wanted to correct people are without number. It would only have encouraged them, so I held my peace."

She took a sip of tea. Nobody spoke. "My father was a rich farmer. Not rich by your standards, but rich enough to be on good terms with the local squire. I met my husband when he came to discuss a matter of business with my father. Mutual grazing rights, I think. I was carrying a dish of cream, one of those large, shallow bowls from the dairy, and I was so intent on not spilling a drop that I did not see him until I was upon him. So much for spilling a drop. I tipped the entire contents of the bowl over his fine suit!" She smiled.

"I remember that story, Mama," Francis said through the laughter.

So did most of society. That story was what had labeled her as a dairymaid, but it sounded as if she was much more than that. And her intelligence had helped to triple the original worth of the earldom.

She had worked with Francis to develop and manage the new opportunities he'd opened up abroad. Dismissing all the well-meaning advisors who had drifted into her sphere, she administered the estate herself. That alone had recommended her to many people who would initially have dismissed her as an upstart, a social climber.

"So, my son, I am delighted that you did not burden me with Combe Manor. I can't help but think that it will make an appalling orphanage. It is far too close to the sea, for one thing. And the cellars…" She shuddered. "Damp, and they're like a warren, winding everywhere. My father didn't approve of smugglers, but I can't help thinking that the house is far better suited to the trade than it is to shelter small children."

"You're right," Virginia acknowledged, "but it is on the list of establishments my late husband wanted to turn into orphanages. I am—was—bound to do it, but other than building a wall higher than Exeter city walls, or locking the mites up all day, I'm at a loss how to do it safely. I was obliged to house fifteen children at each orphanage." She sighed.

"And block up the cellars," her ladyship advised.

"I was forbidden to make major structural changes." She hesitated, but why should she not reveal the whole? "Ralph did not trust me that far. He said no woman had a sense of space, and I would fill the house with plaster ceilings and French wallpaper. His instructions were specific."

"Why did I hear none of this before?" her ladyship demanded.

Virginia had turned into a babbling brook. If she told one person, she should tell them all. It was like playing with fire; if any of the trustees, whose names she did not know, got to hear that she had spilled the beans, then they would take the decision away from her.

"I was not allowed to tell anyone," she said simply, smiling and spreading her hands in a kind of apology. "The penalty for telling someone was severe." Getting up from her seat, she walked to the window. Restlessness filled her. She folded her arms, her lace ruffles tickling her bare skin. "But it doesn't matter now."

But there was something else, something that tickled the edges of her memory. For the life of her Virginia couldn't imagine what it was.

* * * *

The following day was spent in resting, walking in the garden with Jamie, Francis, and Maria. Francis's man of business arrived in the early afternoon, and Francis spent some time closeted with him, dealing with the affairs of the estate.

Just before she was due to go upstairs to change for dinner, Virginia went to the library. She had kept the list of orphanages—not that she needed them. She remembered every one. That had given her the feeling that she was missing something.

Armed with the list she already had, plus the ones Henderson had told her about that morning, she crossed to the table and laid them out. The large, rectangular table was set in the middle of the room, writing implements set in a circular silver writing stand. The moderately sized room was lined with glass-fronted bookcases, all satisfactorily full. The smell of furniture polish and the musty smell of paper wove in the air.

Bitterly she scolded herself. She had slipped into following the terms of the will because at the time it had suited her. After Ralph she had not wanted to marry anyone ever again.

But now she did. She had accepted an offer from the most unexpected place, and he made her happier than she had thought she could ever be. Feelings she had no words for, of such profundity she hadn't considered them possible, coursed through her.

And with the return of the full person, Virginia started to think more clearly. The orphanages were the clue. Everything hinged on them. Ralph's insistence on her establishing them, his careful plans, down to the last penny. Virginia had put that down to his military history, that he was using a method he was accustomed to, but her assumption had misled her.

She recalled the ones she'd already set up. Every site had something in common—they were near the sea, in small communities. None were in towns. But then, Devonshire was part of a peninsula, and no place was too far from the sea.

It all added up to something else.

She had to explore the bookcases thoroughly before she found the atlases, not least because she kept coming across books that intrigued her, that she would return to later. But for now, she wanted the well-thumbed maps she found on the lower shelf under the window. She carried a couple across to the table and laid them open.

Half an hour later she had her answer. Finally she had unraveled the last conundrum. She felt certain she was right.

That was where Francis found her an hour later. Glancing at the clock, she groaned when she saw the time. "Oh no. I'll go up and change for dinner straightaway."

A man stood behind Francis and, at his impatient gesture, moved forward and bowed. "Wait a while, Virginia. My dear, this is Samuel Cocking, a Bow Street Runner."

Samuel Cocking was a man of moderate height, slender, with alert gray eyes and a sharp nose. He did not bow so much as nod, which perversely, Virginia liked. He laid a plain leather folder on the table and undid the strings.

"What is your business in Devonshire?" Virginia demanded, puzzled. "I thought you dealt with matters in London only."

Cocking and Francis exchanged a meaningful glance. Cocking cleared his throat. "When Magistrate Fielding set up the Runners, he always intended us to deal with major crimes like smuggling. We work out of Bow Street, but we may travel to wherever we need to in order to apprehend offenders."

Cocking drew a paper out of the file. "This is part of the Bow Street records on the smuggling activities in Devonshire and Cornwall. In the last ten years the activity has increased threefold, perhaps more. Before that, Essex was the hotbed for large-scale smuggling activities, but the trade from Devonshire is bigger than it ever was."

"Before I moved to Devonshire, I had no idea it was such a problem," she admitted. "Of course I knew it was rife, but not in such an organized way."

Cocking nodded. "The gangs take control of villages, whole stretches of the coast."

Next to her, Francis was leaning back in his chair, appearing indolent, but the spark in his eyes showed him as anything but. He was listening, waiting for the story to unfold before he added his comments.

"When the four footmen were murdered, we were alerted to the possibility that the case was not restricted to London."

Virginia frowned. "Why?"

"Because of their destination. They were not murdered for gain, they had nothing of real worth, and they were strong men, easily able to fight back. They were dispatched quietly and swiftly, and their bodies hidden so they would not be discovered. It was sheer chance that made a stableboy run behind the stables, intent on relieving himself. But he found the bodies crammed there and sounded the alarm."

Virginia would have screamed like a banshee.

Cocking continued. "We learned the intended destination of the footmen. The day after the murders, we were assured by one of our most trustworthy informants that this outrage had nothing to do with the London gangs. Once we discovered who had hired the coach, we knew you were in danger, and we followed you. We lost track of you, but I knew I would find you at your house."

Francis nodded. "I have told you what happened at Staines. After that, we decided to travel covertly and quietly. Someone was pursuing us. There were two attempts on my life in London, one warning and one serious attack. Someone wanted to separate me from Virginia. I assumed it was Lord Dulverton, but now we know it was not."

The Runner nodded gravely. "Indeed. I visited the customs offices at Exeter, where they informed me of the events at Combe Manor. The operation went smoothly, as if the smugglers have been doing it for a long time. The caretakers would leave the premises, close the shutters against prying eyes, but leave the door open. The cellars have internal stairs leading down to the cliffs. There are many caves hereabouts, and in the past they were probably used for storage. They still were, but the storage was illegal contraband. The excise caught most of the gang, but none are talking. But we're not done yet." He tapped another paper.

Virginia's turn. Since the Runner was here, he could see what she had discovered.

"Look at these." She indicated the books and the series of marks she'd made once she found the red ink.

The men stood and leaned over the book. "What have you been doing?" Francis asked.

"I know what Ralph was up to. Why the orphanages were so important to him. That story he told me about the waifs on the battlefield?" She snorted inelegantly. "He didn't care. He used it as a useful excuse."

She pointed at the map. "The red crosses are the orphanages I have already set up. The slashes are in the places where I was expected to establish them."

Silence followed as the men studied the map.

"Damn," Francis muttered. "Dear God."

Cocking grunted.

"I worried I was imagining things, but I'm not, am I?"

Francis traced the lines with his fingers. "Mousehole, Hayle, Padstow, Fowey, Mevagissey..." Straightening, he turned and leaned against the table. "No, you are not imagining anything. Those places are notorious hotbeds for smuggling. And wrecking."

"My thoughts exactly, sir," Cocking agreed.

She shuddered. "And I've been helping them."

"Unwittingly." Francis was too steady, hiding his emotions as he used to. But this time he was not covering them with the insouciant, careless attitude he had used in London.

"It was unwittingly, wasn't it?" Cocking demanded.

A chill crept down her spine. "What do you mean? You think I knew?"

Francis stood between her and the Runner, who shook his head. "I didn't mean it like that, I'm sorry. But the pattern is so obvious when it's plotted out like that. All on the coast or close to it."

Francis folded his arms and met her gaze with a somber look she was not used to in him. "Your late husband was a soldier. His expertise was organization, the necessary part of war that rarely attracts much notice."

"Yes. He enjoyed organizing everyone and everything."

"Including you."

"Including me. And he found something else to organize, didn't he?"

Cocking nodded. "He planned to turn the haphazard smuggling that goes on here into a countywide enterprise. Increase the efficiency. Make more profits."

Turning back to the table, she closed the books. "Nobody else should find these."

"I'll dispose of them. Is this the list?" Francis picked up the sheet of paper on which she'd written the places, studied it, and passed it to Cocking.

"Yes. They were jumbled up, in no particular order. That was why I didn't notice at first. And I don't know the West Country as well as I should. Of course they are near the sea because we're on the peninsula. There's little but coastline here. He never meant me to have the property. He knew that by the time I knew for sure, I would be complicit."

"As guilty as the others," he murmured. "Whoever they are."

Tears stung her eyes. "I thought he was treating me like a child, but he wasn't. He was pulling me in. Making me guilty. Perhaps he thought that eventually I would join in. I will not. Ever!"

She flung herself to the door, but he caught her from behind, his hands banded around her forearms. Without thought, she turned into him and let him hold her while she shook. "My husband was a smuggler. A criminal. He was doing what he did best. Organizing, making profit. Betraying his country."

"Not everybody sees it like that," he murmured against her hair.

Cocking spoke from his station at the table. "Never you mind that, my lady. What is most important is that we have discovered it. Now we have to stop it. Tell the authorities. The trouble is, half the excise men in the county are taking money from the smugglers."

She drew back. "If there is an organization, there must be more people like Ralph. More people of wealth and power. Don't you think?"

Francis nodded and guided her back to the table. "Yes, there must. I had thought of that. Sweetheart, do you object to making the celebratory ball even bigger than it was? We can invite friends but also all the local gentry. Someone will know something. And perhaps we will learn more about what this all means. If a man approaches me and asks me about my plans for Combe Manor, for example."

"I can have men attend the ball, my lord. Dressed as servants. No need for you to get involved. I can handle affairs from here."

"I wouldn't hear of it," Francis said promptly. "We will keep this between us. Only my mother and Lord and Lady Dulverton should know."

"With your permission, I can be at the ball, my lord. Keeping an eye out. You'll have your guests to manage."

After looking at the Runner for a long time, Francis finally nodded. "Very well."

He took her elbow. "Meantime, you have to change for dinner." He nodded to Cocking. "Would you join us?"

"If'n you don't mind, I'll be better in the kitchens," he said. "I'll tell them I'm a new footman, hired for her ladyship's personal use. I can see what's what that way."

"Very well. I'll send word. You may confide in Hurst, the footman. He knows as much about this matter as I do. You will also find a man in bed upstairs by the name of Butler. He has given us signal service, and while I want him resting until he is recovered, you may trust him and listen to what he has to say."

Francis took Virginia upstairs to change for dinner. Outside her room she paused, her hand on the panel. "You won't do anything too dangerous? I don't want to lose you, Francis. Not now." With people trying to kill him, enlarging the guest list would also increase the danger. Although she had sent for one more guest: her solicitor from Exeter, Henderson.

"I promise I will talk and listen, that's all. I swear." He kissed her, making it soft and sweet, a kiss that went with his promise.

She eased out of his arms. "Thank you." She pressed a light kiss to his lips but drew away when he would have caught her close. "I'm glad you know. We have to talk about it, I know, but at least we've found the key."

"You found the key," he corrected her. "Clever woman. I'll go to the drawing room while you change."

Chapter 23

Guests had begun to arrive for the ball. Emilia Dauntry arrived with the remainder of Virginia's belongings that afternoon.

Emilia came into Virginia's bedroom while Winston was still getting her ready. She had not bothered with more than a light knock, but what if Virginia had been engaging in something more intimate with Francis?

Virginia greeted Emilia with a kiss on both cheeks, but also with relief. Emilia was at heart a kind woman, but her inability to think matters through, and a regrettable tendency to make instant judgments, occasionally led her to make pronouncements that made Virginia want to slap her. Now Virginia need not entertain those sentiments, although she would have to find someone else to take Emilia.

"I thought you might stay at Hatherton Cross for the time being, if you would like that."

Emilia clasped a hand to her formidable bosom. "Goodness, that would never do! A woman living on her own is either a servant or a doxy! And since I am neither, I would prefer to remain in a house with other ladies."

She wanted to stay here at Wolverley. While Winston teased Virginia's hair into a glossy knot, with a few loose locks falling into curls that were anything but careless, Virginia stared into the mirror at her companion.

Emilia had made herself at home on the daybed. She wore her second-best evening gown of bright blue satin, which Virginia privately thought was a touch too bright and a touch too shiny for Emilia, but she would never dream of saying so. Emilia declared herself an expert on fashion, as she was on everything else.

But she had a kind heart.

"Well, you must regard my old home as yours," Virginia said desperately.

"Well that is exceedingly kind of you, Virginia, but I will need respectability."

Virginia cast about for an answer. She could not have Emilia here. Sooner or later Francis would crack. He did not have the patience to deal with her. There had to be a place for her somewhere. Would the dowager take her?

Anybody?

"Of course you will, my dear. How remiss of me." She turned her head, keeping still so that Winston could ply the curling tongs. This being summer, instead of heating the tongs in the fire, Winston was employing a small lamp, and the scent of burning oil added to the aromas of lavender, rosewater, and starch.

All scents Virginia was deeply familiar with. Scents of home.

"My dear, I was never so shocked as when I heard you had married Lord Wolverley! Your note took me quite aback. I had assumed you were still at Combe Manor, since you said you would join me from there, but to hear you had taken this step…! When I left London, you were quite resolved on eternal widowhood. I have done my best to explain your sudden decision to your neighbors, but I have been stretched to do so."

Virginia heard the unspoken resentment loud and clear. She had never treated Emilia as her dearest friend, so she had no right to expect it now, and yet this was what she had come to hear. She would have to disappoint her companion. Repeating the legend she wanted to become the truth seemed the most expedient. "Lord Wolverley has been courting me this past year and more. Surely you recall?"

"Ah, oh yes." Emilia had never been slow at reading between the lines. But she sometimes had the annoying trait of taking the wrong ones. "But I thought that was merely because you are neighbors here in Devonshire. He never seemed overly smitten to me." She sniffed. "You could have done so much better, Virginia, if you were set on marriage. Think of the Duke of Watmough!"

Virginia recalled the short, squat duke full of his own importance and did not bother to suppress her derisive snort. "Really, Emilia? The man is a walking parody. He might be a duke, but Wolverley can easily surpass him in wealth."

"Wealth is not everything," the lady said, flicking her fan out with a decisive swish. "Consequence can amount to much more. Lineage and history, my dear. Wolverley is merely the second earl, is he not? His grandfather was a mere baron."

"A clever one who set Europe on its ear when he acted as Ambassador to the French court," Virginia pointed out. "Or are you casting aspersions on my mother-in-law?"

Emilia covered her face with her fan, but not before Virginia had marked her heightened color. Of course that was what Emilia meant. The dairymaid countess.

"I prefer to assess people by their character," she continued relentlessly. "Many a fool holds a title."

Winston stepped back, her signal that she had finished. After a glance in the mirror, Virginia nodded and smiled her thanks. She had performed her usual miracle and made a beauty out of her. Virginia had made herself graceful and elegant, but Winston added the touch that gave the illusion of beauty. She had enhanced the simple way Virginia preferred to dress. Virginia was so glad her maid had not betrayed her.

But others had. People she'd trusted, and she could not deny how much that hurt. And what it had done to her self-esteem. If not for Francis, she might have gone into a decline. Or, of course, been dead.

With that sober reminder, she went downstairs to dinner.

* * * *

The morning of her wedding, Virginia awoke alone in her own bed. She turned over, expecting a pair of strong, warm arms to curl around her, but of course he was not there. She had insisted that they spend this night apart. What had she been thinking? She'd missed him all night, her sleep disturbed by his absence.

A movement told her Winston was already in the room. When Virginia sat up, Winston stacked pillows behind her back and then brought her a tray with tea and toasted bread and butter, her favorite way to start the day. They would have breakfast later. Most of the company who had been arriving for the ball didn't know they weren't already married. Virginia hugged her secret close to her heart.

Today was her wedding day.

Once arrayed in the fresh, pale yellow silk, her hair dressed simply, she went down to the chapel, where Bishop Lavington waited for them, together with the vicar of the local parish.

Mrs. Lavington, Jamie, Maria, the lady soon to become the Dowager Countess, and to her shock, Angela Childers were there. When had she arrived? Angela gave her a warm smile, but Virginia had eyes only for one person. The man standing at the altar, dressed most untypically in ivory.

The light shade made his skin appear darker, his eyes brighter. She had not even known he had something that pale. The gold buttons gleamed in the morning light streaming in from the skylight above, and the candles flickering at the end of every pew. The staff had prayers here once a week, but a long time had passed since the last wedding was held here.

"We are gathered here together..." the bishop began.

Virginia became the Countess of Wolverley in twenty short minutes. Or rather, she was declared the wife of Francis Collingwood. She liked that better, because she was marrying Francis the man, not the title. At last she could leave her previous history behind her.

Almost. There remained one more thing to do. But she would not think of that now.

Apparently Francis thought the same, because in the few minutes before their family joined them to congratulate them, he leaned over and murmured in her ear, "Today is for us. Nothing else matters."

Then she was being hugged and kissed by everyone but Francis. The vicar brought the register to them, his face a mask of impassivity. He probably disapproved of their behavior before their marriage. Or perhaps he had another candidate for Francis's countess. Whatever his problem, he did not cast a shadow on their day.

* * * *

Henderson arrived in the late afternoon. The journey here would have taken him most of the day. Virginia took some satisfaction in that. She saw him in the library.

"You should know that I have married his lordship. I am now Lady Wolverley," she told him bluntly.

Not being a cruel woman, she poured tea and served him herself, while he sat down at the big table, goggling at her. "You have given up your inheritance?"

She nodded. "So you have much work to do."

"I do indeed. I must inform the trustees immediately."

Virginia walked over to the window, gazing outside at the people enjoying the sunny day. She would keep this brief so she could join them. "I don't think that will be necessary."

How much did Henderson know about the ulterior motive behind
the orphanages?

"What do you mean, my lady?" He slurped his tea, keeping his attention
on her, peering over the rim of his tea dish.

"Matters have arisen…" She turned to face him fully. He sat in the
chair by the cold fireplace, watching her gravely.

She started again. "The orphanages were not all they were meant to be.
I am contacting the authorities, so they may look into the matter. I need
you to send all the details of my prior marriage and the arrangements for
his orphanages to my husband's man of business. After all, the terms are
now void, and there is no longer any need to keep them secret, is there?"

His mouth dropped open. He had not closed it when she left the room.

She was done with the orphanages, with the inheritance, with the whole
sorry business. From now on, the excise, customs, and magistrates could
squabble over the will and punish the gang of smugglers.

* * * *

Dressing for the ball was a particular pleasure. When Francis had asked
her what she was wearing, she had said casually, "I thought I'd wear my
new blue." The one she had not worn yet. The gown was in the French
style, and nobody had yet seen it.

The gown was dark blue, the color of summer midnight, and the theme
was roses. Pink roses in raised embroidery rioted down the robings either
side of her bodice, and more decorated the deep flounces of the matching
petticoat. They edged the flounces on her sleeves, too, grazing the triple
flounces of Mechlin lace that Winston sewed to the end of the sleeves on
her shift. She'd even had matching shoes made, and the buckles were pink
brilliants. Her stomacher was a riot of bows in the same color as the roses.

Virginia stood back from the pier glass on the wall and examined her
appearance critically. Winston had dressed her hair in her usual knot, with
curls teasing her bare shoulders.

"Jewelry," she murmured. She glanced at the dressing table, where a
box holding her pearls lay waiting for her. She made a sudden decision.
"No pearls. They stand for tears. I want nobody to construe anything
but happiness."

"I have it, my lady." Winston closed the box and took the pearls back to
the dressing chest that held Virginia's jewels. She had a new one tonight,

a plain gold band on her finger that she would never take off. It was the most precious piece that she owned.

Someone tapped at the door. Winston locked the chest before she went to answer it. A murmur of voices followed, and she came back to Virginia. "Your lord husband sent these. He says they are part of the family collection. He would appreciate you wearing them."

Virginia sighed. "Let us pray they are not emeralds."

Winston opened the lid of the wooden box.

Pink topazes and diamonds. Each large oval pink stone was surrounded by diamonds, and diamonds linked them. The earrings had to have ribbons to support them over the tops of her ears; otherwise, they would have pulled the lobes down too far. There were bracelets for each wrist and a large brooch, which she pinned to the top of her bodice. And hair ornaments, set on tiny springs so they moved with her, shivering when the light caught them.

"Oh my goodness." She had some good pieces but none as fine as these.

"Madam," Winston said, her voice full of awe.

"Do you think it's too grand for a country ball?"

Winston's voice went up an octave. "At Wolverley? My lady, how can you say such a thing? You are the mistress of the most elegant house in the county, the treasure of Devonshire!"

"I'm not sure I like that." She held out her hand. Winston placed her fan in it, and Virginia felt complete. "You took good care of me," she said quietly. "I will never forget that. Thank you."

Without waiting for an answer, she gathered her skirts and left the room.

Only to find her husband waiting outside. He was leaning against the wall, but at her appearance he kicked away from it and came to her, hands outstretched to take hers. "You look like an empress. I am the most fortunate man alive." He lifted her hands to his lips, one after the other.

"In that case you are an emperor. You could pass for one."

He smiled. He'd chosen blue velvet, in a shade lighter than her deep ultramarine. Diamond buttons glittered in serried rows down his coat and waistcoat. A huge sapphire gleamed at her from his finger, and he wore another ring, a plain gold one, the twin of hers.

Startled, she lifted her eyes and met his amused gaze.

"I wanted to. I know it's unusual. I have decided to have two signet rings made, with our seals on them, just in case you want a change."

"I..." She had expected none of this attention, the public signs of affection he was lavishing on her. She put her hand to the large brooch on her bodice. "And this...it doesn't look old enough to be a family piece."

"My father had the gems remade for my mother, but she didn't like it. However, before he died she wore it enough for people to know what it means. It was made for love. They will know."

Before she could answer, he tucked her hand under his arm and walked with her to the other side of the wing, where people were gathering for the dinner before the ball.

Normally a ball this early in the summer would be thinly attended, especially considering the short notice the guests had been given, but her mother-in-law had informed her that they had covers for forty.

The numbers did not daunt Virginia. Although she had never catered for so many before, she took the twenty she had regularly entertained in her previous marriage and doubled it. She would have liked to sit next to her husband, though.

The table in the great dining room had all its leaves slotted into it. The state rooms were all open. Everything was as ready as she could make it.

"So charmed you invited us." Sir Bertram and his family had arrived in good time. Unfortunately, since they lived some way off, they were staying overnight, and the magistrate had brought his whole family with him.

At least he had no children left in the schoolroom; otherwise, Virginia suspected they would have had to find nurses and governesses. Most guests brought their own, but Sir Bertram had only brought a footman and a coach driver. Virginia had located a couple of servants to attend Sir Bertram, his wife, his heir, and his three daughters.

And Sir Bertram had been unhappy with the rooms assigned to them and insisted on moving to the family wing. Virginia had compromised and put them on the floor above. Her other guests included the Duke of Colston Magna, Lord Marston, and the Duke and Duchess of Leomore.

The newly married couple had caused a sensation during their courtship because of the lady's humble beginnings and the way she met the duke. Having been accused of stealing a valuable necklace, she set out to prove her innocence.

Virginia knew her well and embraced her warmly when she arrived. Like Virginia, Phoebe wore her SSL pin. "Y-you look very happy," she said. Not a comment on how fine she looked, as everyone else had said. She knew the difference.

"So do you," Virginia said in the few minutes they had to themselves. "You are happy, are you not?"

Phoebe nodded. "Oh y-yes. B-blissfully."

"Yes," Virginia said softly because she knew what Phoebe meant. "But, Phoebe, I have something I want to tell you."

Drawing her aside, Virginia outlined what she and Francis had discovered. "Will you help?"

"Of course!" Phoebe's face lit up. "I'm d-delighted you asked me. Should I tell the others?"

"I've already told Angela." In a walk that morning in the grounds. "And only the other members of the SSL and your husband. We still do not know who we can trust. We had thought Jamie was involved. Lord Dulverton," she added by way of explanation, "but he is not."

"I see."

Who could Virginia trust but her colleagues and friends from the society?

Now Sir Bertram was confronting her with a familiarity she did not enjoy but would put up with for the sake of peace. "If we had not met you on the road, we would not have had the slightest idea you were married," he said, sliding his quizzing glass out of his breeches pocket. He lifted it, but Virginia, not liking to be stared at, gazed at him, chin up, lids half-closed.

He put the glass back in his pocket.

"We did not wish for fuss until we told his mother," she said. "Of course she knew he was courting me, but when my maid fell ill, we decided to marry early, so we could leave together for the country."

"Hmm." He glanced around and caught sight of the dowager. Resplendent in deep pink, the lady was deep in conversation with Lady Dean and the Countess of Wickham, but she spared Virginia a smile. "I had no idea you were close to the countess."

"I was not," Virginia answered, "but as you know she takes her own path, and I met her outside the ballroom." But not at the society, or at the other places she had liked to go. Not for the first time, a suspicion whispered through her mind.

Had the countess known the smugglers? Did she know them still? But she adored Francis. She would not have arranged to have him killed, or even hurt.

Not knowing which of the guests here tonight were part of the organization made her itchy. Knowing she had been involved didn't change the way she felt about closing it down. Perhaps she should talk to some of the guests, try to find out more. After all, she had the support of the SSL here tonight.

Even Angela.

But before that, she had another job to do.

The quartet from Exeter that her mother-in-law had hired struck up, playing a tarradiddle to announce their readiness. Virginia turned in a swirl of skirts to find her husband waiting. She smiled.

"I'm glad I have that effect on you," he said, taking her hand. "My lady, we are expected on the dance floor. The minuet."

Balls started with a minuet. Elegant, graceful, executed with care, it was the pinnacle of the dance, the height of civilization, as she'd heard it described once. She wouldn't go that far, especially with smugglers in the room. But the dance was important, in an esoteric way. Executed properly, it told people that they belonged. And demonstrated to those who did not belong that they were not part of the exalted few.

Tonight the newly wedded couple who hosted the event would dance alone. Virginia reconciled herself to the necessity.

Until the dance began, Virginia had forgotten the other function of the minuet, until she had performed the first curtsy. When she rose and met his gaze, she saw a man in love. So did everyone else in the room. A murmur went around; fans fluttered as she rose.

She paused before he gave her fingers a minuscule tweak, reminding her to move.

They went through the steps of the dance. Virginia had never performed a minuet like this one, and she'd entirely forgotten that it was a dance of courtship. Until now. Francis made her remember it. Every step was a declaration of love. Every time his gaze met hers, he repeated the message. She could do nothing but respond and then make a declaration of her own.

When she sank into the final curtsy, she made it deep, far more than the dance required. At any other time that would have been seen as gauche, but not tonight. Everyone would know what that final obeisance meant.

The music ended, and a pause fell, so profound they could have heard a pin drop. Or a fan.

But none dropped, and the quartet began to play again as Francis led Virginia off the floor.

"That was rather bold," she ventured, keeping her voice low in case it shook.

"I felt I should make some kind of declaration," he said mildly, plucking two glasses from a passing waiter's tray and handing one to her.

"You did."

"So did you. Or am I imagining it?"

She sipped the cold white wine before she spoke again. "No. I love you, Francis."

He closed his eyes and laughed. "Best of wives."

With a graceful gesture to the dance floor, she answered him. "I told you there as well. What else could I do when you declared your love for everyone to see?"

His smile was somewhat smug. "I did, didn't I?"

Angela had reached them. She fanned herself vigorously. "Goodness, everybody is agog! After this, nobody will ask if this is a love match. You realize the word will be passed around the whole country in the next few weeks?"

"Good," Francis said calmly. "Let whoever is here tonight who wishes us harm know what they are up against."

"Francis?" A thread of worry wove itself through Virginia's happiness.

He raised a brow. "I want to bring matters to a head. If we continue in the same way, we could be years hunting down the people we seek. I want it finished, done with." The smugglers. "They know we're united, and now they know why. We're united. I've sent gossip around, saying we know who organized the smuggling gang."

She gasped. "You're making yourself a target?"

"You could say that. Someone will do something."

He turned her, and the three of them strolled toward the music room, which was acting as a card room tonight. The state rooms had been thrown open so that anyone could see from the entrance right to the end, to the state bedroom, where nobody ever slept.

People moved aside as if they were royalty, but that would not last for long.

"I'm expecting somebody to approach me and ask me to join them. Which, of course, I will not do, but I will at least know where to look."

Virginia sighed in exasperation. "Francis, they've tried to kill you twice."

They had reached the music room, so they continued through. People were sitting at the tables, playing cards and conversing. A few looked up; the rest continued in their play.

"They will not do that now," he said confidently. "Even if someone does, I am prepared. But they will want me on their side, will they not? And they will be anxious to recruit me before the authorities do. They have been asking me for years to play more of a role in the fight, but I have always maintained that the fight should be in Parliament."

He stopped, facing both women. "However, with the danger to my wife, I'll no longer stand aside. They will suffer, and they will do it soon."

As if he had flicked a fan across his face and then closed it, his expression changed. As quick as that. His easy smile returned, and he addressed Angela. "I must claim a dance from you, ma'am. If you will permit?"

And after escorting them back to the large drawing room and taking Virginia to his cousin, Francis did just that.

* * * *

With relief, at the end of the dancing and supper, none of which he really wanted, Francis escorted Virginia to their bedroom. They occupied a suite away from the state rooms, and of course the state bedroom, where nobody had ever slept.

Virginia was his, and nobody had the right to take her from him.

Francis couldn't quite believe it. He had always loved her. And he'd had to wait a long time for her.

That was before he'd learned what Ralph had done to her. Knowing she had spent her marriage dreading the man would have spurred him to approach her sooner, if only to offer his help. Not as a lover but a protector. She'd needed a friend, and she'd had none. That knowledge hurt.

Ralph's taking a young, innocent woman merely because he wanted to mold her into his creature was more than wrong. As well Virginia had resisted in a way that had retained her character and strength. Francis would never treat her so, although he doubted every day of their married lives would be like this one.

Barely able to wait, he led her upstairs, but outside her room, he paused. "Half an hour. No more. I can't wait any longer than that."

Smiling, she leaned in to kiss him but moved back after a brief kiss. "Half an hour."

As she turned to go inside, he added, "Come to me."

She paused before she went in, telling him she knew what that meant. She would have to be the person to leave after they had made love. Every night since they'd arrived at Wolverley, he had visited her. True, he had not left until morning, but the choice had been his. This time he would let her decide. If she wanted to leave him and sleep alone, she could. Otherwise, he would happily keep her captivated all night.

After half an hour, as the clock on his mantelpiece chimed the half hour, a soft tap came on the door that linked their chambers. Francis hurried to it and threw it open, finding his wife on the other side.

He held out his hand. "Welcome to your domain, my love."

"But this is your room."

"Ours," he corrected her. "Always. I want you here in sickness and in health. Remember?"

She could hardly have forgotten what they had sworn to each other in the presence of God. "I remember," she said softly. "This morning I had the most beautiful wedding ceremony in the world."

He felt the same way.

The grand lady of this evening had gone, replaced by a beautiful, desirable woman. Her hair streamed unfettered down her back, in glossy black waves, and her light ivory silk robe skimmed her body, delineating every mouthwatering curve. He put his hands on her shoulders, gazing down at her, still afraid to believe that at last, after all this time, this woman was his. Just as he was hers.

Outside, someone stumbled past, presumably on their way to bed. All the guest rooms in the house were occupied, and some guests, like Angela, would remain for a visit. But only the people he liked, the ones he wanted.

He took the step that brought his body flush with hers. He was not wearing much more than she was. The heat of their bodies joined as he bent his head to kiss her. She cupped his cheek as their lips met, a gesture he loved, and one she was in the habit of doing.

Her mouth opened easily, and he tasted her, the unique flavor that was Virginia flooding him with desire, as if this time was new. Every time they came together was new, their hunger as keen as ever. He would never tire of her.

Francis tasted her, adored her, wrapped his arms around her and pressed her against him, their bodies melding, her curves melting against him in lush promise. He could have kissed her all night, except there were more pleasures he ached to share with her.

Easing away, he took her to the bed. His valet had already turned the covers down, so whisking her out of her robe and night rail, then lifting her onto the sheets, took less than a minute. In another minute he was naked too, and he wasted no time in joining her.

Propping himself up on one elbow, he stroked her, curving his hand around her breasts, plumping them to bring his mouth down to taste and arouse her.

Her nipples, already peaked, hardened even more against his tongue. First one, then the other, taking his time, reveling in the way she stroked his shoulders, ran her hands over his arms, murmuring to him. "Francis, I love you."

He would never tire of hearing that. He kissed down her body, paused to tease the sensitive spot on the inside of her hip, laughed when she flinched and gasped. Her stomach was satin smooth, tightening when he teased her and licked around the sweet indent of her navel. "Every part of you is mine. Every inch. Say it."

"I'm yours, Francis. All of me."

He loved the easy way she could say that, as if finally she had let him in, without stint. "And I am yours. I've been yours for a long time."

Before she could say anything, he nuzzled between her legs, finding what he sought. At the first touch of his tongue, she cried out. Glorying in the sound, he gripped her hip to stop her moving too much, and feasted.

Her babble of cries and encouragement drove him on, and by the time he pushed himself back up the bed to lie over her, she had come twice. He gazed at her. Her eyes were dark, the pupils almost black, despite the candlelight turning her body into a golden goddess. And she laughed, a sound of sheer happiness.

"I want to hear that often," he told her. "Not just in bed, not only when we are making love, but all the time." He dropped a swift kiss on her lips. "Now turn over."

Her luscious lips fell open, but she did as he asked and didn't demur when he raised her lower body and helped her to spread her legs, opening her body completely to his possession. He had never done this with her before, but he'd ensured she was ready.

If he had to make her more ready, he would disgrace himself, and that was not going to happen. Although his shaft was big, straining with his need for her, there was little natural resistance when he slid inside her body.

"Oh, my love," he murmured as he set to work.

A hard slam had her crying his name. He loved her response so much that he did it again. And again. She was soft and silken inside, all he needed to drive himself to oblivion. But that would not happen until—yes.

She shivered and cried out, her body contracting around his. Francis, experienced though he was, had to stop moving, else he would have finished there and then. And he wanted her to come at least twice more before he did.

Touching the most sensitive parts of her body, the nub between her legs, her nipples, and bending to lick and suck the juncture of neck and shoulder, where he had learned she was particularly responsive, made her jolt under him, her backside colliding with his groin and sending him into paroxysms of joy.

Virginia buried her face in the pillow and screamed.

The next time she would scream into his mouth. But he had emptied himself inside her.

"I meant to make you come twice more. I only managed once."

* * * *

Francis said that with such a disgusted tone that Virginia laughed. Snuggled into his body, held close and safe, she had never known such joy. Even though they had made love many times over the last few weeks, tonight was special. Not just because she experienced his lovemaking in a different way, but because tonight they had, in the words of the poets, plighted their troth.

Consummated their marriage.

"You can do it next time," she said, stroking her hand down his chest, relishing her right to do so. Curly chest hairs tickled her palm, and she turned her head to stifle her yawn against his shoulder. "You seem bigger out of your clothes than in them."

"A good tailor will do that." He twirled a lock of her hair around his finger and smiled down at her. "God help me, Virginia, I will kill myself making love to you. But you're tired."

"Aren't you?"

His shoulder moved. If she hadn't been using it as a pillow, he might have shrugged. "I'm still keyed up, excited. We should go away. I have a neat little manor house in Nottinghamshire, well away from the sea. We'll go there."

"Anywhere," she murmured as sleep swept over her in a great wave.

* * * *

The click of the door alerted her. The job door, where the servants entered. The sound of footsteps, heavier than she would expect a maid to make, crossed the floor, softening when the person reached the thick rug.

Next to her, Francis snored softly. They had separated sometime in the night.

Virginia slitted her eyes so as to appear undisturbed. Francis stopped snoring.

A person stood at the end of the bed. Not a servant. A man in shirtsleeves and breeches. He raised his arms. He was holding a pistol in each hand.

Virginia cried out as Francis shoved her hard, pushing her off the bed.

The first explosion rocketed around the room, but Virginia did not wait to find out if she was hit. No pain, which was a good thing.

Someone fired, but she didn't know who. Someone crashed to the floor, rocking the boards under her.

A voice from outside the room called out, "I have him! Put the guns down!" Cocking had kept his promise.

Virginia got shakily to her feet. Only when she was standing did she turn her head, dreading what she might see.

If the assassin had killed Francis, then he was a dead man.

But Francis was standing on the other side of bed, a pistol in one hand and a sword in the other, a saber. Its long, curved blade gleamed wickedly in the light of the wavering candles being held in the doorway. Behind her the job door stood open.

"Virginia! Are you all right?" Francis's voice, tight with shock, boomed out.

Her voice wouldn't work at first. She coughed and tried again. "Y-yes." Trying to think of a way to reassure him, she came up with, "Not hurt."

His long sigh of relief was enhanced by a groan. Heedless of his nudity, he strode to the chair, snatched up her robe, and walked around the bed to stand in front of her. She shrugged into the garment and clutched it around her body as shouts came from outside and people raced up to their room.

Taking his time, Francis caught the robe someone threw to him, wrapped it around himself and belted it, before turning and helping Virginia to her feet. He studied her from head to foot before paying any attention to anyone else.

Cocking took a look outside. "Colston Magna and a few other men are preventing anyone coming in." He gazed down at the figure on the floor.

The man was screaming. A high-pitched, uncomfortable scream that hit her eardrums at exactly the wrong pitch.

With a long-suffering sigh, Cocking pulled off his neck cloth and bent to the man. "Hold still," he said after a moment. "And stop that noise. You won't die. That is, you won't die just yet."

"Who is he?" Virginia demanded. She took a step forward, but Francis held her back, pulling her against his body. She shook him off.

Cocking sent her a warning glare, then addressed the man on the floor again. "If you don't hold still, you'll bleed to death."

A low rumble was the answer, but after that Cocking worked swiftly and soon had the man's arm bound up. He hoisted him to his feet. Francis dragged a wooden chair over, and they threw him in it.

Sir Bertram was still conscious, but at least he'd stopped screaming. In fact, he was totally silent, although his breathing was somewhat ragged.

"We should move him into another room," Francis offered, shooting Virginia an anxious glance.

She waved his concerns away. "He'll only soil another rug. That one is beyond saving."

Francis grunted. "So he has. So, Sir Bertram, we'd appreciate knowing why you tried to murder us in our beds—bed," he corrected himself. "And how on earth did you plan to get away?"

Sir Bertram growled and glared at Francis. "Easy. Once you're dead, I get away in the melee."

Yes, there would have been a melee.

"Or he could have claimed to find us," Virginia pointed out.

Hurst came in, accompanying Angela. "She refused to leave," he said. "I sent the others back to bed."

"What did you tell them?"

"That nobody was hurt, my lord. An accidental discharge."

Angela wore a quite magnificent Chinese-style padded robe, which she lifted fastidiously to step over the mess on the carpet. "You'll have to burn that," she commented. She took in the prisoner on the chair. "Damnation," she said calmly. "I thought you had more sense, Sir Bertram. I've been waiting for an opportunity to investigate the suspiciously large increase in your income."

Sir Bertram glared at her and growled, then whimpered in pain as Angela patted his shoulder on her way past him to stand at Virginia's side.

"Why?" Francis repeated. "What do you have to gain by this rash act? I had thought you would try to persuade me at a more civilized hour."

"What good would that do?" Sir Bertram grumbled. "You intended to wrap up the orphanages, to report everything to the authorities. We couldn't allow that, could we?"

So Henderson had told him. That answered another of her questions.

If they died, there would be no more argument. The trust, where presumably Sir Bertram had a seat, would control the orphanages, and the smuggling. A few years more and the chain would have been set up and almost impossible to break.

Francis leaned over Sir Bertram and dragged his watch out of his waistcoat pocket.

There, dangling as a counterweight, was a gold token.

Chapter 24

The black cloth, like a handkerchief, was reverently placed on the full-bottomed wig worn by the judge. Exeter assizes had elected to try the case, rather than have all the prisoners transported to Bow Street in London.

Virginia sat with Francis, Jamie, and Maria in the balcony of Exeter assizes. The people who weren't watching the man in the dock were watching them. She ignored them. Calling on all her training, she kept her expression impassive while the case took its course. In less than an hour, the fate of Sir Bertram Dean was decided.

Sir Bertram had lied, pleaded, sobbed, claimed that he had no idea what the trust was for, and finally stood silently in the dock, with his bare head bowed.

Without his wig he appeared a much older man, or perhaps that was the result of the six weeks he'd spent in Exeter Gaol. Normally, a prisoner of standing could be released on his recognizance or sent to stay with someone, but the charges were so serious that the magistrates had given him his own cell. He wasn't even allowed to mix with other prisoners, most of whom were fellow smugglers.

The county was in uproar, and Francis and Virginia were at the heart of it. Wryly she reflected that if they were not married, someone would surely have found them out. Next to the tragedy that had hit the Dean family, that was nothing.

Smuggling was an offense punishable by death. Normally someone as senior as Sir Bertram would wriggle out of the charges, but Francis had been determined to see this case through. When he'd accompanied the excise men on their search of Sir Bertram's house, Francis had taken personal charge of the ledgers and files, detailing the runs and the profits.

When he'd first shown them to Jamie, Jamie exclaimed, "What idiot keeps records so detailed without at least putting them in code?"

"Someone arrogant enough to assume he would never be caught," Francis had answered him. "Someone foolish enough to assume they could kill a man in his own home. And take on the task himself."

Their derisory laughter had no humor in it.

There was no humor now. The trial had gone forward in fraught, tense silence for the most part. Villagers had turned the king's evidence to avoid meeting the same fate as one of the principal investors in the smuggling trade, pointing out times when Sir Bertram had accompanied the smugglers on runs, inspecting the contraband personally.

And those gold coins. They had been damning. Tokens rather than coins, struck specifically to give to the people involved.

They had not implicated Ralph in the scheme. When Virginia would have protested, Francis stopped her. "Sir Bertram wants to take full credit for the trade. Let him."

So she had. After all, she did not know who had first mooted the scheme to organize the gangs, link them and concert their runs, so that goods could be sold in the right places for the most profit. The threads had run over the whole country, but pulling them up would take a life's work. Even then, more gangs would spring up to take their places.

Virginia watched Lady Dean sniffling into a handkerchief, her daughters following suit. Her son sat, legs crossed, face grave, paying heed to nothing but the trial. Nobody knew how much he was aware of the business, or if he had any involvement in it. But he was the family's sole breadwinner now.

The magistrate spoke. "You have been convicted of the heinous crime of smuggling. You have also threatened the lives of many people, including a peer of the realm, and you have murdered at least one man, and arranged the murders of others."

He'd paid ruffians to acquire the carriage and put his own assassins there instead of the footmen he'd so ruthlessly disposed of. He'd employed people to kill Francis when he got too close to Virginia.

Witnesses had come forward to place information about the time Sir Bertram had shot a man for trying to steal off the top of the contraband—keeping a portion for himself. The men who'd attacked them at Staines had been traced to Sir Bertram. He was clearly responsible for that, too.

Whether that was true or not, Virginia did not know. Neither did she care. She was witness to a reckless attack that should have ended with the deaths of her husband and herself. That was enough.

The magistrate continued amongst deathly silence. "Your crime introduced many men and women to illegal acts when they might otherwise have led blameless lives. You have deprived the Crown, and therefore the state, of untold sums of money, indirectly causing the suffering of many others. You have encouraged others to engage in illegal trafficking of goods. On the fourteenth of July last year, we have heard that you brought a French spy onto British soil, and that therefore you are guilty of treason. We are still seeking corroboration for that crime."

Everyone gasped. Treason would mean the loss of his title, the family home, and everything they owned.

Francis leaned in to murmur in Virginia's ear. "That's just a warning to keep them in line."

Ah, yes. In the future, if his son strayed, they could revive the charge. Although by then Sir Bertram would be dead and could no longer be tried for the crime, and his son could be implicated. Even if he was not guilty. The threat should keep him away from reviving his father's schemes.

"With the permission of the court. Sir Bertram Dean, your sentence is this: You will be taken to the place from which you came today. You are to go from thence to whence you came from, thence to the place of execution, and there be hanged by the neck, Dead, Dead, Dead. The Lord have mercy on your soul."

The hushed silence lasted a minute until Lady Dean gave a wordless cry that she muffled in her handkerchief.

Her husband stood in the dock, a dead man. The wooden surroundings, more like a vicar's pulpit than anything else, contained him. The chains binding his feet clanked as he shifted. "My lords, I thank you for your mercy. However, if you grant me a stay of execution, I believe I may be able to lay information on my colleagues, men and women who aided me in my shameful trade."

The magistrate, one Sir George Cavenham, a man who had attended dinners, sat on boards with Sir Bertram, now regarded him with the face of death. "There will be no stay of execution. Take him away."

The clerk moved behind him and gently removed the black cloth as the men standing either side of Sir Bertram took him away. He shuffled, the chains too heavy for him to walk properly.

Although they had allowed fresh clothes for the trial, Sir Bertram had lost a great deal of weight, so they hung on him as they might hang on a skeleton. His head hung low, but as he turned, he lifted his chin and, for a brief moment, met Virginia's eyes. She drew back. She had never seen such hatred before in anyone.

"It wasn't my fault," she murmured, but fortunately people were talking again, some of them loudly, so nobody heard her but Francis.

"Whatever he did, he did it freely," Francis answered her as Sir Bertram shuffled down the stairs on his journey to his gaol cell. "The only one at fault is him."

"And…"

Francis touched his fingers to her lips. "Hush, my love. I know. That was not your fault, either. What involvement you had was unwitting."

Sir Bertram had tried to implicate her, but the magistrate would not allow him to speak. Bad enough that a prominent citizen, a magistrate himself, should be convicted of such an act. Worse that a peer of the realm and distinguished soldier should be implicated. And what good would it do? Ralph was dead, and his will was in turmoil, challenged by Jamie, as it should be.

The case would take some time, but Jamie would win, or so the lawyer said. He had promised to restore Virginia's dowry and her widow's portion. Maria's parents had relented, eventually, and Maria was in possession of her fortune. Having inherited a great estate through his wife, Jamie was no longer so concerned, but he had promised Virginia that he would use much of it to revive the orphanages, create suitable establishments for children orphaned through war.

Virginia had other concerns now.

Outside the court, she would have stopped to take in some fresh air, but Francis hustled her away into the carriage that stood waiting. People thronged the area, but a great cheer went up when they emerged. The echoes of it stayed in her ears as they drove through the city.

The place bristled with excitement. The case had caused a sensation and set up a warning to other free traders that they would probably not heed for long.

Francis held her hand and smiled, his public face firmly in place. "Jamie and Maria will come for dinner next week," he said. "I thought to invite the local dignitaries, too. It is time for rebuilding."

Virginia nodded. "It is. I will play my part. I'm lucky they didn't condemn me. Although we kept Ralph's name out of the trial, most must know how deeply he was involved." She paused. "And me."

"Not you." He gripped her hand tighter. "Ralph tried to implicate you by giving you direct control over the houses that received and passed on the contraband, but he failed. You did not know, so you were not guilty."

She recalled a few minor incidents that had no meaning until she had learned of Ralph's involvement. He'd asked her to take letters to Henderson when she went to visit her mantua maker or do some shopping in town, or ensured she was at dinners that she now knew were arranged to discuss tactics and upcoming runs.

"He loved organizing things. He organized me. I had to obey him, and the houses had to be exact, just so. Over time he grew worse, as if he wanted something else to distract him from the central failure of our marriage. He used to show me the plans of the battles he engaged in. He remembered them all. I noticed nothing."

"You were barely eighteen when he married you, and he continued where your parents left off."

They were traveling along country roads now, leaving Sir Bertram and his family behind. While Virginia would keep her experiences for the rest of her life, while what had happened to her in the past would affect her forever, there was no reason she needed to repine on them. Especially with the news she had for him. She would not tell him yet. They needed time to absorb the events of the last month.

As it happened, she could not wait more than two days. They had stayed at Dulverton Court overnight and traveled on to Wolverley the next day. That night, curled up in bed together, still hot from a particularly vigorous bout of lovemaking, Virginia could keep her secret no longer.

"Yesterday Winston pointed out that I have not needed certain—items for some time. Since well before our marriage."

Francis, his chest still heaving, the sweat still sticking to his chest hairs, turned his head and smiled. She saw when the realization hit him, and it hit hard. His eyes widened and he shot up, leaning over her. "You think you're with child?"

Delighted, she nodded.

She had no time to say anything because he sealed their mouths together, making his kiss long and sweet.

When he lifted away, he didn't go far. Just enough to gaze into her eyes. "You have given me everything I needed, even the things I didn't know about. You gave me unconditional love. And I give it back to you." A smile touched his lips. "Now we will have to find more for whoever is in here."

He touched her stomach, so gently she barely felt it.

"You said it yourself, my love. It's unconditional. And boundless. There's plenty for all of us."

"So there is. So there is."

Author Biography

Lynne Connolly was born in Leicester, England, and lived in her family's cobbler's shop with her parents and sister. She loves all periods of history, but her favorites are the Tudor and Georgian eras. She loves doing research and creating a credible story with people who lived in past ages. In addition to her Emperors of London series and The Shaws series, she writes several historical, contemporary, and paranormal romance series. Visit her on the web at lynneconnolly.com, read her blog at lynneconnolly. blogspot. co.uk, find her on Facebook, and follow her on Twitter @lynneconnolly.

References

I do a ton of research for each book I write, too many to bore you with here! For a list of references and books I used, check my website, or contact me directly.

Printed in the United States
by Baker & Taylor Publisher Services